First and Ten

Douglas Anderson

Crown Publishers, Inc.
New York

This is a work of fiction. The characters, incidents, and dialogues are products of the author's imagination and are not to be construed as real. Any resemblance to actual events or persons living or dead is entirely coincidental.

Published by Crown Publishers, Inc., 201 East 50th Street, New York, New York 10022. Member of the Crown Publishing Group.
Random House, Inc.   New York, Toronto, London, Sydney, Auckland
CROWN is a trademark of Crown Publishers, Inc.

Manufactured in the United States of America

Library of Congress Cataloging-in-Publication Data
Anderson, Douglas, 1949–
First and ten : a novel / by Douglas Anderson. — 1st ed.
p.   cm.
I. Title.
PS3551.N3588F57   1993
813′.54—dc20   92-20601
                                                              CIP

ISBN 0-517-58859-5

10 9 8 7 6 5 4 3 2 1

First Edition

First and Ten

Day

four

e could never say the killer didn't warn us.

Friday, day four of the NFL strike, I lay in bed. Lona Nachman, my girlfriend, stood naked in the bathroom. The shower water was already hissing. I could see its steam pour over the walls of the stall.

Leaning over the toilet, Lona sucked on her Merit one last time. Then she flicked it into the water and stepped into the shower. She slid the glass door shut.

In the dark bedroom, I looked away. At least she could have flushed. My bedside clock said 11:03 P.M., so I punched on News-Center2, hoping to hear news of the strike.

To ease my aching back, I got out of bed. Naked, I walked over to my IBM computer and picked the day's mail off the top. At ten, when Lona arrived, well liquored and randy, I'd been about to go through the envelopes and cards. An hour and three minutes later, I could finally continue.

I punched up the TV volume to compete with the shower. With my right hand, I rubbed the elbow I hurt when I collided with Jumbo Smith on Sunday at Rich Stadium.

With my left hand, I sorted the mail. I angled each envelope and card into the bathroom light. The first card that made any sense invited me to Reading, Inc.'s, annual fall picnic. Rain or shine, Saturday after next, out in Clarence.

Then a pink card, same size, again from Reading, Inc. It invited me to the Fifth Annual Gala Awards Banquet. To be held even sooner, the next Thursday at Artists Gallery.

Lona slid the shower door open. She stuck out her soapy head, blinking, and called my name: "Santa!" She lowered her voice. "Oh, there you are. You can't miss Daddy's banquet next Thursday night."

"Just got the invite." I held up the pink card and wagged it. "It's going to be a gala."

So we donors would add another zero to our checks. "I can't plan that far ahead. I go for surgery tomorrow. And the owners could stuff their dicks back into their trousers, settle this strike before Tuesday's deadline. Then we'll be cramming for the Colts Thursday night." I doubted that. NFL owners—with a couple of question marks for those not so endowed—pretty much kept their dicks where they belonged. Except when it came to their teams.

"We'll see." Lona slid closed the shower door. As the daughter of Josh Nachman, she was used to getting her way.

The magazines and junk mail I set on top of my IBM. The yellow and pink invites I tossed on top of them. I kept two envelopes, one from Geraldo, my dealer.

The other had no return address, no postmark. The plain white envelope was addressed to Santa in red and blue crayon. My name. The Bills' colors. Probably another eight-year-old fan. Unsure about stamps, he had flown past on his bike and stuffed the letter into my mailbox. It had happened before. Eight-year-olds write great letters.

Lona shouted over the water, "You can't miss Daddy's banquet."

Truth time, early on. The previous several dozen times—minus one—that I had had sex, it had been with Lona Nachman.

"By Daddy's banquet, you'll be out of the hospital. And you're getting an award."

"I can miss it if Coach says we have to look at Colts films."

I crawled back under the covers and ripped open the plain white envelope. From it I fished a folded sheet of typing paper. Again, block-printed in red and blue crayon:

2

THE STRIKE IS KILLING PEOPLE
I BEG YOU TWO TO STOP IT
IF NOT, FIRST AND TEN GOODBYE

Some eight-year-old. When Lona got out of the shower, I read it to her. "Now what do you do with a mind crazy enough to threaten 'first and ten goodbye'?"

"Call the cops."

"This—" I paused while Lona leaned way over, tucked her long wet hair into a fluffy beige towel. "This is too silly."

"Santa."

"Well, it's silly to call the cops tonight. There's no time limit on this 'if not.' "

I watched Lona drying herself. Body by *Playboy*. Brain, unfortunately, saturated by turpentine and alcohol. She'd been painting with oils since probably three that afternoon and drinking steadily since probably three-fifteen.

Lona had a suggestion. "Call Albert."

"What good can he do? An agent's a civil lawyer. 'First and ten goodbye' sounds more like a criminal threat."

"Then call the cops." Beige turban atop her head, Lona put on my black robe and walked out. She was going downstairs to pour herself yet another Stoly.

When she got back, she set her tumbler on the passenger-side nightstand and took her pack of Merits off the wide ashtray she had been filling. She lit a Merit and flopped back onto the bed beside me.

She wriggled out of my black robe. Then she unwrapped the beige towel and rubbed her hair. No belly. Breasts the size of cantaloupes. Thighs as firm as mine.

Question: would Lona stay the night? Usually I fell asleep and she wobbled off to a bar over on Elmwood for a toot and a whistle. Where she ended up was her own business.

She gulped her drink and got on her favorite subject: the strike. She told me I was crazy to walk away from a paycheck the size of mine. Not just defer it. Abandon it. "Go back to work," she urged. "Cross the line."

3

"Can we change the subject?"

She talked more about the banquet at Artists Gallery for her dad's agency. Next Thursday, a long time away. That Sunday's Dallas Cowboys game had been called off. Just like 1987, the NFL owners were signing scabs. The coaches were training them.

All I wanted was to microwave my nightly concoction, salve and wrap my bum elbow, and go out back to consult Gus about the note: first and ten goodbye.

I promised to call Lona in the morning between team practice and my back surgery. She tapped off half an inch of ash and took a sip of Stoly, no mixer, no ice. She asked about visiting hours at Buffalo General and promised to drop by. Her eyelids were already drooping.

She would not remember a word of that conversation the next day. Didn't matter what I said. And come down to it, I didn't care whether or not she stayed over. Next time she'd be conscious, I'd already be fifteen miles north at morning practice, working up a sweat.

I often wondered how Lona could eat at Wendy's, drink at the trough, get so little exercise—and still look so terrific. Finally, her eyes closed and she went limp.

I got out of bed and put on jeans and a red Bills practice jersey with my number: 31. Yeah, yeah. I never was a good boyfriend during the season. At least I covered her before going down. Slid the Merit from between her fingers and stubbed it. Picked the sopping beige towel off the sheets and flung it toward the bathroom. Not much I could do about her wet hair.

I picked up the envelope from Geraldo and, using my birch cane, hobbled down to the kitchen. Oh, my aching back. After I put a mug of skim milk into the microwave, I opened the letter—Geraldo's quarterly, typed neatly on the usual form.

Sold: eight oil paintings on paper, various prices, totaling six thousand dollars.

Minus: one hundred dollars per frame.

Minus: Geraldo's 40 percent.

Minus paint, brushes, and paper. Geraldo would have to do

better than that if painting were to maintain the premises after I retired from football.

When the skim milk almost boiled, I stirred in one scoop of decaf Nescafé and two scoops of protein formula. Birch cane in my left hand, I carried the mug—and four vitamin capsules and a codeine tablet—into the TV room to look at sports news on the cable. They'd have strike stories.

The phone rang. I shifted to my left butt, washed down the four vitamins and the codeine. The phone rang again. I picked it up and grunted.

"Mr. Arkwright? This is—" Sounded like Ja-make-pee-something-or-other. "With the *Buffalo News*. Like your comment on a story we're working on."

"Yes." Of course, about the strike.

"About your back. I hear you're going under the knife. Is it tomorrow or Sunday?"

How'd he find out? "Nonsense. I'm not going to talk about it. If you call again, you'll only get my machine." I hung up, punched the button. It'd play my answer but not bother to record him. How'd he get my number?

The phone rang again. The machine cut in, and I didn't hear another thing.

Anyway, I was hobbling out to the barn. To me, the front half was my painting studio. To Gus, it housed his jungle and his critters.

The back half of the barn—two rooms, kitchen, and bath—was all Gus's. For a social call, I always traipsed all the way around and knocked on Gus's door.

No answer. I pushed the door open. "Gus?"

In his little living room, I heard voices in the front half of the barn. Sounded like a ball game on the radio. What else?

The door in the far right corner stood open, so I pushed it and stuck my head around. "Gus?"

He wagged his poop scoop. "You won't believe it. Pirate pinch hitter got a double. My man! They're coming back in the ninth." He dumped a scoop of poop into the white plastic bag hitched to his belt. He wore slippers, jeans, and an old Bills practice jersey. An ex-Bill, he was one of the few entitled to.

Gus's jungle. Lush ferns hanging under the skylights. Dark bromeliads filling the corners. Ficus and palms you wouldn't think could grow that tall that far north. Flowers everywhere. He was partial to geraniums. Somewhere in that jungle were two speakers wired to the radio in Gus's living room.

And Gus's critters: birds, reptiles, fishes in dozens of cages and tanks. Rodents and other small mammals, too. Gerbils, hamsters, and rats. They had names like Roger Maris and Yogi Berra— ballplayers who Gus thought had been overlooked for the Hall of Fame. Gus turned from me to scoop the poop out of the cage of Leo Durocher—a light brown gerbil.

Of course, a half-full Bud sat atop a parrot cage. Knowing Gus, it was long since warm. "You come to paint?"

"Nah." The rest of the front half of the barn—my painting studio—was a sore spot. I'd hardly set foot in it since training camp started in July. I told Gus about the reporter's call. "How'd he know about my spine surgery?"

"So what? Reporters call all the time making guesses."

"But only three people know. Aubrey Stennis." Our general manager. "And Hacksaw." Our private nickname for the Bills' orthopedic surgeon. "And Harvey's specialist." Dr. Geoffrey Barraclough, who was going to do the procedure.

"Wrong." Gus held my eye. "Besides those three and myself and Albert and Dr. Harvey?" He raised all the fingers on his right hand. "Buncha persons know."

"Lona, of course. I stressed she had to keep it secret."

"That can make Lona all the hotter. Who knows who she told?"

"All right, Gus. I get the idea."

Gus nodded. He liked solving my problems. He turned back to his game. The crowd clapped in quick rhythm, urged by the organ. I couldn't pay any mind, so I walked toward my shelves of paints and brushes. The previous Sunday at Rich Stadium, my tackle on Jumbo Smith late in the game held him to a four-yard gain. But we collided so hard I was going to have surgery on my spine.

If we'd been having regular practice, the Bills' coaches would have seen that I couldn't stretch my back fully. After the doctors poked around, I wouldn't have played in the Dallas game, anyway.

But that hit on Jumbo Smith forced me to make a choice. No longer did I ask whether I would have surgery. I asked when.

So the strike came along two days after the Smith hit. Up high, in the downtown office of Albert, my agent, I sat with him and Dr. Harvey Laurel, my doctor. And Gus.

We had two items to vote on. Should I go out on strike?

Albert said, "Yea." The strike would lead to higher salaries.

Harvey said, "Nay." He got long-winded on the futility of strikes. The violence they bred. The moral stature I had on the Bills. The responsibility of leading the younger players.

Gus said, "Yea."

I made it three to one. Sorry, Harvey.

So on record, I hoped the strike would end. But I wasn't going to play for a couple of weeks in any case.

Next item. When should I have the surgery? Harvey called it a lumbar laminectomy. Geoff Barraclough would slice down my spine. He would scrape out the disk between two spine bones and encourage them to grow together. He'd done it so many times.

Short-term, I needed surgery because my spine hurt like crazy. Codeine time—and one more when Lona came over. Birch cane time.

Long-term, I needed surgery to play the couple of years we might need to get back to the Super Bowl. After playing the game so long, I wanted to at least win the big one.

Plus, my contract was up after the season. And yes, sir, I'd like a raise, please. So I stood to squeeze another couple of million bucks out of Mr. Hanks. If I wanted to spend the rest of my life oil painting, those millions would come in handy.

On Gus's radio, the Pirates' shortstop sliced one to right that made it to the wall. Two runs came in to put the Pirates ahead.

Gus celebrated a moment. Low fives. High fives. A toast of

warm beer. I unfolded the red-and-blue-crayoned note. "Look what came nameless in the mail." I read it aloud.

Gus tied the drape around a bird cage. "Say what? The man be serious? 'First and ten goodbye'?"

While we talked, we visited each cage down the line and fed, draped, tidied. Put the critters to bed. Whatever needed doing.

"Hey," I told Gus. "I agree with the nut. The strike means no games on Sunday. So, yup, the strike's killing people. Like the restaurant and motel owners near the stadiums. They make a killing eight Sundays a year. Like the fans. They'll have to kill time some other way. Like the TV sponsors. Like the players."

"Like yourself," Gus added.

Like me. The strike cost me sixty-four thousand and change when I missed Monday's paycheck. It looked to cost me another sixty-four thousand the next Monday. And the next Monday and the next.

Gus said, "Then there be all the guys you don't think about. The little guys."

I thought about them: the little guys. A couple of years earlier, Josh Nachman, Lona's dad, started a place called Reading, Inc., to teach adults to read. A part of Reading, Inc.'s, budget came from me. I wasn't happy about some of the praise-the-Lord stuff that Josh did, but I gave a thousand bucks every time I intercepted a pass or fell on a fumble or sacked a quarterback. Josh then had a local suit match my thousand.

But I got only four turnovers and sacks, maybe five or six, per season. So Josh also signed up Greg Bowsk. Bowsk gave a thousand—matched by a local suit—every time he threw a touchdown pass. If you figure twenty throws each year, Bowsk gave a large part of Reading, Inc.'s, budget.

Josh Nachman dealt with Bowsk and me, not with whoever happened to be playing quarterback and free safety. To get the local suits to match the donation of the scabs would be one thing. To get the scabs to donate that much of their teeny salaries would be impossible, even for silver-tongued Josh Nachman.

So Josh stood to lose a couple thousand each Sunday we stayed out on strike. The little guys like Josh Nachman you didn't think about. They were really getting killed. And look how much good Josh did with the money.

"What's this line again?" Gus stabbed at the note.

" 'I beg you two to stop it,' " I read.

"Who two?"

"Yeah, Gus. Me and just who?"

Gus turned from spritzing a hanging asparagus fern and showed his teeth. "And if you two don't stop the strike, what the bozo say here?" He stabbed again.

" 'First and ten goodbye.' "

Day

five

early early, I called Albert. His service took the call: he'd been held overnight in Toronto, due back by evening. If I knew Albert, a young lady had turned his head.

I packed my gym bag for at least two nights in Buffalo General. Harvey had set surgery for the middle of the afternoon, so I had plenty of time for the team workout at Erie Community College. I was still not sure what to do about the nut's note. But I'd probably want to show it to Shrimp, our strike leader, so I stuffed it into my bag.

Before our workout at ECC, we had a team meeting in the field house. Five days into the strike, most everyone had stayed in town. We believed our guy and the owners' guy, both honorable men, would settle the horrid thing soon. Then I wouldn't have to worry about the nut's note.

The classroom, green cinderblock, had fluorescent lights set into the ceiling. I leaned on my cane in the back. Up in the rowdy front row, Jimmy Roma, crammed into a little desk, waved to me. Jimmy was a decade younger, a hundred pounds larger than Gus. But the same thick neck, tiny ears, wide mouth. Jimmy looked to be talking trash with the fat guy on his right, Eddie del Greco.

Eddie del didn't even try to sit; he straddled his tiny desk. I hobbled up. "You guys hear about this note I got last night?" In the noisy room, we had to shout, too.

10

Jimmy, a goofus, had a mind to match. "Was it seven numbers? A dash near the middle? It's her phone number, choirboy."

Eddie gave a sneer and wagged his bushy eyebrows. "But if it had just words, I'd be happy to help you spell them out." He and Jimmy fancied themselves a comedy team.

I said, "The note was something about first and ten goodbye."

Jimmy's turn. "What?" Palm to ear. "You got it firsthand when he'll die? What you got, Santa, a warm hand on someone's nuts?" Jimmy elbowed his partner, Eddie del. "Santa says he feels like a hot, smelly jockstrap. Pass it along."

They laughed so hard they must have thought they were funny. In fact, I could hardly hear, what with the packed room's roar of gossip, outbursts of laughter, and slap of high fives.

Except for the Puritans. Those half-dozen guys—third-string quarterback, the kicking teams' kamikaze, our premier wide receiver among them—sat off to the side. Quiet, sober, hands folded on knees. The role-model crowd. Determined to set a good example, which meant HNF: have no fun. My opinion? They were all scared to death. Religion gave them something to cling to.

Still, the team was the best we'd had since 1991 and, some thought, the best Bills team ever. But such children. Sometimes I felt like their den mother.

None of us was exact about why we were out on strike. For sure, we couldn't believe the papers: the negotiators' posturing and the analysts' pontificating. But as ballplayers, we fell back on our instinct and training, a.k.a. teamwork. If we went on strike, we went as a team; if we went back to work, we went as a team.

Greg Bowsk, in the third row, was our leader, period. Not because he threw the TD passes. And not because the check he'd miss every Monday the strike lasted would read a tad over two hundred thou.

Know why he was our leader? Greg Bowsk was most gullible. Let's say we were down three TDs, two minutes to go. Bowsk was the only guy who believed we'd still win. He couldn't convince us, the defense; we weren't stupid. But the offense? Those dummies pulled out enough games to at least make us keep trying.

In every other sense, Greg Bowsk was just another brash, cocky kid. An ego the size of the Old West. But give him time. He—not I—would make the Hall of Fame.

To start the meeting, Shrimp announced that a Captain Byzant, Erie County sheriff's office, wanted to yat at us.

Byzant, short and skinny for a cop, looked puny standing in front of Jimmy and Eddie del and the other linemen in the front row. He was clean-shaven, but he kept rubbing his cheeks as though trying to detect the first hint of stubble.

He spoke in general. ". . . the heightened emotions on all sides. Now we don't want you men to hesitate . . . report the slightest suspicion of any trouble. We would much rather have you cry wolf daily than . . . any trouble while it's still brewing."

Then Byzant asked and answered a question. "Now exactly . . . do I mean by . . . suspicion of any trouble?" He paused to stroke his cheek. "I mean any threats you may hear, any notes, any—"

I can't swear he emphasized "notes," but I don't believe in coincidences. As soon as he finished, Byzant wished us all the best and left. I hobbled for the door he'd taken.

Byzant was the only person in the green cinder-block hall. "Yes?"

Even though he was a cop, I held out my hand. "Howdy."

"That's right. You're, uh, Arkwright. One of the veterans." Not a Bills fan. "Pleased to meet you." He shook my hand.

"Captain. Listen, last night I got this note"—I held it up—"and I think you should take a look at it."

He needed only a glance. "Let's wait here a minute to see if anyone else comes out. Maybe the asshole can't count, sent more than two notes. Then we can go downtown."

Two notes? Cop shop? "No way. I can't miss practice. Team solidarity is all we've got, Captain. I'll come down later. But I can stay only a minute. After that, I'm seeing a doctor."

"Sorry, Arkwright. I must insist."

Don't you love 'em: cops who expect instant obedience?

I started walking away. "Visiting hours this evening at Buff General. Why don't you catch me then?"

*   *   *

Saturday afternoon, the lush top floor of Buff General. Harvey Laurel came into the procedure room after the saddle block had taken effect. He wore black wing tips—Italian, no doubt—and a white lab coat, ID badge pinned to the pocket.

I was lying on my stomach. The nurse spread my gown, pulled a sheet over my bare ass, and doused the area Dr. Barraclough would cut.

Harvey Laurel had a strong handshake. I saw the Spanish in his olive skin. He was in his mid-forties. "Santa, how do you feel?"

"Below my chest, nothing." I let my arms dangle over the sides of the table.

"Good, good, good."

Then Geoff Barraclough came, gowned and gloved. About sixty, he had white hair and a fat pink face. He slipped an X-ray out of a folder and held it up to the window. Then he brought a lamp down to the floor and held the X-ray over it so I could see, too.

I could discuss X-rays, especially my own, in medical jargon. Geoff had realized that soon as we met and so told me the what and why of my lumbar laminectomy in about thirty seconds.

He smiled broadly, showing a gorgeous set of teeth. "Any questions?"

I had half a dozen very technical questions on neurology, about which I had read a great deal.

Geoff worked while he and Harvey answered my questions. Geoff said I must keep talking and keep moving my toes. "When you can't do one of those, I'm in big trouble. You, too."

So I asked my questions and pretended I was playing Chopin with my feet. Either Geoff or Harvey answered every question directly. Both were way ahead of me a good portion of the time, so they seemed to know their game. Geoff was the most articulate spine doctor I'd ever talked to. And I'd talked to a lot of spine doctors.

Harvey, of course, was one of the most intelligent people I'd ever known. He trotted out his new angle on the strike. "If you cross the line, you won't play anyway, postsurgery. But you'll get paid."

"I'll get paid because the owners will be able to point to me as a scab. Give the other guys less reason to stay out."

"That's what I had in mind."

"Harvey, whose side are you on?"

"Yours."

So I told Harvey about the nut's note. Shouldn't have. I could tell Harvey anything, of course, but Geoff, his nurse, and the anesthesiologist heard, too.

Harvey got back on his soapbox. "Here it is again, starting already. Strikes and violence. This strike could go on for months. Who knows what violence it'll lead to? Why don't you just go back to work?"

"Enough, Harvey!" At least I added, "I shouldn't have told you what I just told you."

Geoff said, "But keep talking. Why the nickname Santa?"

"When I started at Pitt, the coaches had too many Williams and Billys to holler at."

"But why that name?"

"The Pittsburgh papers said, quote, He came with all the gifts, unquote. Then they listed them. The guys ragged me for weeks until they hit on that name to always remind me."

"Keep talking. Exactly how did you make this mess of your back?"

He hadn't been at Rich Stadium or seen it on TV, so I told him. Early in the fourth quarter, the Oilers led 30–27. They took their time in the huddle, ran a lot of sweeps and screens, and took forever to untangle themselves after the whistle blew.

Around midfield, a third down. My job as free safety was to cover the wide outs if Sonny Trapp tried anything so foolish as a long pass. As soon as the ball was snapped, I backpedaled three steps.

Our front guys yelled, "Screen, left! Fuckin' screen! Left!"

Forget the wide outs. I started running toward Jumbo Smith, their Heisman Trophy winner, and the three linemen pulling out to form a screen in front of him. Sonny Trapp tossed the ball and it fell into Jumbo's arms. He tucked it in and turned downfield behind his blockers.

First, our left cornerback and two linebackers hit the screen. Three Bills versus three Oilers. I raced up, and our right cornerback closed fast beside me. Our guys tried to get around and their guys tried to get in the way, which created a jumble of bodies Jumbo tried to slice through. Then he would encounter me.

High-stepping Jumbo did his famous juke—threw a head, threw a shoulder—as I'd seen him do many times on film. But one of his blockers hit our right cornerback. The cornerback, arms flailing, channeled Jumbo out of his juke and straight into me: head-to-head, helmet-to-helmet. Both of us running full-speed.

"You heard it before," I told Geoff.

The crack—so loud and so sharp—silenced the fans. Then they roared; they loved it. The coaches, both teams, jumped up and down; they loved it. The viewers at home saw the replay from four angles.

I missed it all. And not only the crack, which I saw on film, but the next hour, too. Even though I left the field to thunderous applause, I had a guy on either side propping me up. They didn't want me to vomit on the field. In truth, I was out cold.

"They said they asked me, 'What day is it?'

" 'The twelfth of never,' they said I said.

" 'Where are you?'

" 'Kansas.' "

Nary a chuckle out of Geoff or Harvey. But the anesthesiologist laughed. No pain, but I heard the scraping. Geoff was peering very close and scalpeling out every last bit of laminal tissue between the fourth and fifth lumbar vertebrae. The trick was to get all the laminal tissue and none of the spinal nerves, which was why Geoff wanted me to keep talking and moving my toes.

I complained about the scraping noise. Harvey told me to try humming. Pissed me off.

Harvey'd heard it before, but I said it for Geoff. "Concrete's the most crucial issue in the strike. The NFL owners got to jackhammer that asphalt and concrete out from under their artificial turf. They got to haul in rich black soil and plant real grass, St. Augustine, for instance. A little Kentucky Blue. Even frozen, they give a bit when my tailbone whacks down."

Harvey made a "tsk-tsk" sound, like some schoolmarm. "Whacking your tailbone too often on that concrete carpet has nothing to do with it. It's your overdeveloped quads. Your back's not strong enough to work with them."

He meant my quadriceps. But I needed those thighs to jump, to make up for my short six feet one-half inches. If I couldn't run forty yards in 4.3 seconds and if I couldn't extend vertically way past eleven feet off a standing jump, it didn't matter what shape my back was in. I was going to get beat the next Sunday.

And Coach Fort had a depth chart full of underpaid, lightning-quick, strapping young defensive backs fresh out of college who panted for my starting job. Panted for my paycheck. Panted for the old man to fall apart.

* * *

At eight, Byzant, the Erie County cop, came to my room. He had a lot of questions, but I made him wait until Albert, just in from Toronto, came to listen and take notes. Because Albert wasn't sure what it could lead to, he asked Harvey and Gus to listen in, too.

Then Tex Branger showed up; he was from the security company employed by Danny Hanks, the Bills' owner. The questions were friendly. No one read me my rights. I hadn't done anything wrong except sleep on a nameless note, but I still felt I'd better be careful. And Albert, Harvey, and Gus were always there to make sure I didn't slip up.

Then Aubrey Stennis came. He was general manager of the team: the boss. I was out on strike. So, in theory, Mr. Stennis and I should not have been within sight or sound of each other. But Mr. Stennis had received a red-and-blue-crayoned note, same wording, same day I had. So that was the two the nut wanted to stop the strike—me and Mr. Stennis.

One of Buff General's rent-a-cops stood outside my door. I lay flat on my stomach. Harvey stood at my right shoulder, Gus at my left. Captain Byzant sat at the foot of my bed—and in my face. Mr. Stennis and Tex Branger sat against the far wall. Albert perched on the radiator, pen poised over note pad. Quite a crowd.

Byzant led the way. "Focus on the final line. 'First and ten goodbye.' Exactly what's this nut threatening to do?"

The saddle block was wearing off and my back was killing me, so mostly I swallowed my questions and listened.

"Right off," Byzant said, "the nut's playing mind games. We have two ways to read that line."

Gus grunted.

"What do you mean?" Mr. Stennis lit another Salem. He had curly black hair, sallow skin, and long black lashes. Sorta pretty.

Byzant said, "Let's take the first and ten in terms of football. First down, ten yards to go for us to get a first down."

"Or," I said, "the other team has the ball and we have to stop them. So the players' strike will kill the whole tradition of 'first and ten'?"

Tex Branger broke in. "Who said 'goodbye' means 'kill'?"

Nobody answered.

We had agreed to call the nut a he, for convenience. Mr. Stennis asked, "But he sent the exact same note to a player and to a general manager. Which side's he on? Or is he on a third side, threatened somehow by the strike, needing it to end?"

Not even Harvey had a good answer. He might disagree with me about the strike, urge me to cross the line. But that was in our huddle. On the line of scrimmage, Harvey and I were on the same side.

Then we tried thinking of first and ten in terms of anything except football. On my own, I played art critic, tried to get some hidden picture or message out of the pattern of reds and blues and the shapes of the letters. The nut probably wrote with the opposite hand or by holding the crayons like knives. He left no fingerprints; the papers were so clean that Byzant guessed the nut must have worn gloves whenever he touched them.

Mr. Stennis and Tex Branger left my room first. After holding the door for them, Byzant turned to ask my guys—specifically Albert—to keep it from the papers for a day or two.

Harvey disagreed. "You don't want to give every detail. But won't public disclosure make people wary? Help them protect themselves?"

Byzant stuck out his lower lip. "Sorry, Doctor."

While the door swung closed on Byzant, Gus muttered. Even without hearing the words, I knew they didn't speak well of Captain Byzant or his toilet training.

Then Gus and Albert left. Told me to get some rest.

Harvey knew me better. Fresh out of surgery, I wanted exercise. For half an hour, under Harvey's baleful eye, I stretched. Dead bugs, supermen, one-leg bridges, two-leg bridges. "For lumbar stabilization," Harvey said.

"For pain," I said.

"That's how you know you aren't dead."

Day

t e n

That chilly, rainy Thursday, Lona and I went to Reading, Inc.'s, gala. The Bills who'd been invited—plus girlfriends and wives—gathered in the courtyard of Ice Station No. 5 over on Essex Street. When had the good burghers of Buffalo's West Side last needed ice? Well, the horses to draw that ice had needed stables and tack rooms, long since hollowed out for artists' studios and apartments.

The high-ceilinged old ice room itself was Western New York Artists Gallery.

As a group, five of us Bills were a bit inbred. Shrimp, me, Jimmy Roma, Eddie del Greco, and Greg Bowsk, in order of seniority. But not in order of inanity.

Jimmy Roma had dated my Lona. Greg Bowsk's girlfriend was after me, big-time. I sorta fancied Shrimp's main squeeze, Barbara Benson. Eddie del Greco had that summer married Shrimp's sister. And around and around. What else were teammates for?

The sixth Bill, Alex Lamar, was our third-string quarterback and leader of the Puritans. Alex and his wife stood near us but not with us. He had explained many times the extent to which he disapproved of our life-styles and values. He stood tight-lipped, in control. But Mrs. Alex Lamar, of the same born-again mind, glared her disapproval.

19

The ten of us heathens passed Barbara Benson's flask. Bumps and hugs and slaps and laughs. Jimmy said, "After practice, Eddie del an' me cruised a few Southtowns bars."

"Cocktails at Jimmy's," Eddie added. If you carried their body weight, you'd need a six-pack, too, just to get your motor started.

I knew what happened next. I'd been there before. Jimmy and Eddie del and their wives always took Jimmy's Mercedes, boys in front, girls in back. That chariot came with a wet bar. Jimmy's wife poured. The boys pretended they were sponges. Eddie del's bride, trying to get pregnant, was designated driver home.

By the time they got to Artists Gallery, they were well lit. Bowsk thought they were funny. Shrimp thought not. He knew what it took to survive as long as he had in the NFL. And he told them.

"Aw, ol' man," Jimmy said, "it's this self-destructive streak Eddie del's got in him."

Leaning on him, Eddie del said, "Jimmy figgers 'is bum knees won't outlive 'is sodden liver, anyway."

They laughed and laughed. And passed the flask.

Shrimp, I noticed, drank deeply. He'd started on the offensive line for eleven years. Then, the past summer, he got cut in training camp. But he still had the body, the skills, and the appetite. Why cut him?

He was "old." About to turn thirty-three. Excuse me. And his salary was high.

Bye-bye, Shrimp. It about killed him. He was in such a funk. What? Life without football? He couldn't imagine it.

Six weeks and one injured rookie later, he was back on the team. His salary was still high. He had just turned thirty-three. But the trading deadline had passed and he was content to play at the end of games we were winning by a very large margin.

Next year? He didn't stand a chance. He knew that. And so he held the flask and kept drinking and drinking.

On the porch across the courtyard, I saw someone I recognized. Squinting, I poked Shrimp.

He took the flask from his mouth and squinted too. "It's what's-his-name, the reading guy."

"Josh Nachman," Lona said. Her father.

Greg Bowsk poked Shrimp's belly. "He's your host for the evening, fat boy."

"Well, I think it's time for chow, way he's wavin' at us."

Eddie del had an idea. "Why'n't we call him down here."

Jimmy's wife said, "Too lazy to walk that far, Eddie del?"

"Besides"—Bowsk shuddered—"Josh'll have to say grace, every sip you take."

Except for Mr. and Mrs. Alex Lamar, we all laughed with Bowsk while we made our way across the wide brick courtyard.

Reading, Inc., had no one room large enough for such an affair, so Josh Nachman rented Artists Gallery for fund-raising dinners. With Josh, everything, every breathing moment, was fund-raising.

Inside, we had to shake and smile. Listen to people mutter their secret opinion of the NFL owners, predict the strike's end. In a crowd like that, I wasn't real good with names of people I saw only twice a year.

The dozen paintings on the walls were large city scenes in fire-engine reds and pumpkin oranges. They looked as though the artist tried not to draw well on purpose. Located somewhere between dreck and kitsch. And they'd sell? Probably.

Finally, the waiters came out and we could hunt for our names written on our memento. The waiters served us cold roast beef, gristly and dry. They were students at Reading, Inc., so they came in all ages and sizes and both genders. Each wore dark slacks, a white shirt, and a clip-on black bow tie.

I opened my memento—a tiny gift-wrapped book about two inches high and an inch and a half wide. Front cover said Dictionary. Back cover said Reading, Inc. That much I could read. I'd need a trip to Mount Palomar to read the words inside. Very useful. Lona gave me hers.

She and I sat at a huge circle of a table. Five other couples—all strangers—ate with us. At the table beyond, Jimmy Roma sat with his wife and Eddie del Greco with his sober bride.

Two tables over, Bowsk sat next to his date. She sat next to Shrimp and his date, Barbara Benson.

Barbara Benson was Shrimp's type; he liked older women. They didn't expect ever to marry him, he claimed. Barbara was recently divorced, two kids in college. Forty or so, an age in women I had recently begun to appreciate. She had a slender body, a foxy, close-eyed face, and frosted hair cut in a fashionable shag. She sold real estate.

And she had a bad influence on Shrimp. She smoked cigarettes. And when he was around her, he smoked.

Barbara and I couldn't hear each other, but we nodded and smiled a few times and took a good look at each other. Her face had been tanned too much. It was beginning to wrinkle and slacken.

Shrimp, né Charles Gibbon Dawson Coleman IV, was a round, balding no-neck. He could bench-press a heifer, but he had a dainty, fleet way of dancing around a blocker before he smashed into the ball carrier. The kind of physical specimen that made me glad I wasn't big enough to play on the line. He looked out of place at the table: outsized and out of proportion. His secret—now don't tell anyone—was steroids. Not for me.

Barbara slid an endless duet of True Blues out of a brown leather snap-purse. She held them deep between her first and second fingers so that when she lit them, her thumb and forefingers stretched from ear to ear.

Then she passed one to Shrimp, the idiot.

After clearing the plates, the waiters brought around the pumpkin pie and Spanish coffee. Reading, Inc., had a reputation for downplaying alcohol, one reason Jimmy and Eddie del knew to get lit beforehand. Josh's waiters had given us one glass only of cheap rosé with our meals and then the one Spanish coffee with dessert. Lona drank my wine; neither of us would touch a Spanish coffee.

So the serious boozers, like Lona and Barbara Benson, brought their own. "Conditioned drinkers," I once heard a cop call them. Made Jimmy and Eddie del look junior varsity. Lona kept running to the ladies'. I watched Barbara Benson several times pull the shiny silver flask out of the purse at her feet. She poured something amber-colored into her water glass.

Then, damn her, she started filling Shrimp's and he started gulping. Getting into condition, I guess.

Our host, Josh Nachman, made the rounds during dessert. Too excited to eat, he visited each table, shook every hand. A smile and a cheery word for all.

Josh had put on weight around the middle. He wore a dark brown three-piece suit and a yellow tie dotted with small brown diamond shapes. He slapped every man's back, squeezed every woman's arm.

At the table next to ours, Jimmy and Eddie del were getting bored. And thus rowdy. During the season, the coaches kept us on a short leash. But during the strike, it would be up to the wives. Jimmy's wife had lots of such experience. The banquet would be a good test for Eddie del's bride, however.

If she could get him through the next hour, we could cart him, longside of Jimmy, over to Elmwood Avenue, slip their leashes, and let them run and howl.

Shrimp had scarfed down his beef, mashed potatoes, and baby carrots. But he didn't touch his dessert. He talked more to Greg Bowsk and his date on his right than to Barbara Benson on his left. Bowsk said later that Shrimp's references to female anatomy made his date want to leave.

So then: well-liquored, sort of flirting all around, Shrimp probably died happy.

*   *   *

The night Shrimp got murdered, Josh Nachman bounced back up to the lectern and started the program. He was a junkie for affection.

The camera lights opened fire, flooded him. Two of the network affiliates had sent crews, partly for the politicians and ballplayers and partly for Reading, Inc.'s, becoming news in its own right.

Josh was so short the microphones blocked the lower part of his face from where I sat. Balding straight across, he began to sweat under the TV lights.

"Ladies and gentlemen."

Everyone ignored him.

Louder: "Ladies and gentlemen." That time we fell quiet.

He looked unslept and unkempt, his mind elsewhere, not himself at all. He looked scared. "Let us pray."

Josh always prayed. His prayers, always different, challenged us to give up our old selves and dedicate our lives to the living Christ. He always spoke of sin and damnation and eternal life. Especially when he spoke of sin, I got the feeling he spoke from firsthand experience. But he did it in a couple of sentences and then said "Amen."

"Amen," we all echoed.

"Praise the Lord." Josh unfolded his hands and raised his eyes. "I'm delighted you can share our meal tonight."

He had Mr. and Mrs. Alex Lamar on his right. He had a local politician and wife on his left. He had the awards to present to the likes of Bowsk and Shrimp and me. And we all had to say a few words, so he kept his openers short—for Josh.

He summarized Reading, Inc.'s, year: more staff, students, contact hours, contributions, and—ta-da!—numbers of graduates enrolled in a college or university. "Our successes." He named them. "And we honor them all tonight." He reminded us that Erie County still had twenty-three thousand illiterate adults.

To Josh's immediate left sat his wife, Lona's stepmother. Her name was Charlayne Daniels, Ph.D. and former nun. Of the three in Josh's family, Sister Charlayne was my favorite, by far. I had been sleeping with Lona since the night after the final game of the previous season, long enough to know I didn't want to marry her. And I sometimes got a kick out of Josh's pomposity. But the real reason I gave my time and money to Reading, Inc., and the real reason Greg Bowsk gave, was Sister Charlayne.

Where Josh and his daughter were dark and gabby, Sister Charlayne was pale, shy, and rail-thin. She and Josh had started Reading, Inc., same time they got married. Sister Charlayne wrote the curriculum and trained the volunteer teachers. She was the registrar, the dean, and the principal teacher. Josh was the book-keeper and head cheerleader.

A good marriage. Sister Charlayne never had to worry about

First and Ten

der; he needed someone to address it publicly. "Cramer McKensie," he told me, the new director at Artists Gallery, "she doesn't even admit that anyone died there."

Makepeace, middle name Vulture, didn't mention the note outright, and I gave Lona Nachman the benefit of the doubt; maybe she hadn't mentioned any note, either. But she must have been snitching to Makepeace if he even tried to link it all.

Denying everything, I clicked him off. Gus had heard it all over the speaker. He said, "Why don't you call the *News* to check up on that joker?"

But I got another call. Captain Byzant.

"I must stress to you the importance of confidentiality regarding the note you got and our conversation in Buff General after your surgery on Saturday. Did you get your mail today?"

"He usually comes around noon. But, Captain, for me to get a note today, the nut had to mail it before the banquet last night, in which case—"

"I know that, Sherlock. Still, if you get anything, don't open it. Let me stress that. Don't tell no one. And call me right away."

Asshole. "So you think the note and Shrimp had—"

"Yes." Hard to tell over the phone what that meant. Yes, you stupid idiot? Or yes, we're checking all possibilities?

"Then what about the other nine? Were they all the sick people?" After Shrimp went down, confusion led to panic led to drama at Artists Gallery. Cops and ambulances came to sort it all out.

"We have your cooperation?" Byzant asked.

"Of course."

Another pause. "Most of the sick people were imagining symptoms. As usual in a case like this."

"Does that mean nine more are coming?"

Byzant didn't answer. What did he mean by "most of"?

"What killed Shrimp? Had the food gone bad or was something deliberately put into it?"

"Department policy, Arkwright. Nothing personal."

Yeah, sure. With that tone of voice, it was personal.

"You have no use for any of those answers. So call me ASAP if you get any more mail. And don't open it."

Fat chance. "But Captain—"

"Listen, Arkwright. I don't tell you how to play your game, and you don't tell me how to stop this nut. Got that?" And he was gone.

"Stop this nut"—not "find this nut"—sure made me think that Captain Byzant thought he would try to kill again. After clicking off, I looked at Gus, skimming a fish tank, who had heard every word. He reminded me to call Greg Bowsk and catch him up.

Bowsk and I had both skipped morning practice, Shrimp dying on us. "I was up half the night myself," I told Bowsk, "too pissed off to sleep. I kept raging at the nut."

"But the cops—" Bowsk began.

"Byzant, the jerkoff, doesn't give answer one about how Shrimp died. I just talked to him." I told the story.

"Santa, from a cop's eyes, it's so what? We ain't cops. We ain't reporters."

"I want to know."

"We got every right to know, man. I'm so pissed off I could suck a snake."

"Me, too. It's the kind of angry I gotta do something about."

"Do what?" Bowsk had such a logical mind.

"Shit if I know."

"We could start with some details about what killed him."

"Good point. Let me get back to you." I pressed the button for a sec and then called Dr. Harvey Laurel at his office. I told him what I was looking for. He said he'd get right on it.

"You can call me back at home. But for sure, you can find Lona and me at the Blue Note later tonight."

"Too bad," Harvey said. "Now that my daughter's in town, I was hoping to fix you up with her."

Her name was Cramer McKensie, the new director at Artists Gallery. A cow. A horse. "Sorry, Harvey. My dance card's already full." I clicked him off.

Gus lifted one of the newly potted spiders onto a hook under the skylights. "Doc Harvey still trying to fix you up with his gal?"

"As usual."

"Santa, you need her. Ask him to invite you two to dinner at his house."

"I've never been there. And she won't even look at my slides."

"Take them with you. Or invite father and daughter over here. You know how to cook. Then over dessert, ask her to hang your paintings on those big white walls at her gallery."

"I've asked her to come for a studio visit. She refuses."

"Well, do something. All Geraldo's doing is getting a paper piece in some dentist's waiting room. Artists Gallery can get the splashy review in the Sunday paper. Get the sales of the big canvases. Get your painting career zoomin'."

I changed the subject, but we both knew Gus spoke the truth.

* * *

The Blue Note. Even after my eyes adjusted, the light was too dim for me to read all the photos and posters on the walls: jazz greats and jazz concerts, every one.

The room, already in a smoky orange haze shot with blue spotlights, held about a dozen tables. Along the far wall stretched a bar, eight stools long, waitress station at the right end. Stemware hung from a wooden rack above the tiers of liquor bottles. A curlicue-painted mirror stretched behind.

Lona and I got there a little before eleven, when the house quartet was warming up on some original tunes. We sat at a table. A few folks took a long look and a few fingers pointed, but no one bugged me.

I nodded to the bassist. He looked like Che Guevara: beret, ponytail, and scraggly beard. He and Lona were buddies.

About eleven-thirty, they brought on the fat lady and cranked it up a notch. She had one of those huge brassy voices that made it impossible to talk except in screams. Nights when I really listened to "God Bless the Child" or "Since I Fell for You," she gave me goose bumps. But that was not one of those nights.

Not up for screaming, Lona smoked and gulped, jiggled her knee, and blew streams of smoke barely over my head. She scowled.

I fiddled with my second club soda, twist of lime. Amazing how the death of a teammate clarified the mind. Made me want to get my house in order. I should confront Lona about snitching to John Makepeace, the reporter, though I still hadn't seen his by-line, sports page or anywhere else.

Hey, dummy, pop a quarter into the phone in back, call the *News,* and simply ask, "John Makepeace, please."

Or should I break up with Lona before I confronted her? I didn't want her to think her snitching caused the breakup. But if I broke up with her first, she'd be angry and I'd probably never find out whether she was the snitch.

When the singer took her first break, for sure, I'd do it.

On the other hand, the solution to all our problems was a sustained bout of passion. Did either of us know where to buy passion? Remember how to feel it?

Harvey Laurel walked through the doorway and stopped at the woman behind the cash register. He had toned down on the silver and gold, but he still wore silk, summer and winter.

Fair enough for a forty-five-year-old orthopedist who earned—I'd guess, after he paid his malpractice premium—in the mid six figures at his own practice and was also assistant professor of surgery at UB medical school. While he paid the quartet's two-dollar cover at the Blue Note's door, I caught his eye and he raised a finger: wait a minute.

In the quartet's quiet vamp between songs, I sat thinking while Harvey took a detour to the bathrooms.

It was too much effort for us to shout at each other, so Lona had been sitting there smoking Merits, drinking a third and fourth Stoly martini, and stewing. Shrimp's death had left her bug-eyed, contemplative. A rare Lona.

She shouted, "What's he doing here?"

"Harvey? So don't talk to him. Just listen to the band."

She raised half her upper lip. "I'll still slip on his slime." She snatched her pack of Merits and shoved them into her purse. "I'm out of here. He's a worm."

I chuckled. "Anything else you don't like about Harvey?"

"I don't like his wardrobe."

What had Harvey done to make Lona hate him so? How would I know? Until that moment, I hadn't even known they knew each other. Which told you how much business stuff I discussed with Lona and how much personal stuff I discussed with Harvey.

By the time Harvey got out of the bathroom and made his way to the bar, the fat lady was socking out a titanic third chorus of "The Lady Is a Tramp."

While Harvey carried his Labatt's to our table, Lona slung her shoulder bag and walked off. She had friends at other tables.

Harvey sat down. He was good-sized, a bit bigger than his daughter. The same broad torso, Harvey all burly, Cramer all breasty. Back during the '89 season, I had a thigh bruise Hacksaw didn't take seriously. So Albert, on a referral, asked Harvey to his office to check it out at our usual Monday meeting.

A couple Mondays later, we called on Harvey again. He disagreed with Albert and had fine cause to do so. The Monday after that we called on him again; he gradually became a Monday regular.

Not that Harvey and I were friends or anything; we had a professional relationship. After he sat, I shouted, "So what killed Shrimp?"

His smile spread. "Nicotine in the Kahlúa. I hear they found the bottle. A couple sips of that Spanish coffee'd kill anyone."

And Shrimp had gulped his. I looked three tables over at Lona, smoking Merits, and remembered Shrimp's True Blues. "Nicotine?"

Harvey took a sip of Labatt's and nodded. "Take tars, tannins, cellulose out of a tobacco leaf and all you have's nicotine. It's a clear liquid. Not half a dozen drops, if it's pure, a little sip. You'd be dead in an instant. The stuff's so strong you could hold your hand over it and the fumes would make you sick. If you drink it in coffee, it might take a couple seconds. Might not."

"What actually kills you?"

"Usually your heart stops. Sometimes another organ controlled by the autonomic nervous system fails first. Pure liquid nicotine's classified as your basic supertoxic, like strychnine, atropine, cyanide. That crowd."

"But what about tobacco smokers? They do nicotine all day."

He lifted his Labatt's as though offering a toast. "I'm doing alcohol. I assume you're doing codeine off that scrip I wrote. All poisons. But in low doses, many poisons are rather pleasant."

I nodded. "Pain-relieving."

"That, too. Downright medicinal."

"So if you relieve enough pain . . . ?" I let it hang.

"Bingo. You're dead."

I felt my anger surging. "Shrimp didn't deserve that."

"Who does? Final lab reports won't be in until Monday. And they'll be sealed for the courts. But Shrimp was alive one moment. And painlessly dead the next."

"How do you know all this?"

"How else? The nurse talks to the ambulance driver, who talked to his buddy the cop at the scene. The pathologist holds forth to a rapt crowd in the cafeteria. And zap! A dead Bill's all over the hospital." Harvey had a twinkle in his eye. He hoisted his Labatt's. "That's some killer."

The song ended. The quartet slid down a half tone and into a blues. A quieter song, I hoped.

When Harvey leaned close again, I could talk without shouting. "So what we have here is not an outbreak of food poisoning. No."

Harvey nodded.

"What we have here is murder."

He nodded.

"It couldn't have been an accident?"

He twisted his grin. "Now what fun would that be?"

"Someone at his table? Barbara Benson?" She fed him cigarettes and Johnnie Walker as it was.

Harvey rolled his eyes. "Where's her motive?"

I went fishing. "What about some wacko back at the Kahlúa bottling plant? Like the one who spiked the Tylenol. Remember?"

"Still a murder. Once the lab pegged the coffee, the cops brought in every cup. Shrimp's had nicotine. So did nine others."

"Hey, the note said ten. Mine? Bowsk's?"

He frowned. "Don't know."

"Wait a minute. A Kahlúa bottle has more than ten shots."

"Not one that's been emptied of all but, say, ten ounces and has one of those gadgets so you can pour only one ounce at a time. Tossed bottle and said gadget also tested for traces of nicotine."

Wow. Talk about cold-blooded. The killer didn't care who sipped first. One of those poisoned coffees could've been the one I pushed away. Or Lona's. Or Greg Bowsk's. Or—I shivered. "Any ideas?"

"My man, think it through. Build a conspiracy. Who could slip a doctored bottle of Kahlúa among the bunch needed to pour out a hundred Spanish coffees?"

I had thought about it. "Start with the guys who worked at the restaurant that catered. The staff at Artists Gallery. The staff and students of Reading, Inc."

"And everyone at the banquet. Santa, the cops'll probably question the whole of West Buffalo before they're through." He chuckled. "Wait'll they get to you."

"Me?"

"You got the note. You link the strike and the dead body."

"Me?"

" 'Ten goodbye' doesn't mean he's going to wave at you. It means he's going to kill. Got it?" Harvey's eyes held mine. Wouldn't let go. That was what he'd come to the Blue Note to tell me. "You go back to work, and the Bills will follow."

"You think that'll stop the strike? Stop the killer?"

"Yup."

"Why can't I stop him on my own?"

"You? What can you do?"

"He killed my teammate. I gotta try."

Harvey chuckled. "This isn't the first half of a game."

"So you think this nut will kill again?"

Harvey sipped his Labatt's before he answered. "Don't you?"

Day

t w e l v e

home from Saturday-morning practice, I called Cramer McKensie, Harvey's daughter, at Artists Gallery. No answer. Nor at home. Not even a machine at either place. So I called Becky, the assistant director, at home.

Becky's boyfriend answered. "Cramer ain't here. The crime lab snoops, finally this morning. They wiped butt and got out. Told Cramer she finally could clean up. She's still pissed. Had to put off tonight's opening and all."

"But the free publicity?" Whenever she rescheduled the opening, art lovers would spill out the door onto the green wooden porch and down into the brick courtyard.

"Cramer don't see that. Says it pulls in the wrong types."

"She doesn't know people very well." Also, she'd just moved to Buffalo from Texas, of all places.

"Tell me about it. Becky and me, we're over there helping her. Goodness of our heart. But Cramer picks an argument with Becky and they're screaming at each other, so I drag Becky on outa there. Now Cramer don't even answer the phone."

* * *

Up a step behind Artists Gallery's green wooden door, Cramer McKensie stuck out her head.

36

I had to look up into her eyes. They were gray. The whites were clear. I saw not a trace of makeup.

"Another cop?"

I hoped I looked hurt and offended. It'd be hard to find something worse to call me.

"They said you guys were done."

"Not me."

She opened the door farther. For two beats, she squinted. She wore a dirty cotton shirt and baggy jeans. She had pulled her hair into a ponytail and tied it with a scarf. Some of the light brown hairs had come loose around her face.

"Oh, hello." A pause while she searched. "Uh, Arkwright?"

"Yup. Call me Santa."

"I hope you're not here to show more slides."

"Nah." On Gus's advice, I had a strip of them in my shirt pocket. But I wasn't about to admit it.

"Listen, plenty of galleries do celebrities' hobbies. They'd be thrilled to hang your stuff."

"You don't know me until you've seen my work."

"I saw your slides."

"The six old ones on file? They're not—"

"And it's been done before, ad nauseam. Somewhere between de Kooning and Pollock and their trillion imitators. But that was decades ago. Why don't you try something different, something no one's ever seen before? Original art."

"You never saw my new stuff. Or don't you like any abstracts?"

"Will you listen if I'm rude? Dilettante abstracts do as much for me as a limp—"

"Dilettante?"

"Yes. It's an Italian word that means amateur. Superficial."

"So you're saying I'm—?"

"I don't know anything about you. I'm saying that if you're still doing abstract expressionism at this late date, yes, you can't get it up artistically."

My, weren't we charming? "Let's set a firm date for you to

come over to my studio. You take your shots, I defend myself, and then you schedule me for a show."

She stared at me, chin cocked. "Not likely."

"You're pretty feisty for a lady who's in a lot of trouble."

"Are you threatening me? To like your work? Or you'll bring your bully boys over here and do what?"

Instead, I wanted to ask her nasty questions. Who on your staff wrote me a nameless note? Who jacked around with the Kahlúa? "I'm talking about Captain Byzant. He has to consider you a suspect. All your staff."

"Suspect?" She pushed open the green door and started ticking them off on her fingers. "I did not touch any food. And I checked with the gallery's lawyer right away. I am not liable and the gallery is not liable if I rent out this space and a caterer comes in and gives everybody food poisoning. The food wasn't bought here, it wasn't cooked here, it did not go rotten here. It was simply served and eaten here. It . . ."

I let her run on a moment, let the hook sink in. "It wasn't food poisoning. The Kahlúa contained a lethal amount of nicotine. It could easily have been added by—"

"Kahlúa?" That threw her off-track. Her eyes darted away, darted back. "Same thing. No way I'm liable for a batch of bad Kahlúa. Talk to the distillery."

My turn to be rude. "It was murder."

Maybe I'd watched too many cop shows on TV, but hers looked like a genuine drop of the jaw. Innocent.

Cramer McKensie shut the green door in my face.

*   *   *

One P.M., I went to the funeral home. People on the sidewalk, in the parking lot, solemn, crying. They'd never met Shrimp, but he'd been a Bill for a decade, so he was like family.

Inside in the a/c, a packed crowd and more tears. Not mine.

Lona was there, but I don't think she saw me. Her eyes were red and inflamed, her makeup long since wiped by the tissues balled in her hand. Did she always cry like that at funerals? Or what was special about Shrimp?

Barbara Benson, looking spooked, leaned on Eddie del. On Eddie's other shoulder leaned his bride, Shrimp's sister. Eddie del wore his game face, ready to tear apart some poor quarterback.

Soon as I saw Shrimp's corpse, I got angry. They'd dressed him in a white shirt, a red tie, and a blue wool suit. What had I expected, his uniform?

They'd put powder on his face, too yellow. They'd put some pink gunk on his cheeks. I reached out and touched his fat beefy hand. Hard as a rail. Cold as his casket.

He was my teammate and I loved him. But I wasn't going to cry. I was going to get even.

So I waded back through the crowd. Heard my name but didn't turn. Outside, I got into my Jeep and raced off.

But where?

I could shake the shit out of the waiter who'd served Shrimp. Or I could visit the caterer who'd made the Spanish coffee. What about the liquor supplier? For that matter, what about the nicotine?

At a pay phone, I found only forty-three entries in the yellow pages under Chemicals—Manufacturers and Distributors. Ruling out the swimming-pool folks and the specialty places, I could probably have visited half of the area's nicotine sources before five, caught the rest on Monday.

Problems. First, I could only assume Captain Byzant was on the same trail. But he had a badge to encourage law-abiding chemists and distributors to show him their records. "By all means," they would tell Byzant, "you may officially question our employees."

I didn't have a badge. I could go far on my name if I ran into Bills fans, but Byzant would hear about it. And he would feel very unhappy, I was sure.

Second, who'd elected me to solve the world's problems? The nut had probably picked me at random from the team roster. I'd never ordered a drink with Kahlúa in it, so the nicotine wasn't intended for me by a guy who knew my habits. How had he targeted Shrimp? He hadn't, obviously. Anyone would do.

I wanted Shrimp's murderer caught. But that's what we taxpayers paid Byzant to do, and I had no sign that he was not up to his job.

My job was to get healthy, body and mind. The healthy body was easy: take it slow but keep pushing. The healthy mind was not so easy. That new gallery director—that Cramer McKensie—called me a dilettante? I'd show her. But Lona first.

So Saturday, Lona and I met for our six-thirty reservation at May Jen on Elmwood. When I touched my fork, it felt cold and hard, like Shrimp's hand. But I picked it up and pretended to enjoy my meal.

I said to Lona, "I think the spicy red sauce should have gone on the tiny shrimp and the subtle white sauce on the jumbos."

She tasted both. "Your tongue's jaded. All that pepper you pour on everything." Lona ended up eating the jumbo shrimp. She was dark, which is what I think I didn't like about her if I had to put it in one word. Dark.

Black hair graying, dyed blacker. Dusky skin. Eyes the brown of milk chocolate. Five nine and in only her own eyes getting plump, which horrified her.

"I saw you today at Shrimp's—"

That wild-eyed look again. "Why didn't you say something?"

"In that crowd? Besides, I just wanted to get out of there."

She sniffled, brought her napkin to her nose.

"It really broke you up?"

She nodded. Looked about to say something but gulped her Stoly martini instead.

I waited her out.

"Listen." She dabbed her napkin at her eyes. "I hate to bring it up in a place like this where you can't yell and pace and wave your arms."

"What?"

"It."

Ah. The C word. Commitment. "I'm happy you brought it up. I've been thinking a lot about it, and I think we should stop seeing each other."

She looked me right in the eye and pursed her lips as though she were going to spit.

I stared back.

It must have got through that I wasn't joking; she gulped the rest of her Stoly and looked for the waiter.

"You're a real ambusher." That time she was the one who couldn't yell and pace and wave her arms. "What do you call that in jockland, a blindside hit?"

* * *

Somehow, we ended up back at my place by eight o'clock. On the floor.

I shouldn't say "somehow." I know how. I was in attendance the whole time and had my wits about me. We had a quiet argument at May Jen's. We had a loud argument during the walk toward her house, which took us down Elmwood past my block. Then she wanted to pick up a novel she'd left, which got her in the door.

When I got back downstairs, trashy novel in hand, she'd poured herself a Scotch. "You're out of—"

"Yes." Stoly, of course.

"May I have some ice?"

"Just one. Then you go." Big mistake.

When I got back from the kitchen, glass full of cubes, she'd stripped to high heels and panty hose. She was crawling around on all fours, her butt in the air, her head down, her hair dragging the gray carpet. Her breasts swaying.

An hour or so later, exhausted, I rolled over onto the carpet.

One more time. "Lona, I can't commit if I don't know who and what I'm committing to."

"You can't stand to write anyone a blank check, can you?"

"No. Of course not."

"You simply can't—"

"This is a stupid argument, even for us. Lona. It's over."

"It wasn't over thirty seconds ago."

"Just because we roll around on the floor doesn't mean—"

Her sneer stopped me. "Asshole. Jerk. Then why don't you drive me home?"

She lived only a short walk away through a very safe part of

town. But it was raining. And driving meant I had to get dressed
and find my keys. Which was the reason, of course, that she insisted I drive her.

In my Jeep, Lona kept shivering and hugging herself. Her
I'm-so-alone-scared-and-vulnerable act. She stared straight ahead.
"You're only the second man I've gone out with, draws more stares
than me. At least it's not because you're prettier."

"Was the first guy?"

"Angel? Oh yes indeedy."

"Angel?"

"Angel Ramirez. He just moved to Houston."

"I thought you lived in L.A."

"Then Houston awhile before here. Downhill all the way."

"How old were you?"

"Angel's my first boyfriend. I learned that lesson early; never
date a guy prettier than me."

"What happened to him?"

"Spent all night trying to get my bra off."

"Did he?"

"Yes. But that's all. I's only fifteen."

"So you had a good time."

"Brought me home. Argued with Daddy. Then he went home
and killed himself."

"Angel? What'd he do?"

"Handful of pills."

Why had she told me that? "What do you intend to do?"

"Not kill myself. You're not worth it."

"You're right. Please don't forget that."

Her top lip began quivering. "I'm gonna go get drunk. You
jock-jerks are all alike."

Before me, she'd dated Jimmy Roma for a while. "Hey, on the
basis of Jimmy and me, you can't—"

"Jimmy and you and . . ."

"And?"

She spat it out. "And Shrimp."

"Shrimp?" No wonder she was so broken up. "When did you
go out with Shrimp?"

She kept silent.

"Just wondering. Not that I really care."

That got her. "Last spring."

Oh ho. After she and I had started sleeping together. But I wasn't exactly in a position to protest or do the jealous number.

When I turned left onto Allen, not two blocks from her house, I figured she was building up for one more round before she'd leave the car. So I'd better ask her about the reporter.

"You talk to that reporter for the *News?* John Makepeace?"

She didn't respond.

"In addition to my private phone number, he knows about my aching back and my daily schedule."

"I don't know what you're talking about."

"He even knows about this note I got. The one I promised the cops I'd keep out of the papers."

She turned to attack. "And the big jock hates to admit to the cops that he can't control his girlfriend."

"Ex-girlfriend. Just tell me if you're the snitch."

She started to sniffle. "You really don't love me, do you? I'll get Daddy to dump you from Reading, Inc."

"He dumps me, he loses my contribution plus that of the local suit who matches it."

"Uhn-uh, jock-boy, you got it wrong. He'd get all those matches anyway."

All those matches? I slid the car to a stop in front of her house. For what it's worth, F. Scott Fitzgerald spent much of his boyhood on that block. And look what happened to him.

"Want me to walk you up?"

She widened her eyes as though I'd suggested some unnatural and painful act. Rain slid down the window; tears slid down her cheeks. "You need Daddy far more than he needs you. And I'm going to make sure he dumps you." She opened the door and got out. "Because all you jocks are such ego jerks." She slammed the door.

Then she opened it again. "Daddy does whatever I want. You're a jock-jerk. You know what's wrong with you? You don't trust anyone but yourself." Slam! And she was gone.

All those matches? I'd have to ask Josh about that. Right away.

Meanwhile, Lona still hadn't admitted she was snitching to John Makepeace.

*   *   *

Back to my third year in the NFL, my second training camp with the Bills. On the first day of two-a-days, I lay in my college-green cinder-block dorm room. Rib-sore, oxygen-deprived. Furiously scratching my scalp. As usual, training camp meant psoriasis. A clear cause and effect.

Only one guy had a shot at my free safety job—Delta Gustavus Green, an All-American drafted in the sixth round. His college numbers were mind-boggling, even allowing for his playing in a minor conference. He ran the forty-yard dash in 4.31 seconds, only a hair slower than I did. I'd seen his college films: indeed, the guy's timing was split-second impressive.

So why was he drafted in such a late round? Some such guys had been red-flagged by the scouts as potential head cases. Which usually meant they thought for themselves and expressed opinions.

When the alarm clock said 12:27, I roused myself and walked down the hall. Coach's office, where I was due at 12:30. Why? I expected Coach to be there, of course. Maybe the general manager if I'd been traded and it affected the incentives in my contract. Maybe the defensive backs coach if they were going to cut me but it was still discussable.

Coach's secretary told me to go right in.

The office had the same college-green cinder blocks as my room. Coach Fort sat behind his desk. Across it, to the right of an empty chair, sat Delta Green, cross around his neck, Bible on his lap.

"Sit down, Santa."

That powwow most decidedly was not a trade or a cut. Not with Delta there. Not with the three of us alone.

"You boys met?"

"Yeah." We smiled and shook hands.

Coach tossed his cap onto his desk. "I'll spare Delta any pro-

44

longed embarrassment here. The young man has a reading problem. Since y'all have the same playbook and get the same xeroxes, you could help him out."

I scratched my left temple. "What's the story, man? You dyslexic?" That was the only reading disorder I could think of.

He paused a moment, then said, "I'm 'lliterate."

I wouldn't say Delta was the brightest guy in the world, but he wasn't dumb. So I knew why he'd been drafted so late. I made circles with my hand while I phrased my next thought. "But you got a college degree. I see you sitting there reading that Bible at chow."

"I'm a defensive player, man. I went to church so long, the Bible's my only book. Fooled you. And I don't have no college degree."

A lot of pro players didn't. Most went to schools where maybe a tenth of the players on athletic scholarship would graduate. To go on to the pros, though, they had to be smarter. So the wannabe pros had no trouble keeping within the NCAA's very loose guidelines.

Delta's college coaches no doubt enlisted another player to read for him. Wasn't Coach Fort trying to enlist me? The logical thing to do. The Band-Aid solution.

Did Delta Green even know the alphabet? Could he dial a phone or did he work from patterns?

So I told Coach, "Sure, I'd be happy to help out."

Coach held out his hand. "I knew we could count on you."

I smiled and shook. "But don't you think, Coach, we got a long-term solution here? Like teach Delta to read?"

Delta snorted. "You can look far down the line of bodies behind me. Teachers thought they could get me to read."

I tried, in vain, to teach Delta Green, who made the team and got a nickname, Gus, out of his middle name, Gustavus. For help, I went looking for the best reading teacher in Buffalo and found her—Dr. Charlayne Daniels at St. Celia's grammar school. She was a former nun, but everyone still called her Sister Charlayne.

After thirty minutes of talking to Gus, she had the answer. He didn't want to learn how to read.

About when I first met her, Sister Charlayne married Josh Nachman, and I donated some of the seed money so they could start Reading, Inc. I was the very first volunteer tutor—during the off-season. We got Gus to volunteer, too, cleaning up, watering the plants, hanging out. Sister Charlayne, crafty like a fox, waited him out.

It took a year. He watched welders, housewives, janitors, cooks. He heard their stories, how learning to read as an adult was the hardest thing they'd ever tried to do.

One cold winter night, Gus and Sister Charlayne were locking up. Just the two of them, and he said to her, "I'm ready."

She told me the story, but he and I never did talk about it, even after he moved into the barn back of my house. But I noticed that a book or two appeared in his living room. A magazine in the john. A cookbook in the kitchen.

Then the great day came when Gus pointed out something he'd read in the newspaper. That Sister Charlayne sure made a fan out of me.

*   *   *

So Saturday night, way after ten, I slid the Jeep into a space in front of the Nachmans'. Downstairs lights on.

"Why, if it isn't my favorite football player." Sister Charlayne swung open the front door. "The house's a mess. I'm not dressed. But you didn't call first, so it's your own fault."

"Sorry. Can I come in anyway?"

She grabbed my elbow. "Now I got you here, I'm not letting you go."

By "house is a mess," Sister Charlayne meant the light bulbs weren't recently dusted. Everything else was spotless.

By "I'm not dressed" she meant in her Reading, Inc., uniform—floppy white bow tie, dark suit, padded shoulders. No. She wore pressed jeans and a bulky sweater. Small gold cross on a chain. Furry slippers on her feet. First time I'd seen her in dishabille.

"Josh home?"

46

"He's at a meeting. Now what can I get you? Glass of something? I have pie in the fridge. I'm having a glass of cider myself." She picked it off the coffee table. "Sit down, Santa."

I sat but my back hurt, so I stood right up and leaned on my birch cane. "Back's a little too tender at the moment. Why don't you give me something I can take a pill with?"

She nodded and went into the kitchen. I could hear the fridge door, the tinkle of glasses, a plate scraping.

Josh was at a "meeting" that late on a Saturday night? Exactly his style. An around-the-clock fund-raiser.

Sister Charlayne brought my juice and a piece of pecan pie the size of Greenland.

"Thanks. I broke up with Lona tonight. Or at least I tried to." I set the plate on the coffee table and knocked back a codeine tablet. Then I slowly sat on the couch.

Staring at me, Sister Charlayne sat in the stuffed chair and lay on the carpet the Bible she had been reading. "It's best for both of you." Finally looking down, she sipped her cider. "Much as I love that girl, she needs to pay some serious mind to reining in her emotions."

"What do you think's wrong with her?"

She looked me back right in the eye. "She doesn't have the Lord in her life. Neither do you."

Josh was nutty religious, but Sister Charlayne had bailed out. She was in free-fall: daily Bible study and hourly prayer and going to church for more Bible study and prayer. I wasn't. What troubled her so much? I didn't like to sing, either.

"How come Lona never talks about her past?" I asked.

"I don't think she's very proud of it."

So what did that mean? "I don't think I can help her."

"No one expects you to. Even her father and I have given up all but prayer. No one can help Lona except the Lord. Please pray for her with us."

I set the pie down. "Mmm, that's good."

"Thank you."

"Listen, Sister. I know Josh takes my contribution to Reading,

Inc., and Greg Bowsk's contribution and has a program to get them matched by local businesses. How many businesses, would you say?"

"Oh, I couldn't tell."

"Reason I ask, we had this idea a Ford dealer matched Greg's check and Westside Drugs matched mine. We're in the same photo on the wall in Josh's office." I could have told her what Lona said—all those matches—but it would be too easy to dismiss Lona as a babbler. So I lied. "Then at the banquet, this older gent introduces himself and says his firm also matches my check. Now, I don't mind Josh does that. But if he told me, I'd be a better smile-and-shake man if I ever run into any of those other matchers."

"That makes sense. If Josh were here right now . . ."

"I can ask him tomorrow or the next day. I thought I'd stop by on the chance. So really, this football strike is hurting Reading, Inc., pretty bad." I studied her face.

"Yes," she said. "Josh must secure other sources of funding, which he has already begun doing."

She sang it like a press release, so I kept studying her face. I had the moment before lied easily about that older gent. But Sister Charlayne, former nun, even more devout, did not lie as easily. She thought about lying, I think, but looked at me first. I wanted the truth.

"So Josh needs Greg and me that much?"

She bobbed her head. "If the funding dries up, Reading, Inc., could be a failed memory by the time Josh comes up for confirmation in Albany."

Albany, Albany. "Why hasn't he come to Greg and me? We put our heads together—" I had more, but her expression stopped me.

"Josh is at a meeting tonight."

"You told me that. Do you know where?"

"Fund-raising has been difficult enough during the Republican years." She lowered her eyes. "Josh will be at the game tomorrow."

Whoa. Where had that come from? To get time to think, I

asked for a second piece of pie. Sister Charlayne jumped to the task. Josh was going to the scab game?

Not treason, but it did cross a line. A dozen empty stadiums all over America and the strike would have been settled by nightfall and all the first-and-ten nonsense would have faded away. But if staunch, stalwart, never-say-die Bills fans like Josh Nachman were attending, I stood the possibility of never going back to work.

When Sister Charlayne brought my pie, I said, "I need something else. A list of all your current students and staff."

She looked up quickly.

"And all the guests at the banquet. And all your donors." I'd bet a lot that Shrimp's killer appeared on one of those lists.

"Whatever for?"

"Well, I feel real bad about Shrimp."

"So do I. Are you going to the service tomorrow evening?"

"I'm doing more than that. I want to take all those lists and send out a letter to everyone telling them that I personally still support Reading, Inc., one hundred percent. Copy to the *News*." Not a bad idea, for spur of the moment.

"Oh, Santa, wonderful! But don't go to any trouble. I'll draft the letter, you can add your personal touches, and we'll run it through the computer to our whole mailing list."

"Could I have a copy of that list?"

"Whatever for?"

I couldn't think of another excuse. "Because someone murdered Shrimp at that banquet two nights ago by putting nicotine into the Kahlúa. Chances are the murderer is on your list."

"Murder?" She crossed herself. "The detective asked for that list, too. But he didn't say anything about murder."

"You mean Byzant, the little guy?"

She nodded. "How did you, uh—"

"Nicotine? A supertoxic. A doc at Buff General where they took the body for autopsy told me. Listen, Sister. Give me the keys. I'll copy your mailing list and bring the keys right back."

She set her cider on the coffee table and leaned close. Her eyes searched mine. "Josh didn't have anything to do with it."

"I know that." A lot of things I didn't like about Josh. But he did not seem a man to deliberately murder one of my teammates. Not when-in-doubt-say-a-prayer Josh.

I finished my pie. And Sister Charlayne gave me three tarnished brass keys to speed me through the night.

* * *

Reading, Inc., was a ten-minute ride south on Bailey, west on Genesee. Half a block down a side street. In an old storefront— once a liquor store, before that a grocery—stood Reading, Inc., spiffiest building on the block: new paint and signs, bright colors.

The plate glass was covered inside by posters because adults learning to read didn't want passersby gawking. Some were Bills posters. One showed Shrimp fresh off a sack, both arms raised in triumph. I wanted to rip it down.

The glass was covered outside by two steel grilles, the accordion types pushed out of the way during business hours and stretched across at night. The brass key Sister Charlayne had said fit the padlock didn't get even a quarter-inch in. Well, maybe I mixed them.

The smallest key went in if I forced it but didn't get close to turning. The third key went about halfway in.

Give me a break. I served on Reading, Inc.'s, board, or the portion excused from regular meetings for "professional activities." I sat bored through the annual budget wrap-up meeting and maybe one other. So I had earned the right to peek at those mailing lists. Come Monday during regular business hours, I could.

By giving me bogus keys, keeping me out, Sister Charlayne was, at best, giving Josh Sunday for fair warning. Which meant I had probably come to the right place.

But I had no intention of giving Josh all Sunday to clean up his act. If he wasn't on the up-and-up, and I was contributing to him—I mean, our pictures in the *News* together—the NFL would not be happy. The No Fun League. A tainted Josh meant a tainted Santa, and my bank account didn't need any p.r. tainting.

I could go back to Sister Charlayne's and confront her, try to get the real keys. But all she'd need to do was tap-dance until Josh got home.

So I walked around to the back of the building. The rain fell a little harder. In the cold, my spine was down to only aching sore; the codeine I'd taken at Sister Charlayne's had shaved the nasty edge off it.

Except for petty cash in a lockbox and an IBM-compatible, the copier and Josh's vast mahogany desk, what did Reading, Inc., have worth stealing?

The board had voted for a grille to keep the plate glass intact and, attached high on the side of the one-story building, an alarm that made a rude ugly noise. A passing cop would have to hear it, or a light-sleeping neighbor would have to dial 911. It might take the cops twenty, thirty minutes to cruise past and shine a light.

That would give me time to copy the mailing lists but none to look for a record of local suits who matched my contributions. So smashing glass and breaking in wouldn't fly. I was going to have to find a more clever way into a room where I had every right to be.

The building had no side windows because it had been built so close to the building on the right, which had been torched, and the building on the left, which had been torn down for a parking lot. I found the back door, a small high window on either side of it. But all were boarded up. The planks over the door were not nailed; they were riveted into the cinder-block walls. Hammered rivets. I'd need a chainsaw to get through the planks.

Looked to me like a violation of the fire codes. I should do something. My civic duty. I parked my Jeep two blocks away and took the tire iron from under the backseat. Back of Reading, Inc., I pulled railroad ties from the border of the parking lot. I laid four atop some garbage cans to make a platform.

At the high window, prying off the wet old pine boards was easy. No alarm sounded. Breaking the cobwebby old glass was easier. No alarm. Crawling through the small window was awkward and painful.

The same desks and file cabinets I'd seen back in 1990 toppled easily, a thunderous crash, and I was in. Felt my way around in the light from my broken window. Felt the door to the basement. Felt the door to the rest of the building.

The storeroom door was locked from the other side. The tire iron came in handy again. I punched a hole and stepped through into the hall. Along the wall, I groped my way to a switch that clicked on the ceiling lights.

To my left, three doors: men's room, women's room, closet for paper and supplies. To my right, two doors: Josh's office (plate: Executive Director), then Charlayne's (plate: Program Director).

In the main room, I turned on a desk lamp, sure that no one would notice from the street. In the file cabinets, I soon found the mailing lists I wanted and in ten minutes had them copied.

Next, the list of matchers. Sister Charlayne would have all the academic records. Josh would have the financial.

His office door was locked. For the fun of it, I tried the three brass keys she had given me. Hah.

The bolt lock was rigid and the door thick. Not thinking real clearly, I put my shoulder into it and it didn't give. I couldn't tell whether I hurt my spine: too full of codeine. When I woke up the next morning, I'd know.

A couple yanks of the tire iron and I was in. I left two hundred-dollar bills on Josh's desk under a note: "Sorry. You needed new doors anyway."

Josh's office had no window. It wasn't big, but then he wasn't there very much. His mahogany rolltop dominated the room like a ship in a bottle. Even after taking the legs off, he'd had to widen the doorway to get it in. It had dozens of drawers. I didn't find what I was looking for in those unlocked. Those locked were not very large, so I turned my attention to the file cabinets, heavy-duty and well locked.

Again, none of my keys fit. I tossed them onto Josh's desk and sat in his swivel chair behind it. Cool off. Think. What did the rookies call it that year? Goose? Hey, Santa, goose out.

Josh had four file cabinets; each had three drawers. If I were going to believe the labels on the drawers, I needed to break into but one of the four cabinets. That one had drawers labeled "Administrative," "Financial," and "Fund-raising," top to bottom.

I sat there contemplating the file cabinet. Once I busted it open, I had hours of reading in front of me. Who all was matching my contributions? Why hadn't I met them? And how much was the strike really hurting Reading, Inc.?

While I thought, I slowly slid the swivel chair toward the file cabinet. How heavy was it? More than my spine could take. But if the chair could transport me, it could transport that cabinet.

The silver label on the corner said the cabinet was made by Wisconsin Security. I love textures, so I leaned forward and ran my finger over the label. Felt something funny.

A vibration. The cabinet was humming—only slightly—as a refrigerator might hum. I crouched down and put my ear to it. A fan in the middle drawer? Then something in there was making a lot of heat.

The file cabinet directly to the right of the Administrative Fund-raising one was stone cold, dead still. The thin carpet on top of the floorboards was stone cold, dead still. So electricity actually ran through the first file cabinet. Made only it shiver. So it must be plugged in.

I didn't see any cords to unplug or wires to yank, so I tried to move it. Did a cord run out the back? I only gave the top a shove to get some idea how heavy it was.

But I couldn't budge the cabinet more than a quarter-inch or so. I jammed my tire iron between the middle drawer and frame. Put my weight and leverage behind it. Let gravity help.

Immediately, the cabinet's vibrations stopped.

Which made me worry about alarms and think I had the file cabinet I had come looking for. Which also made me think I had better skedaddle. The Reading, Inc., board sure hadn't okayed that wired file cabinet.

I pulled the swivel chair until its back was wedged against Josh's desk. After I got the seat where I wanted it, I tried harder to topple the file cabinet onto it. Thing wouldn't budge.

Was it bolted to the floor? I stepped through Josh's broken door and went into the storeroom. That time, I turned on the light. If the cops were gonna come, let 'em.

But I hurried. The basement door had a padlock. I snapped

the metal assembly out of the doorframe with one push of the tire iron.

I clattered down the rickety wooden steps. The basement had a low ceiling. I found the place under Josh's office where the bolts had been drilled through—through the wood floor and into a concrete slab that the bolts held to the ceiling.

My, my. Oh, my, my. What did Josh so not want to leave the building? The junk underneath had not been moved in years, if I could judge from the dust.

I stood wobbly on some of that junk while I thought how to attack the wood floor around the concrete slab bolted to it. Out of the bottom of the cabinet and through the floorboards and concrete ran two lines: a power cord plugged into an outlet in the basement and a smooth cord thick as my index finger and stapled to the basement ceiling. I followed the smooth cord to an outside wall. Much too thick for a telephone line. Cable TV? No time to try to figure it out.

First, I piled junk snug under the concrete slab so it wouldn't fall onto me. Then, throwing in a few curses, I applied the tire iron to the boards around three sides of the slab.

Ten minutes later, I could treat it like a very heavy trap door. Playing Hercules, I put my shoulders under it and pushed. Heaved the cabinet and the boards underneath and the three-by-two slab of concrete it was all bolted to. Toppled them against Josh's desk, which took a deep gash.

I needed the exercise, anyway.

After hoisting myself through the hole, I even remembered to stuff into my pockets the mailing lists I'd copied earlier. I tell you, that night I had it all together.

Day

t h i r t e e n

When I got home, the wee hours, I parked the Jeep—with file cabinet and concrete slab—deep in the driveway.

Around at the front door, I fished Saturday's mail out of the box. The usual: magazines, bills, and junk. And a white envelope, no address, no postmark. I knew right away.

Captain Byzant had told me not to open it. So I did.

> SCRUB DOWN
>
> I BEG YOU TWO TO STOP IT
>
> IF NOT, STARS KABOOM

Call Shrimp a scrub? I wanted to kick something. Hit something. Make something hurt as much as I did. Not a doubt, though; it was the same red and blue crayon, the same nutty "I beg you two to stop it."

And the asshole had been to my front door. Close enough to shove his shit into my box.

At the phone, I had a mind to call Byzant as an obedient little citizen would. My instinct said, Go to Gus when you have a problem. My other instinct, common sense, said, Don't be home when someone—for instance, Captain Byzant—comes a-callin'.

So what was close, warm, and private? And had hot coffee?

The Artists Gallery. The old icehouse didn't open until one o'clock on Sundays, so I'd have plenty of reading time.

At Artists Gallery's green door, the tire iron helped me pull the whole padlock and hasp from water-damaged wood. The alarm—an electrical job wired to the door—started hooting. I yanked it out.

I marched into the big room—the old icehouse—where Cramer had finished cleaning the cops' mess and hanging the new show. A year's worth of work by Ronnie Bogdanovich, who'd been one of my teachers at UB graduate school. I took a long, slow look. The canvases weren't painted badly, but I couldn't see them very objectively. Flat grounds, not much depth or movement. Lots of symbolic little figures. The same technique Ronnie had been working out for years. I owned a couple and for sure would buy one out of that show. But which?

I had half a mind to go home and lug some of my canvases over so Cramer McKensie could see them on her walls. About the only way I was going to get them hung.

I walked into Cramer's tiny office. Oh, yes, we're a hip arts gang. Very low-tech: brick walls, concrete floor, some posters of recent shows, and a lot of dust. A file cabinet stood next to the cluttered desk. Amid the clutter sat a PC.

I ground some of Cramer's Swedish coffee beans and stuck a crusty heating coil into a Perrier. The alternative, mind you, was tap water. In the corner sat a stained sink full of her dirty sable brushes stuck into jars full of turpentine. She painted portraits.

In her file cabinet, I found a manila folder that had my name on it. Inside was my application and a plastic sheet holding six slides. The work was two years old. Had Cramer even glanced at them before she formed her famous judgment? Dilettante, my ass.

While the Perrier boiled, I found Cramer's tools. Back outside, I sledgehammered the concrete slab off Josh's file cabinet. Dragged it up the five steps and into the gallery's big room.

Cramer's Black & Decker drill was my best friend. After I sprung the drawers, I found a lot of file folders in the top and bottom drawers and a big surprise in the middle drawer, labeled "Financial." Finally, I knew what had been humming in Josh's office: a Tandy computer. But not the whole thing. No printer, no screen, no keyboard. Only the processor and a smaller plastic box, a multiplexer from some little high-tech company I'd never heard of. It had sixteen regular phone jacks that got bundled into the smooth, thick cord stapled to the ceiling in Reading, Inc.'s, basement.

The hum? The computer's cooling fan. And then a little black shock box, which had made my prying tire iron shut down the whole system. That alone was very odd.

In Cramer's toolbox, I found screwdrivers. I took the casing off the processor and found two cards in the slots. One led to the multiplexer through a jack labeled "MUX." It also had a jack labeled "MIC" and a volume knob. The second card had a couple of chips I'd never seen before.

Now why did Josh need info twenty-four hours a day through sixteen phone lines? And to keep it hidden? Locked tight and primed to shut down at the slightest budge. How did that raise funds for Reading, Inc.?

After clearing the clutter from around and atop Cramer's PC, I attached her screen and keyboard to Josh's processor. I got a blinking cursor and nothing else. What was it doing, asking me for a password?

Reaching around the back, I turned off the machine. Then I pulled out the second card and turned the machine back on. That time I got a system prompt. Some security system.

From the system prompt, I called up the hard disk's directory and found only a couple of files, the standard one for the operating system. They'd tell me nothing, and their total size accounted for only about 10 percent of the bytes unavailable on the disk.

Same story with the unlabeled floppy disk in the single drive. So both disks had lots of hidden files. I would have to know the magic word to get to them. Or go home and get my utilities disks.

What was Josh hiding in that machine? I spent half an hour reading in the cabinet's file folders I stacked neatly on the floor. They looked like Reading, Inc.'s real books. Records of donors and the standard financial statements. In need of much more reading time, I grabbed Cramer's long yellow legal pad and wrote two notes: one on Cramer's office door explaining the mess on her floor, the other on the green outside door telling her I'd be right back.

At home, I stood in the TV room and listened to my messages. A friendly-as-ever Josh asked me to call. A stern Sister Charlayne. "Sorry, Santa. That key thing . . . very cowardly of me. But if you can see it in your heart to give him some time . . . He wants that job in Albany so much. We can do so much good."

We? So Sister Charlayne wanted the education part of the job in Albany. It was partly to protect Josh that she had given me bogus keys. But also partly for herself.

Next message. A drunk, abusive Lona explained my problems. I was afraid of life. She promised to kill me, to make sure I'd never be happy. Atrocities she'd commit on my firstborn. I kept the phone at arm's length through much of it.

Again, Josh. "You bit off more than you can chew this time. Let's hear from you soon." From the tight, cool tone, he'd been to Reading, Inc. He almost sounded amused. I wished he expressed his feelings as clearly as his daughter did. Hey, Josh, why do you have a computer and multiplexer locked up in a drawer labeled "Financial"?

And last, I heard the call I didn't want. From Captain Byzant.

He shouted, so I reached out and turned down the volume. "Call me immediately." Didn't sound very friendly, but it made sense. If two notes went out the first time, one to Aubrey Stennis, one to me, then two notes the second time. Assuming that obedient Mr. Stennis had called Byzant right away, then Byzant had called me.

Know who I called? Albert, my agent, to tell him everything. I got his machine and left a message, call me ASAP at the gallery.

Too early to call Harvey's office. Too early to call Cramer.

Gus, of course. But I called Greg Bowsk first.

We talked about what we were going to say that afternoon at Shrimp's service. Then I warned him. "Greg, the cops got this theory that says Shrimp got killed on purpose. And we're next because we're star players."

"How many late movies you watch, old man? Why would anyone want to kill us?"

Good question. "I think he wants us to go back to work, end the strike."

"This ain't in the papers. And I know no cop's gonna say—"

"I got a note."

"Oh, yeah? You hear what else about last night? Our team's been busy. Jimmy and Eddie del almost killed each other."

"What else is new?"

"No, for real. Jimmy gets a call, this young lady he knows is at Millard Fillmore, sick unto death. Turns out he's been poking this young lady for years and—"

"But," I interrupted, "Jimmy's married."

"Santa, you inhaled too many paint fumes. Anyone ever tell you? Of course Jimmy's married. So Jimmy goes to visit his pokee and guess who's already there at bedside?"

"Jimmy's wife?"

"No."

"The girlfriend's husband?"

"Nope," Bowsk said. "It was Eddie del."

"What's he doing there?"

"Turns out he and this young lady used to go together."

"You mean Karen, the blonde?"

"You knew her, too? Don't tell me you two are—"

"No. I just met her with Eddie."

"Any rate, Eddie del, when he got married last summer to Shrimp's sister, he officially stopped poking Karen."

"But not really?"

"You got it, fume-head. Meanwhile, she takes up again with Jimmy. But Jimmy don't know about Eddie del. And Eddie del don't know about Jimmy. Until last evening."

"So what happened when they both showed up?"

"They worked it out on a physical basis."

"They would." After more chitchat, I hung up.

Up the stairs for the utilities disks. The bedroom was too chilly and then I saw why. The window was broken. Glass had spread in a six-foot arc. The rock, when I found it, had rolled under the bed. To throw it, the guy—whoever—had stood in my driveway.

Stood there when? After stuffing the second note into my box?

I dialed Gus and didn't have to ask. "My man, welcome home. Know what came down last night?"

"Someone threw a rock through my bedroom window."

"Don't say, now. I'm coming to take a look." He hung up.

No time to wait. After grabbing the utilities disks I needed, I dashed back downstairs. I made it as far as the kitchen.

Gus came through the back door, trash bag and whisk broom in hand. "I didn't hear no rock. How bad is it?"

"Nothing. Take you two minutes to sweep up." I showed him the second note and read it to him.

He was breathing hard. "I'd be pissed off."

"I am. Now tell me what you heard."

Facing me, he leaned against the countertop next to the sink. "Out in the drive? Lona stood there shouting. But your lights were out."

"I wasn't here."

"So I tried to tell her. She had a wee bit to drink."

I'd been at Artists Gallery, merrily discovering Josh's secrets. "You know what I want to believe. Lona hurled the rock. The nut stuffed this note."

Gus poked the whisk broom at me. "Another idea. The nut delivered both."

"No problem. And then Lona's serenade was, as the newspapers say, an unrelated event."

"Here's another idea. Lona delivered both." Gus grinned at such a triumph of reasoning.

"Lona's a nut, but is she the nut who poured nicotine into that Kahlúa? Nah. She never drinks coffee anyway." Allergic, she'd told me, since she was a kid, to any uppers, caffeine included.

Gus stuck out his lower lip and shook his head. "I don't spend much time feeling sorry for folks. But that gal."

The phone rang. Byzant again? Gus said hello, listened a sec, then thrust out the phone. "That gallery lady. And is she hot."

I took the phone. "Yes?"

"Okay, buster, you have ten seconds to tell me why I shouldn't phone the cops."

I left a long pause, at least ten seconds.

Cramer asked, "What about the paintings?"

"Looked just dandy when I last saw them an hour ago."

"They're all slashed. You attacked them with this knife."

Shit. Lona on the warpath? Rocks and knives. What had the note said? "Stars kaboom."

"Sit tight, Cramer. I'll be right there."

Gus followed me to the back door, where I grabbed my green parka off a hook. When I hopped past the Jeep toward my studio, he asked, "Where you going this time of night?" He had a good point—it wasn't yet dawn.

"To get a couple bucks out of my drawer and some slides to show that dilettante gallery director."

Not much later, Cramer McKensie barred the gallery's doorway. "Well?" She held the note I'd left on her office door.

"This is for repairs." I held out more than enough.

She took it. "This won't pay for the paintings."

"I don't understand what—"

"Someone slashed them all up."

"Gotta be Lona."

"Who?"

"My, uh, this woman I know. She's a painter, too. While I was here, she was in my driveway, waking the neighbors, until the cops shooed her. While I went home, she must have made her way here. It's only five blocks. She read the apology I left on your outside door."

"I didn't see any apology."

Down in the muddy courtyard, we found my note. Cramer read it.

"Lona must've torn off my jerry-rig lock with her bare hands."

"Then she found this knife?" Cramer held it up for me.

I'd seen it before. "No, she brought that from home. See, Lona's problem is I broke up with her last night." Lona's problem?

I had trouble thinking of Lona as the killer. Lots more trouble even mentioning it to Cramer.

Who had a question. "And she's that demented?"

"Yup." Walking beside Cramer up the steps, I asked, "You always get to work this early, Sunday A.M.?"

"No. Got a call." She pointed across the courtyard. "The actor who lives over there. Kept hearing screams over here."

I told her about the rock through my window. "See, Lona gets screaming drunk. She won't even remember doing this." In the big room, I looked at the paintings.

"The woman's dangerous." Cramer swept her arm to include them all.

I winced. Each painting had taken from three to a dozen slashes. No whole pieces of canvas were gone, and all were still stretched around their wood frames. But they'd lost their tautness. Some wedges had peeled back and other slashes gaped open.

The files from Josh's cabinet I'd read and stacked up? They'd been flung, scattered, and stomped on.

Cramer asked, "The artist will probably sue us for damages."

"Ronnie? It may cross his mind."

"It's early, but I better call him."

"He's a late sleeper. Why don't I break the news? Then you can get on and work out the details from the gallery's end."

"I'd appreciate that."

I went into Cramer's tiny office. I'd want Ronnie to call me. And I could see why Cramer'd be shy.

My call woke him. Husky voice—"No! No!"—but he took it well. "Who did it?"

"We'll never know, buddy." We didn't, after all, have real proof.

"What about I sew the rips? Add texture to the surfaces."

"Come and look. But get ready for the worst." I gave the phone to Cramer and walked back out of the office.

It didn't take her long. I was trying to sort the scattered paper into the file folders.

"So tell me."

I told her everything.

She listened. Then she asked questions. While I talked, her face relaxed; her arms fell to her sides. I figured that must signify a truce.

She knew not-for-profits better than I, so she started slogging through the stack of file folders, yellow legal pads at her side.

I turned on Josh's machine hooked up to her screen and keyboard and ran the Norton Utilities, starting on Josh's floppy. I slid it in and held my breath. Bingo. The Norton Disk Doctor program not only listed Josh's hidden files, it told me how to unhide them. Same with the files on the hard disk. So I called some up.

As I discovered what Josh was up to, I made little noises that finally distracted her. "You sure know a lot about computers."

I shrugged. "An easy three credits."

"What's this line?" She pointed a pencil at the screen.

"It looks—I mean, I think this is a voice messaging system, is what they call them. Look at the name: ANSERBAK."

"A voice what?"

"Like when you call Citibank to check your Mastercard balance, you get this computer voice telling you what buttons to push."

"Yes?"

Reading the ASCII text files with PC-Write, I showed her some of the menus. "See? 'Answering machine functions.' 'Playback outgoing messages.' ANSERBAK answers the phone, gives each call a unique number and date-time tag." I then called up another menu. "See? 'Enter ID.' 'Enter event code.' 'Enter amount.' "

She gave a low whistle. "An electronic bookie?"

It took me a second because I didn't want to believe it.

"Wow." She shook her head. "A business in a box. I should get me one of these."

I pointed to the card in the back. "One of those chips is a voice synthesizer. It tells the guy what phone buttons will record his bets. And 'event' says it's more than football." While I spoke, my mind raced.

Ever since I'd found the Tandy, betting had lurked in the

back of my mind. But it took Cramer to drag it out of me. "Josh, a bookie? Impossible."

After a pause, she grunted. In agreement? I didn't want to think about it, didn't want to talk about it. She went back to reading files while I made a copy of Josh's floppy and copied onto floppies the files on the hard drive. Then I hooked up Cramer's printer and started printing everything.

Cramer put the backups in a safe place and got another yellow legal pad.

I pointed to the pages jerking out of the printer. "All numbers on Josh's floppy. Not one name, but I'm starting to see a pattern in the sequences."

"So Josh Nachman runs his place on bookie profits."

"Slow down. All we know for sure is he keeps a computer plugged in. It had three levels of security, the locked and bolted cabinet equipped with shock box, the password card I had removed, and the hidden files. All that may be there to keep everyone out—including Josh."

"Someone downloads the data. Money must change hands."

"Doesn't have to be Josh."

"Then what's illegal about Reading, Inc.?"

"Maybe nothing, thank goodness." No need to mention the NFL's draconian policy on consorting. As in banishment throughout the universe in perpetuity. "Say you pickpocket ten bucks from a student there while he's intent on learning to read. You then donate that ten bucks to Reading, Inc. Hey, Reading, Inc., didn't commit the crime. You did. IRS has no problem with Reading, Inc."

"Which"—she held up the yellow legal sheets—"makes Josh what, the perfect laundry? Some pickpocket's dirty money comes out as a clean donation."

"But still a donation. That profits Reading, Inc., not the pickpocket. So it's not a laundry. How do his books look?"

"They look legit."

"So maybe Josh just serves to keep the illegal stuff at arm's length from the real bookie."

"But what if the pickpocket is also the one-and-only Mr. Reading, Inc.?"

Another question I couldn't answer, so I chewed on my pencil. Could Josh do all that bookie stuff and spike Shrimp's Kahlúa, too?

"What's bothering you?" Was that a friendly tone I heard?

"Josh is up for this big job in Albany. So the state cops will check him up, down, and sideways. He's inviting that scrutiny. And how does Josh run a book without his wife knowing? She wouldn't tolerate it."

Cramer nodded. "Go on. Unless she . . ."

I shook my head hard. "Not Sister Charlayne."

"So the whole family's crazy?"

Not wanting to think about that, either, I felt a lump in my jacket. "Here, I have something else to show you."

She leaned forward, brows raised, eyes alive.

I pulled out a plastic strip, two inches wide. It had six pockets, each filled by a white cardboard-mounted slide. For all Cramer knew, I had shot the Bible-spouting bookie and his alcoholic daughter al fresco in delicto.

Cramer held one to the lamp and paused. She turned slowly and gave me that hostile look again.

"It's recent work." I pointed to her file cabinet. "To replace my slides in your file there."

"How do you know what's in my file cabinet?"

"I looked because I wanted to see if you'd—"

"You wanted? So whatever you want, you just do?" She, too, pointed at the file cabinet. "Breaking into buildings, stealing stuff. Who cares what's on these slides?"

"I do." I tried to look flattered.

"Don't bat your eyes at me, buster. All I've known since you walked through my door is trouble."

"Let me explain."

"You already did." She ripped a yellow sheet off her pad, pulled out a pen, and began writing. "Here's a receipt for the money you gave me. Pays for the door and services rendered. So hit the road. Now."

Why did I blush? What had I done wrong?

"If you want any of this stuff back, you can nose through our trash cans. Pickup day is Thursday, so don't be late."

She told me all that while she put the receipt into my hand. I grabbed some of the printouts. Then, her hand on my upper arm, she pushed me to the door.

Whoa, whoa. "What's your problem, lady?"

"You. Far as I can tell, you're an arrogant bully. You figure you can throw around enough hundred-dollar bills to right any wrong. You're meddling and being a—"

"I'm angry, yes." That didn't stop her pushing. "I have a dead teammate. My personal not-for-profit group is up to its ears in gambling on football games. And you're giving me a hard time for bashing in your door?"

"If you don't get out of here, I'm calling that runty cop and telling him everything you told me."

"Feel free. If he doesn't already know it all, he should."

That made Cramer pause.

"Call the NFL if you want to threaten me to—"

"I want you to go away. Now."

"Yes, ma'am." I let her push me out the door.

"And don't come back," she called.

"Don't count on it." Yes, I left Josh's files and disks. But I also left my slides. Recent work.

*　　*　　*

People asked me later, "Whatever did Jimmy Roma and Eddie del Greco have in mind when they ran after that guy?"

My answer: "Who knew with those two?" And by then, they weren't around to ask.

Jimmy wore a strike sign like an apron over his Windbreaker. In huge sunglasses, he looked like a curly-haired, slope-necked nightmare. Species: offensive lineman.

Eddie del had dressed the same but without the sunglasses. To cover his half-bald head, he wore the cap of one of the local trade unions supporting our strike.

The three of us joined the two dozen Bills milling on one side of Bills Drive, the entrance to Rich Stadium. Over a hundred anti-union picketers marched on the other side of the drive. A couple dozen sheriff's deputies stood elbow to elbow along the curbs.

Lots of signs and banners debated the merits of strikes and scabs. The Jesus freaks were out, too. "God hates Buffalo!" they shouted.

I had pulled a sailor's knit cap down over my ears and put on reflecting sunglasses. Parka collar rolled up and body hunched over my cane, I backed off a way and watched.

Between the gauntlet of pickets and cops came all the cars, vans, campers, and pickups. They only trickled through, which was a good sign. Fans yelled from their windows, "Why don't you goons go back to work?"

One of our guys yelled in response, "Enough of you go to these scab games, we'll never go back." Another bellowed, "You want us back, you do your part to keep that stadium empty."

Counterfeit fans to watch the counterfeit Bills.

Still, our guys did all they could to persuade the drivers to turn around. Some tried logic. Others tried facts.

Not Jimmy Roma. "You fuckin' bums! Takin' food outa my babies' mouths. I'll shove your nuts up your butt you don't turn around and drive home."

Not Eddie del Greco. "Go home, mothers! You limp dicks! You hairless assholes! I'll kill you, suckwad!"

Never mind that Jimmy had no kids and Eddie del was the gentlest guy on our team.

The pickets on the other side cheered on the paying fans and refuted our guys word for word and curse for curse.

Then an anti-union picket got over to our side. Jimmy and Eddie del chased after him. Their signs flapped. From their grins, they were more amused than angry. The picket weighed maybe half what our guys each weighed, but it took them only a few strides to catch up.

The rest of our guys circled close around them. No one outside the team would ever see. No one on the team would ever say.

Trying to keep out of sight—prudence and all that—I watched from afar. Here's what I heard happened.

Jimmy ripped off the picket's sign. Then Eddie del tore it through, put the halves together, and tore it through again. Eddie del flung it to the ground, and Jimmy jumped on it a few times to make sure it was dead.

All our guys were laughing. The little picket wasn't. And if Jimmy hadn't been wearing those huge sunglasses, the picket would have seen that Jimmy wasn't really laughing, either.

Jimmy put out his hand to shake. The picket offered his. But just before their hands met, Jimmy pulled his back, oh, so slowly. His laugh melted into a sneer and he slowly shook his head. Turned his back on the picket. Jimmy played football the same way.

That must have made the picket snap. He started waving his arms. And then he said a few things he shouldn't have. Rather vivid descriptions of various parts of Jimmy's wife's lower torso.

I didn't condone what Jimmy did next. But what the picket said about Jimmy's wife was really gross.

Jimmy wheeled back on the picket. Eddie del, from behind, lifted the shoulders of the picket's jacket. The picket came with it and Jimmy stepped up close. Lips tight, nostrils flaring, he blew a long hot breath into the picket's face.

I didn't see it. No one did because Jimmy stood close and his hand hung low. But the picket later complained that Jimmy cupped his nuts and squeezed.

Quite hard, I'd say, because the picket screamed. Oh, did he scream. Eddie del let go of his jacket and he crumpled to the ground.

After my teammates walked away, the picket writhed, still screaming and sputtering. All I could make out was "I'll kill you, cocksucker. I'll kill you!"

Eddie del walked past me and grunted. Jimmy followed, muttering, "I expect I did some tissue damage."

I didn't see the rest. While everyone with a camera was aiming it toward the downed picket, I figured to slip through the gates and into the parking lot. I walked as fast as my birch cane would let me.

In the stadium ticket line, I found the perfect disguise. A guy was selling paper bags, the eye and mouth holes already cut out of them. Fans were snapping them up to wear as a joke. Not only would they be counterfeit fans, they'd be nameless fans.

I bought two bags, to be safe.

*　　*　　*

Rich Stadium had over eighty thousand seats. I guessed not a tenth of them were filled, mostly near midfield.

Josh went to all the home games, and I guessed he had season tickets. But I didn't know where he usually sat. Problem was, thousands of fans were wearing paper bags, as I was. Maybe even Josh.

The press boxes were first on my list. The press I had to avoid. But not David, the guy who taped our games from his own tiny booth. David was officially a scab. I told him I wouldn't mention that if he wouldn't tell anyone I was there. Deal.

David let me use his extra binoculars. I studied the fans from there most of the first quarter while Dutch Regan, the Colts' quarterback, threw the ball short and Scott Hill, receiving, ran half the field for a score, 7–0. The scab pretending to play my position and wearing number 36 got beat on the play. I wouldn't have.

The paper bag was working nicely. A few people glanced at my cane, but other than that, I was invisible.

Second quarter, I took the elevator up to the private business suites under the upper level. At the top, the doors slid open. I turned left—and almost bumped into Josh Nachman. He had been waiting for the elevator, and because of my brown paper bag I had no peripheral vision. I turned to stare at the woman who got onto the elevator with Josh. Neither wore a bag.

The doors closed quickly. Were they together or only going down at the same time?

The woman had a very beautiful face, even if she also had shiny bottle-red hair teased high. She wore a skin-tight sheath dress and very high heels. Saturday night at a hotel bar, she might look a tad overdressed. But Sunday, coming out of a Rich Stadium private business suite, she looked like some local suit's cheap date. Obviously, a private businesswoman.

Would Josh return soon? I waited. He did, with another private businesswoman. That one I knew for sure because one of the guys on the team had private business with her about once a month. Later he gave us the play-by-play. Guess it was Josh's turn. I sure wouldn't tell Sister Charlayne.

That one was not overdressed at all. She was barely dressed. Tank top and skirt so short she probably had to powder four cheeks before she left home.

Josh said goodbye to her and turned back to the elevator. I trotted after. Two guys were waiting. The doors slid open, so I had to go down with them all.

Inside against the railing, I got a good long look at Josh from the depths of my brown paper bag. What did a killer look like? Not Josh. My heart and mind denied it. Josh's public face: tranquil, slightly bemused, and oh so earnest.

But I recalled Josh's private face: angry. I'd seen the anger a few times when he'd had too much to drink.

As soon as the elevator door opened, the other guys stepped out. I motioned away the couple waiting to get in.

"Hey!" Josh shouted. "What the—"

I pushed him back and pressed the button labeled CLOSE DOOR. It was an Otis elevator, modern and efficient.

"Hey!" Josh shouted. "You can't do that!"

By then, the door halves had met and the two of us were headed down. "Hey!" Josh lunged at the button panel. He hit STOP. Thank you.

It worked right away. I tore off my bag.

"Santa!" He choked it out; I'd grabbed his tie and twisted it around my fist.

"Howdy, Josh." Fist first, I escorted him into the far corner. "I need to have a little chat. Got a moment?"

*   *   *

Josh lied, denied, shucked, and jived. Talked the horrors of fund-raising under the greedy Republicans. Talked his love for Sister Charlayne. Talked religion, of course. Gave forth the latest Reading, Inc., propaganda.

"You're a fake," I told him, over and over.

After a while, I put on the second bag and escorted Josh out of the stadium. Why did he keep talking? Talking? It was a torrent. Verbal diarrhea. I wasn't hurting him or threatening him or doing anything except keeping a firm grip on his elbow and asking questions.

Then I stopped listening to Josh and started watching him. Detached myself. We were walking in the half-filled parking lot toward the main gate.

At worst, I was watching a big-time gambler covering up a murder committed to restore his gambling profits. At best, I was watching a timid do-gooder paid to keep a computer plugged in.

Which was he? I'd known Josh for so long, and all of a Sunday I didn't know him at all.

Still not believing, getting nowhere, I tried Cramer's idea: that the gambling money funded Reading, Inc. I pulled out the pages I'd torn from Cramer's printer and read the numbers to Josh.

"You show the board a summary budget that says donations are steadily coming in. As long as Reading, Inc., is running smoothly, no one looks too closely."

His eyes darted.

"What disappoints me"—I stared through the bagholes—"is that you didn't come to Bowsk and me. Your fund-raising is all hot air. In reality, you get paid to front for a bookie. Why? Bowsk and I would've worked with you."

No response, so I went for broke. I brought out the nut's second note and showed it to him. Soon as he recognized it, before I got it close enough for him to read it, he backed off, sliding between a dark blue sedan and a yellow Blazer.

I stepped in after him. "White paper. Red and blue crayon. 'Stars kaboom.' "

The note finally brought on his private face: anger, sneering resentment, a flash in his eyes. "No, you wouldn't have helped me. You and Greg are pros, won't really talk to me. And I don't blame you. I don't congregate like you graces."

"Us whats?" A bunch of baloney, but it sounded like Josh's truth, finally. "Bowsk and me?"

"I mean all of you graces. The congregation of money and power. Look how you treat women." By then he was looking into my eyes. So hard he never blinked.

I looked back. And he wasn't there. "How I treat women? Are you berserk?"

"When it comes to protecting my daughter, yes. You graces get away with murder."

Oh-oh. Steer him away from Lona.

"If you want the truth, yes, I'd like to kill you." He was spitting saliva. Yet his pupils weren't dilated or pinpointed. The whites were clear. He wasn't slurring his words. So no drugs, far as I could tell. "You've toyed with my little girl. I've never seen her so miserable. And I pity you for that, young man."

"Pity?"

"I let no man treat my Lona so sinfully. You'll rot in hell."

Maybe hell was why he babbled and prattled. No doubt the shrinks had some six-syllable word to explain it. I knew only the vernacular: the man wasn't home.

"And you won't rot for killing innocent people?"

"Innocent? What you did to my—"

"What about Shrimp?"

"Innocent? Everyone knows about Shrimp."

My heart sank. Fans fleeing the travesty in the stadium were getting into their cars and driving away. "Josh, I'm starting to see. But why kill? Why not blow up an empty building? Or even try to persuade people with words?"

He grinned. His face cleared and his eyes wandered far away: he'd a thousand times answered that question and was resigned to answer it again. "I'll tell you something. I've used a lot of words in my day, and they no longer serve the Lord. This time, not only Byzant but also the newspapers will link the next death and the strike. Because you know who's next?"

"You already told us. 'Stars kaboom.' "

"Not only stars. You."

I laughed. "And you're threatening me?"

"Informing you. You're a dead man. You can't eat, drink, touch anything or anyone. You can't sit down, breathe, even walk, let alone think—without dying. It's going to happen."

"And you're going to kill me?"

"It'll be exciting for you, the anticipation. What a gift. Most people who know they are going to die soon are deathly ill. But you, Santa, you are a wealthy athlete in great shape. Go to confession and get straight with your God."

It was my turn to point the finger at him. "If you're only keeping a bookie at arm's length, I'll let you get away with that. But if you are in fact the bookie. And if you poured nicotine into that Kahlúa. And if you come near me, I'll . . ."

"You'll what? If you feel that way about yourself, think what you'd do to protect a daughter."

I started to laugh but checked it.

"Ah. Yes. You'll lose not your life, only what you love most. Just as you've taken what I love most."

"And what's that, Josh?"

His face twisted. "My little girl."

Fantasy land. One moment, I die. Next moment, a better idea. "What stops you?" he asked. "Why doesn't it stop me? I'm special, in that way. I do your killing for you. What you let happen only in your imagination or your dreams, I do. What you do accidentally or do deliberately and slowly, I do on purpose, with method."

Ol' Josh was getting too creepy for me, but he had more. "If you weren't such a pus of a human being, I'd pray with you."

Tally it up. Josh hadn't given me anything new, yet he'd shown me a crazy, demented side that I'd never seen in him before. Could it explain murder? Could anything?

A family of four—young couple, boy around ten, girl a little younger—came to get into the yellow Blazer. They broke the spell. In the tight space between the Blazer and the dark blue sedan, Josh and I had to excuse ourselves and let them open their doors.

It was the ten-year-old who spotted me. Tugging on his dad's jacket, he looked straight into my bagholes. "Dad. Dad. Look who it is. Isn't that Santa?"

Leave it to a kid. What could I do? I ducked and hurried off.

Josh called after me. "Repent." He waved a fist. "Save your soul while you have a chance. The end is near."

*   *   *

I went to Shrimp's service. The whole team was there except Jimmy Roma and Eddie del Greco. Purty strange, because their wives were there. Who knew the dive those two bastards ended up crawling into?

I got home around ten. Excited to discover Josh's bookie in a box, I'd had not a wink at Artists Gallery the night before. So sleep was next on my Sunday-night dance card. In the morning I would hit the coffee shop and think about the Josh threat.

My house had a small front yard on an upward slope. The geranium-lined walk was broken in the middle by three slate steps. I usually hopped them all at once.

It was two hops for the rest of the walk. Another hop usually got me up the next four slate steps to the little porch.

Gus had glassed in the porch the previous March. I'd filled it with plants; by October, the cold nights were starting to get to them.

But I did no hopping that Sunday night. With my cane, it took me a while to get to the top step. I swung open the screen door and fumbled for my keys in the pocket of my green parka.

I was so tired I wasn't going to listen to my machine. I wasn't going to wait for NewsCenter2 to learn about attendance figures from around the league. If they were as paltry as those from Rich Stadium, if the football was as bad as that at Rich Stadium, the strike was going to be over by morning. I'd never have to think about stars kaboom or Josh Nachman's threat that I was next.

Through the glass porch door I was about to unlock, I saw a football.

I kept footballs in the house. Many of them I intercepted during games. Some of them were autographed gifts. Some the defensive team captains awarded me after a game.

The one on my porch was an official NFL football, for sure. Bumpy brown pigskin, "Wilson" in black script. I hadn't left it there. Gus? Nah. I kept footballs on shelves and in closets. That football was sitting dead center on the bristly brown mat in front of the wood inside door. And it was too fat.

I had my key out, but the porch doorknob turned easily and the door swung open. Well, it wasn't unheard-of I'd leave a door unlocked. Previous time I'd used that door was when I fished the second note out of my mailbox. No surprise that I'd been too distracted to lock it.

But what if someone other than I had come to my front door? Gus or Lona or even—it made me chuckle—Byzant.

Hmmm. So who laid a fat football on my bristly doormat?

I shouldn't have picked it up. But I was exhausted. And it turned out that picking it up saved my life. Poking it could have killed me, maimed me for sure.

Right away, I could tell the ball was way too heavy. Air just doesn't weigh that much.

But my instincts had already taken over. I thrust the football through one of the glass panes.

Falling anyway, I tucked my head, brought my arms in, and let my left shoulder thunk against the door.

I didn't see, but from the way the glass blew toward me, the football must have shattered it a split second before exploding. The couple dozen glass frames and the sturdy oak lattice took most of the shock in my direction.

Not a bomb designed to blow me and the porch to oblivion, it was only strong enough to blow apart anyone holding it or poking it with his cane.

And if it somehow hadn't blown me apart, would it, as Josh threatened, have taken away what I loved most—playing football?

What did the real damage were the nails and screws that made the ball so fat. They shattered almost all the glass panes.

A dozen nails and two screws pierced my jeans and parka and broke into my skin. My precious bag of skin. I got a couple scratches from flying glass.

My jeans and parka were full of glass. It would be easiest to throw them away. One screw really hurt when I gently slid it out of my thigh.

The neighbors started running onto their porches. "Hey!" "What's going on?" "What was that?" Different voices.

When I looked around, I saw lights coming on.

I was hanging the Swedish ivy back up when I heard the sirens. An ambulance dispatched, most likely, from Children's Hospital, two blocks over. A patrol car out of the station on Ferry Street, east of Grant.

Second-story windows slid up. Heads came out. "Santa? That you?" called Priscilla. She was the old lady next door. Probably she had called the cops on Lona's rampage only the night before.

This night was it Lona's dad, Josh, on the rampage?

The cop cars came roaring up Ashland, lights spinning, sirens wailing. City cops hopped out and drew their guns, one in front of me, one behind.

After I explained, they lowered their guns. Grinned and introduced themselves. Told me what fans they were.

They saw me as victim. I did, too, which is why, figuring I was headed for a hospital, I didn't do anything about the nut's second note in my back pocket. Stars kaboom.

But after the city cops talked to Byzant on their radio, they arrested me. None of that night-sticks-and-handcuffs stuff. Oh, I got the VIP treatment.

"Sorry, Santa. It's a courtesy to a brother who works for the county," said the larger cop. But it was still an arrest.

Gus came home during the to-do. He seemed to care more about the porch than about me. But then he wasn't going to have to rebuild me. Getting arrested instead of hospitalized struck his funny bone. He agreed to give Albert a call ASAP.

In the car going downtown, the cops asked a lot of questions about football. I made sure to rub blood into their Naugahyde seats.

At the Holding Center they threw me in with the rest of the night's haul. Pissed me off, but what could I do? A dozen other guys and I got marched into a shower and strip-searched. And we all emptied our pockets into manila envelopes. A bored cop sealed each one for us. The other guys all had to sign away their envelopes and then they got herded off. For me, more VIP.

Still holding my manila envelope, but not cuffed, I got escorted between two cops down a hall, up an elevator, and down another hall into a little room. Was that a good sign or a bad sign?

The jail doc was in there. He cleaned and dressed all the punctures. Gave me a tetanus shot. Jabbered about the Bills and the strike until I wanted to scream. But I was a captive audience.

I ripped open the manila envelope and took out the orange plastic vial. It held the last two codeine I had. The doctor looked at it and recommended I take one. I needed two.

Then, stroke of midnight, the doc opened the door and let in two guys who'd been waiting.

Byzant and partner.

Day

fourteen

Silly me. I thought I had to decide whether to tell about my visit to Josh's Reading, Inc., office. But Byzant and partner wormed that out of me quickly. I didn't get as far as the Tandy bookie-in-a-box before I came to my senses. But it was embarrassing, so I ain't saying how they did the worming.

I crossed my arms. "I'm done talking until Albert gets here."

They'd read me my rights, so they tried to keep me going. I did my best to doze off but keep an eye on them. They wore sports coats and ties, probably to make them appear professional. They relaxed enough to let me see the straps of their shoulder holsters.

The room was painted green, nothing on the walls. The metal door had a big lock. The wide window was black when I tried to look through it but no doubt gave a clear view of us from the other side.

Byzant brought some coffee and asked about my back. Simply talking about it made it throb. After that bomb blast, I ached in more places than I could list. So I pulled my narrow orange plastic vial out of the manila envelope.

"What's that?" Byzant's partner asked.

I shook out the last pill and gave Byzant the vial. "Doc knows I have it." To help swallow the pill, I sipped some coffee.

Byzant held the vial's top and bottom between his straight

thumb and forefinger. Seemed to read every word. Then he set it on the arm of his chair.

Before they could get any more out of me, Albert and a law-yer from the D.A.'s office got there together. Byzant gave out copies of the police reports and everyone sat quietly while they read.

The interrogation room was hardly big enough for chairs for the five of us. Straight backs, hard seats. Mr. Dingleberry, as I thought of him, from the D.A.'s office, wore what looked like the day before's shirt. He hadn't shaved all weekend. He probably took notes to keep from falling back to sleep.

Albert and I wore jeans and sport shirts. Mine were a little holey. After he finished the reports, Albert advised me not to say a word. No problem there.

He wagged the police reports. "What do you end up charging my client with?"

Byzant said, "For starters, we're thinking about arson and breaking and—"

"Arson?" I spurted.

Albert stretched his arm across my chest and repeated it. My freedom seemed to be at stake, so I listened carefully.

Byzant read, " 'Using an incendiary object or device, suspect tried to ignite a fire at an address he claims as his residence. Then said object or device backfired, apparently exploding.' "

Albert turned to me.

Who needed to worry about cops when they were that stupid? "I came home, found a football on my porch. It blew up when I tried to move it."

Albert turned to the guy from the D.A.'s office, Mr. Dingle-berry. "My client seems to be the victim here."

Dingleberry shrugged while he flipped through the reports from Byzant.

Albert talked reality. "Name the magistrate who would set a bail beyond Mr. Arkwright's means. On attempted arson? The paycheck the man's missing for not playing in yesterday's scab game is more than your yearly salary."

Dingleberry said, "There's always the risk he could flee."

"Flee where? Soon as this strike's settled, he'll be on national TV every Sunday. What do you expect Mr. Arkwright to give you tonight you can't get at deposition? I assure you he will be extremely forthright and cooperative. But tonight, let him go home to get a little sleep."

"Aw, I wish I could," Byzant said. "But we got his verbal confession to breaking and entering. He makes claims that, if true, implicate him directly in grand larceny, withholding evidence, obstruction of justice, et cetera."

Frowning, Albert turned to me. Such a pessimist.

I repeated what Byzant had wormed out of me. "I let myself into Josh Nachman's office at Reading, Inc., where I'm on the board of directors. And I borrowed a little material to review for the next meeting."

After a pause, Byzant urged me on. "Tell him, 'little material.' "

"I took a file cabinet."

"The whole thing?" Albert asked.

"Come on. It was bolted to the floor."

Byzant asked, "What did you use to free said file cabinet?"

"Tire iron."

Albert winced. "You told them this after they read your rights?"

"How bad is it?"

Albert gave me one of those looks he gave during my salary negotiations when I said something stupid. Shut me right up. He played the game to the max. "It seems you're down thirty-five to nothing late in the fourth quarter deep in your own territory, and there's nothing but shit between you and the goal line."

Dingleberry looked to Albert with wide eyes and half a smile. "Well put, counselor."

I asked Albert, "What about I tell them everything in exchange for which they give me nothing?"

"What?"

"I'll make bail in the morning. What's the big deal? Meanwhile, I haven't done anything wrong. What I've learned will help them, not harm me."

"Anything you have to say can wait for a deposition, for cooler heads."

"Not if Josh blows me up first. Albert, I'm here to file a complaint."

Byzant warned, "But you have to tell us everything."

I would have liked to leave out Cramer, but why not tell them everything? "Albert, I want to help remove their suspicions and get them pointed toward Josh."

Albert kept trying to earn his dollar. "As long as you relay it through me and I get to characterize it."

Byzant gave Albert a tape recorder that he could turn on and off. I reported everything I'd done minute by minute since leaving Sister Charlayne's. Albert put it all into lawyerese for Dingleberry, Byzant, and his partner.

Lona's performance at my house, they already knew about.

To prove myself, I took the second note out of my manila envelope and read it aloud.

Byzant glanced at it and set it under the pill vial. Then he looked carefully at everything else in that envelope.

I lied only a little bit about how Cramer had urged me to go to the cops and how she warned how much trouble I would be in if I didn't. She wasn't my favorite person, but she had helped a lot. No sense getting her in trouble, too.

They made me call Cramer—way after midnight, mind you, on the night I'd been too exhausted to call her four hours earlier. Keeping my voice as cold as I could, I asked her to meet the cops at Artists Gallery. Whatever she heard in my voice, she agreed immediately.

Byzant sent a couple of uniforms to get the battered file cabinet, the files, the Tandy, the multiplexer, and the floppy disk.

After they left, I asked, "What are you going to do about Josh?"

"What about him?" Byzant asked. "If we did to you what you did to him, an esteemed attorney"—he nodded toward Albert—"would slap a civil rights suit on us fast."

"What did I do?"

"You allege that you strong-armed Mr. Nachman at Rich Stadium this afternoon."

I looked high on the walls and ceiling. "I walked into this building in handcuffs. I'm not exactly free to leave. My every word is being recorded. Two lawyers are taking notes. No doubt someone's watching through that window. This is not strong-arming?"

"Not legally," Byzant said.

"Then what is this?"

"A chat."

I asked, "What about Josh's bookie box?"

"You say it's his. But say we find it where you last put it. That makes it yours."

"What about the boards I knocked off the concrete base? They'll match the floorboards in Josh's office."

"You already admitted breaking into his office and smashing up the floor. Did you take a picture of the file cabinet? Do you have any witnesses can place it in that office? You're in trouble, son."

"If you show it at Reading, Inc., they can identify it."

Albert said, "And Josh's defense team visits offices all over town. They find the same style and color of file cabinet. In court, ask your witness to tell the difference between them."

Byzant added, "The difference other than the tire iron and drill you took to the one you claim you burgled from Josh's office."

"However." Albert had dark, baggy eyes. He slowly turned them on Byzant. "In fairness, you should let me tell him." He waited.

Byzant rubbed his cheek back and forth. His whiskers scraped. Aubrey Stennis must have showed him the same stars-kaboom note I had, because Byzant hadn't mentioned it after his first glance.

"Tell me what?"

Byzant nodded.

"Jimmy and Eddie del." Albert took his usual time. "They got blown up tonight, too."

"What?"

"They're dead." Albert pointed his arthritic forefinger toward the nut's note on Byzant's chair arm. "Kaboom."

* * *

The uniformed cops came back with the hardware for me to identify. They had the hard disk and Josh's one floppy but not the backups. Good old Cramer. The cops' computer wiz came in. After spotting the voice synthesizer chip right off, he asked me a few questions about the directories and the hidden files to save himself some time.

Before magistrate's court a couple hours later, I dozed in a holding pen. The rest of the night's catch ate cold cereal and Kool-Aid. Called it breakfast.

In court, the cops' computer wiz confirmed everything about Josh's voice messaging system I'd told Byzant. Hey, it was all written out on Cramer's yellow legal sheets. Dingleberry kept up his end and asked for five thousand dollars' bail.

So Byzant had to let me go, but he made it clear he didn't want to.

"Hey, I gave you a big jump on Shrimp's murder," I said.

That didn't seem to excite Byzant. He gave lessons. "No more holding on to notes for longer than it takes to dial a phone. No more amateur detective. And remember that judge's order: no leaving this jurisdiction without my permission."

As soon as I got into Albert's Volvo, he told me, "About nine last night, Jimmy starts his car, puts it in gear, and, well . . ."

"Kaboom."

He nodded. "Eddie del was in the passenger seat."

"It was quick?"

"Very."

"It must have been bigger than the one in the football."

"Much bigger. But the bomb squad's still sorting it out."

Albert's top-of-the-line Volvo had plush leather seats. Like a live wire, I slammed my elbows back into the leather. Again and again. Doing no harm, but thinking about doing some. Albert kept quiet until I stopped.

"Last time I saw them, they'd just hassled this picket outside the stadium."

"The picket complained to the cops and they took Jimmy and Eddie del to the station. Orchard Park."

"The cops arrested them?"

"They were in custody about five hours. An officer drove them back to the stadium, where they'd both come in Jimmy's car. They got into the car and gonzo. Officer saw the whole thing in his rearview."

"The picket accounted for?"

"Either a cop or a nurse had an eye on him all afternoon."

We drove back to Albert's house in silence, except for my furious breathing. I knew that Albert lived alone—wife dead, children grown and gone. But I'd never been to his house. Turned out that he lived in a sprawling hacienda in Eggertsville. Very suburban, very sterile. But very safe.

Albert offered a bed.

"No, thanks."

"It's no trouble."

"Nah. I need to sit quiet a bit and think."

"Make yourself at home." He limply waved his hand. "Kitchen, et cetera. I'm going to take a shower and go to work."

I made a pot of herb tea and sat alone on the couch in the family room. On the UB station, I listened to my buddy Vic Loveland, who billed himself "your communicator and your navigator." In the background, a mellow Charlie Mingus and friends were playing my tune. A dirge, as it turned out.

I did a lot of communicating but not much navigating.

The nut had killed three of my teammates. I didn't need a formal declaration of war. All I needed to do was listen to my heart. And it was pumping tha-wumpa tha-wumpa tha-wumpa.

The stupid idiot. Bad enough having the Byzants on his trail, no doubt. But after killing Shrimp, Jimmy Roma, and Eddie del Greco, he'd have all the Bills and most of the rest of the NFL.

Second night running, practically no sleep. By Monday noon, I had a very short list. Two places to go. Lona's. Sister Charlayne's.

And, of course, I had my usual Monday three-o'clock checkup

with Dr. Harvey Laurel. I needed him to write me another codeine scrip.

I turned off my navigator and lay on the couch.

Time out.

When I woke not long after two, Albert had laid a blanket over me. He'd taped a note to it: "See you and H.L. at 3, my office." Did I have a choice? I yawned and wandered off toward the bathroom.

My parka a bit ragged and holey, I dressed in Albert's pea coat and a dark blue knit cap. I flipped the collar up and rolled the cap low. At the Rite Aid, I bought sunglasses and a *Buffalo News*.

Albert gave sound advice: stay away from your house; stay away from your Jeep. I could rent a car, but then I thought about my short list. As easy for me to catch the bus to the Metro station and take the train downtown.

In the front car, I sat frozen, eyes buried in the paper. Page A-1, the bastards ran a photo of a burned-out 1990 Mercedes. Looked like a convertible, but I knew different. It belonged to Jimmy Roma. Sunday afternoon, while Jimmy, Eddie del, and I leaned against it talking about Shrimp, had the bomb been in place? Underneath? Inside?

In that car, said the *News*, Jimmy and Eddie del "died instantaneously" when a "bomb" blew up. A construction worker's TNT? An Army Reservist's land mine? What made it go off? The cops hadn't told the reporter and she didn't speculate.

So how could I find out? Albert was spending the P.M. calling in his chits at various cop shops. Maybe he'd have more when I got to his office.

"Died instantaneously." Six syllables, so "instantaneously" had to be hiding something. A Mercedes is a solidly built car. The top was gone and the seats were gone. What happened to Jimmy and Eddie del?

Did the cops find the car seats transported elsewhere, intact? Or did they find lint and scraps of charred leather and sharp bits of spring?

Don't do that to my teammates. Okay? Got that?

With or without the cops' help, I was going to stop that nut.

At Theater Station, I got off the train. A gusty wind slapped my cheek with rain. The cold made me huddle into Albert's pea coat. Helped by my cane, I marched, raging, down Main Street to the bank building where Albert held court.

* * *

Albert thought I should take a vacation. He always had my long-term monetary health at heart.

Harvey poked around. The two vertebrae were fusing perfectly. The bomb had left only superficial cuts. The puncture wound in my thigh would heal fast. He thought I should go back to work. He always had my long-term physical health at heart.

And Gus? "Find the joker. Hand him his dick before he kills again. May make him think twice about what you be handin' him next." Gus always had my long-term mental health at heart.

After leaving Albert's, I took the Metro back up to Allen/Hospital Station and walked over to Irving Place. Lona lived a couple of houses up. The last I'd seen her had been Saturday night after I drove her home.

And there I was, late Monday afternoon, back already. But not on an affair of the heart. Nor did I intend to accuse her of slashing Ronnie's paintings.

I stood in the drizzle and knocked on Lona's door. She took one look and started to shut it on me.

"Lona."

She opened it again. "Santa? I didn't recognize—"

"Can I come in?"

Her voice shot right up. "You son of a—"

"About your dad."

"—bitch." She let the word trail off. "Daddy?" But she let me in. She looked and smelled ready to go out on a date.

She didn't sit or ask me to. We stood in the living room while I pointed to the *News* photo of Jimmy's charred Mercedes.

She sniffled and carefully dabbed at the inside corners of her eyes. "What a horrible way to, to . . ."

Catch her off-guard. "Did I hear you right on Saturday?"

A quick, squinty look. A tilt of her head.

"You slept with Shrimp last spring?"

Chin up. That haughty raised lip of hers. "Yes."

"Anyone else?"

Another quick change. Nostrils flaring as though I'd let out a long greasy fart.

"You slept with any Bills other than Shrimp, Jimmy, and me?"

"You jock-jerks still keeping score? Wanna know which positions we played? Who scored the touchdowns?"

"Answer me. Anyone else?"

She started spitting out names. Greg Bowsk and every other teammate she could think of. Then she got to Alex Lamar and the Puritans. Right.

Going nowhere, I asked, "Who does your dad like least in the world?"

"Daddy?"

I asked again and she ticked off a few. I'd heard most of them before. But one made me stop her. "Harvey 'the Worm' Laurel."

"Harvey? I didn't think they even knew each other."

"Yes. Daddy saw him when we first came to Buffalo."

"So it's a malpractice thing?"

"What do you want to know about Daddy?"

I told her what I suspected: a bookie, no doubt losing a fortune because no one would bet on scab football games.

"What?" Her face got red.

"Who knows who that'd drive him to kill?"

"Kill?" She started breathing deeply, chest heaving. We'd never had an argument where I hadn't outtalked her. So that time she didn't even try.

Letting out a banshee's wail, teeth gnashing, she came at me with both fists and her pointy heels.

I'd had a lot of practice keeping at bay folks a lot larger and more motivated than she. But she still got a couple good licks in on my shin.

I heard a sharp knocking on the door to the rhythm of "Shave an' a haircut—two bits." Lona kept on flailing and wailing. Then the knocking came louder. That stopped her. Her date?

Taking the opportunity, I opened the door and slipped out.

Guess who knocked? Che Guevara, the guy who played bass in the house quartet we heard on Saturday night at the Blue Note.

Fine by me. Let him start learning to deal with her rages.

The Harvey Laurel idea wasn't going anywhere. Josh thought everyone on Lona's list, including Harvey, owed him something. I needed someone Josh owed something to.

But I knew this: Shrimp, Jimmy, and I had something in common other than being teammates. Lona. Who had a jealous dad.

*   *   *

I took the Metro up to Utica and then the 12A bus east. A couple of blocks' walk to Reading, Inc. Most of the students had day jobs, so Reading, Inc., was busiest in the evening. Sister Charlayne got there every morning early to answer the phone and do her administrative work. She stayed until the last tutor and student left late at night.

When I arrived, she was explaining the phonic system to a new student. She liked all new students' first couple of lessons to be with her. She could explain Reading, Inc., assess their needs, and assign them the most effective tutor.

I told her I'd wait. I wandered down the hall, where I heard noise. At the end of the hall was a brand-new unpainted door to the storage room. They hopped right to it, didn't they?

The noise came from Josh's office, so I opened the door, also brand-new. All but the desk I'd gashed was gone. The dusty room was covered in thick, paint-splattered plastic. Guys were stripping the walls and tearing out most of the floor. It wasn't a crime scene. Who had reported one? Another couple of hours and no one would know that either the file cabinet or I had ever been there.

I shut the door and went back to the front. Then Sister Charlayne led me to her office, the one before Josh's.

She pulled two plastic tubs out of the little refrigerator on the bookshelf. The one tub had a green salad, the other cottage cheese and chunks of pineapple. "Care for anything?"

"No, thanks." I shut the door and sat down.

She sat behind her desk. While she closed her eyes a moment

to say grace, I stared. She wore her padded-shoulders, floppy-tie uniform. Not a woman much for long nails. But that evening she wore eye makeup. She looked up at me. Instead of concealing, the makeup drew attention to puffy skin and bleary whites. "You did a lot of damage in here Saturday night."

"Not so you have to tear up the floor and totally remodel."

"I'm not talking about that damage. I'm talking about the damage even you can't pay to repair." She and Josh must have had a long, hard night.

"Is Josh here?"

"No." She fished a silver fork out of her pencil jar. "What do you want to do to him now?"

"To him? I almost got blown up last night. By him."

She lowered her eyes. "I pray for your health and safety."

"I told the cops all I know."

"Not the one who was here."

"They've been here already?"

She poked her salad. "At noon."

"Did this cop try very hard?"

"No." A nod toward Josh's office. "The workmen were at lunch. The officer asked if we'd been having trouble lately. I said no. Other than you, that's true. Praise the Lord."

"Oh, thanks."

"That's what the officer said. He said thanks and give us a call. Wasn't in the building two minutes."

What a neighborhood. "A guy wearing a uniform?"

"Yes." She stabbed a tomato slice and put it into her mouth.

While she ate, I told a short version, the same story I had told Lona and my guys. The same story I had told Byzant and Dingleberry.

Except for the theory about all of Lona's dead boyfriends. Eddie del hadn't been in Lona's bed far as I knew. And even for Shrimp I had only the claim by a spurned Lona. Could I assume Josh knew about every man his daughter slept with? No.

Too flimsy for me.

After Sister Charlayne swallowed, she looked up. Silent, but her jawline was fluttering.

I explained her role. Busy teacher and administrator. Dutiful wife. The success of Reading, Inc. So easy to look the other way.

When I got done, she asked, "Is that why you came here, to bear false witness?"

"No. I came here because I believe someone has something bad enough on Josh to persuade him to keep an electronic bookie at arm's length. My guess is Josh gets paid enough to keep Reading, Inc., going. Perhaps even to murder when the strike messes it all up."

She jumped to it faster than even Lona had. I admired the loyalty Josh inspired in his wife and daughter. Where Lona screamed, Sister Charlayne started quoting relevant Scripture. Commandments and proverbs and Christ's parables.

To stop her, I folded my *News* to the picture, put it on her desk. "My teammates, Sister. Look at this charred hulk. Blew them to bits."

She put her hands together to pray. Bowed her head.

"And I believe you know who planted that bomb. If I can figure out who that someone is, then Josh is in much less trouble. So why don't you just tell me?"

She stood and gave me that stare, the one that reminded me she'd been a nun most of her adult life. "You're ruining many lives, chiefly your own. But God loves you, young man. Even you. Now get out of here."

*   *   *

Time to blare it from the rooftops. I found a phone book in a laundromat around the corner from Reading, Inc. No Makepeaces in it, John or otherwise.

I called the *News* and asked for Stan, a guy who covered the Bills. I was one of his "sources." It always made me chuckle to read one of my tidbits paraphrased, quotation marks around it. But I thought he was the best writer on the paper, and I told him so every time we talked.

"Thanks, Santa. Your usual gracious self. What can I do for you? Thinking about coming in? Out of the rain?"

"It's not raining in this part of—"

"I meant, thinking about rejoining the Bills? I bet you'd've had six interceptions yesterday. The Colts' quarterback lobbed softballs. Receivers were a joke."

I knew not to take his bait. Not unless I wanted to see it, misquoted, out of context, on page D-1 the next day. "John Makepeace. He work there?"

"On the *News*? We'd like him to. Right now he's a stringer. He does maybe one long article a week."

"What's he cover?"

"Whatever we can't spare someone for. What we like to cover when we can do it cheap."

"And he's cheap?"

"He's cheap."

"He could get on full-time?"

"Our next opening, I assure you. He's a good writer."

"So how does he support himself? No real job?"

"He teaches at Agassiz Institute." A local college.

I gave him the number of the laundromat's pay phone. "Have him call me. I'll wait here half an hour. After that, have him call Albert." I gave him that number.

"Wait a sec, Santa. This is strike news? You can tell me."

"No, Makepeace's been patient with me. Polite. For some reason, I kinda like the guy. The best thing to do now is get a front-page spread. And it's Makepeace's story."

"Is it hot?"

"Hot enough that if he does it right, he'll win an award."

"For what?"

"Investigative journalism."

I could hear him panting. "Now that doesn't make sense. If you like my writing as much as you say. And it's my—"

I hung up. It's because I don't like you as a person, I didn't say. And your present line of bullshit is an example of why.

On the laundromat's wooden bench, I settled in to wait. Hadn't even unbuttoned Albert's pea coat when the phone rang. "Hello?"

"Santa? You ready to talk?"

I told him where to pick me up. "How long will it take you?"

"I have my coat on and I'm fumbling for my car keys."

In no time, Makepeace got from wherever to the deep East Side. He drove a black 1993 Grand Prix. Not bad for a college prof.

He was tall, thin, and pleasant-looking, as best I could tell. "Damn shame about Jimmy and Eddie."

I grunted.

"Doesn't it piss you off?"

"I'm here talking to you, ain't I?"

At Main Street, he turned left and headed for downtown. I started telling him.

He didn't say a word until we stopped at the light next to the Summer Street Metro station. "I was going downtown, but I don't need any editor over my shoulder at this point. They'd get some front-page guy to write it. Pay me a kill fee. You know anywhere close to get to a word processor?"

"My house is out. Any of my teammates'. Your house?"

He shook his head. "Too far." Then he snapped his fingers. "Here's an idea. Total privacy."

He made a U-turn and drove back up Main Street. At Canisius, he turned into the old Mount St. Joe's parking lot, which was the back way into the Agassiz Institute, where he taught.

The college had only a couple buildings. In the basement of the main building, he led me to an office. Tiny and cluttered. But it had a word processor and a tape recorder.

He snapped on the light and took off his trench coat. He was wearing slip-ons, pleated wool trousers, and a crew-neck sweater in pastel blues and pinks. No socks or shirt. He pushed both sweater sleeves up to his elbows. Gold watch on a loose chain around his skinny right wrist. Very European haircut. Lona's type indeed. Would I be doing him a favor to encourage him? No.

The office had desks, phones, and clutter atop everything. Layout tables. They were laying black-and-white glossies into a book of poems. I read some and shuddered. Looked up: crowded bulletin boards. Concert posters on the rest of the wall space.

And did I have stories?

Before I recorded even a few, Makepeace broke the article into five: a teaser, full of rumors, for Tuesday's Sunrise. For the evening edition, the first of a three-parter based, but not solely, on my story. No names, please. The rest of the week, he'd get corroboration. And finally a Sunday wrap-up, the cops' response. Of course, his editors would probably see it differently.

He wrote the teaser right there. A couple hundred words using "allegedly" a lot. He told the world that a sports "terrorist" was "allegedly" holding Buffalo hostage. Where would he strike next? "According to sources." "An unnamed local man." "Reportedly connected to the NFL strike, currently in its fifteenth day."

When Makepeace finished the teaser, I proofread it. A couple of places, he waxed poetic about fear and death and Jimmy Roma's body. He predicted panic in the streets. Pointing to those parts, I suggested he lean on the delete key before his editor did.

He sighed, did as I suggested, and printed it out. "On any other story, my editors wouldn't run such a speculative piece. Not even the name of the main source. But when they hear this tape . . ." He held it up and shook his head.

In the student lounge, a small crowd was watching scab *Monday Night Football*. Makepeace led me to the college radio station. The DJ, playing a Neil Diamond tune for an empty cafeteria, was a slender girl, maybe twenty, who lit up a thousand-watt smile when Makepeace walked in. She tore off her headphones and ran to him, arms out. "John!"

He gave her a sideways hug and pressed a kiss into the top of her head. She backed off right away when she saw me.

"Oh, hello." She had a breathy little voice and a cute little face. Flat-chested, slim-waisted.

"Santa, meet Sally Hall." He looked at her. "He was reading your poems a bit ago."

I had, while he wrote. The poems were dreadful. Lots of four-syllable words. Lots of forced rhymes. Nary a concrete image. Sally looked up at me, full of hope.

Women looked at Greg Bowsk like that when they met. Sally must have looked at Makepeace the same way. Perhaps they spent late night after late night working on her poems at his house. Maybe when he dumped her, she'd be able to write a more specific poem. About pain.

On the WAIB equipment, Makepeace made a second copy of my tape. He put it in an envelope he addressed to his mom in the Catskills. On the way out of the building, he dropped it off at the mailroom.

I thought he was being paranoid.

Day
f i f t e e n

In Albert's office, where I spent the night, the fat leather sofa did not help my back.

At morning practice, only Greg Bowsk and ten other guys showed. Alex Lamar and the two remaining Puritans were mumbling about crossing. They called it "respect for authority."

Everyone had read Makepeace's teaser in the morning paper. Had any of them slept with Lona? I asked the only three she might possibly fancy. I mean, she did have standards. No, no, and no. Had they said yes, I would have warned them. But they already had plane tickets for far away.

The rest of the team had scattered to various vacation and hiding spots. Safe enough. Who could blame them?

John Makepeace and I spent the afternoon in Albert's sixteenth-floor office. Harvey dropped by to sign some papers but couldn't stay. Gus popped in and out, running errands on Main Street.

Makepeace sat at the fancy computer. He made notes when he wasn't on another line trying to second-source my story as much as he could.

Albert and I sat in stuffed chairs across his glass table. It held a tall cut-glass vase stuffed with ferns and Albert's favorite flower, day lilies. A skinny sixty-year-old, Albert wore a white shirt, an off-red silk tie, and the regulation gray three-piece. He had short gray hair, a short-cropped gray beard, and huge bags under his eyes.

I told Albert about my Lona's boyfriends idea.

Way too often, Albert had gone to the Caribbean to roast his bronzed, creased skin. But not his mind. Quickly, he poked holes. "What about Eddie del Greco? One of Lona's lovers?"

"Not that I know."

"Are you sure about Shrimp?"

"I have only Lona's word for it. Why would she lie?"

"To get back at you with someone who can't deny it."

"Good point." I'd pursue that on my own.

The gray vest wrinkled deeply over Albert's flat belly. He had more. "Does Nachman keep track? Does Lona tell him about every single boyfriend?"

"I'd thought of that problem."

"Hmmpf." By which Albert meant, so much for my crazy idea. "Nachman's no killer, not in my opinion."

Albert had a speaker phone, same model as the one in my studio, so we all could hear. The wire services had picked up Makepeace's article. Sportswriters from every NFL city called. My teammates, the union guys, and my friends around the league loved the story. I got tears and outrage over Shrimp, Jimmy, and Eddie del. Curses and threats.

Some of the old guys offered to come to Buffalo, assuring me that no one would get near me again. We would play ring around Santa. But I had another play in mind: the free safety blitz. I was on my own on that one.

I poked the numbers for my next call: union HQ in Virginia. Lance Bishop, Pres., said he'd met with the twenty-eight player reps all night. Dead players piling up in Buffalo, who was next? More players? Owners? Fans? The reps gave Lance the okay to soften the union's stance on free agency.

Lance wanted to talk about my owner. "Danny Hanks? He's flipping out. He called the governor of New York. He tried to call the White House. Send in the militia! Do something! They're killing my team! Do anything!"

Made me chuckle.

Lance wanted Albert and me to fly to the next bargaining session to tell my story in person. "Santa, you'll bring the owners to their knees."

"But won't that be the owners' line? That the killings will do the same—bring us to our knees?"

"You should hear Danny Hanks howl those very words."

"So ask it this way. Shouldn't it bring all of us to our knees—owners and players?"

A pause. "I hear you, man."

"So best thing for me is stay low. Best thing for you, settle this strike. Right now. You can tell my story as well as I can."

"It's better from someone on the spot. What about Albert comes down by himself?"

I looked at him.

He nodded. "I can't leave until tomorrow."

"Whenever," Lance said. "Just call my girl. I'll have a car waiting at Dulles." He hung up.

John Makepeace turned in his chair. "So that's Lance Bishop's reaction."

"Yeah. He may be too into this strike to see the big picture."

Albert said, "Dead people and labor strikes are no strangers to each other, Santa. You may be the one not seeing the big picture. People will literally kill for a steady paycheck." He tapped his outstretched fingers together, ready to give me his best, considered advice.

I waited.

"Take the next plane to Jamaica until this strike is over. You love it there." You'd have thought Albert knew me better.

"I'll think about it."

"Do it."

I stared at him. Neither of us mentioned the judge's order. Then I turned to Makepeace. "I'm done for the day. You want to go get some Greek? I want to know what you've been hearing on the phones."

"About what?"

"How the good citizens of Buffalo reacted to your article."

"I can tell you in one word. Petrified. Close to panic." Just like my teammates.

Fifteen minutes later, Makepeace and I rode up Elmwood in his Grand Prix. He had pale blue eyes and light brown hair to below his ears. Very easy to talk to. Why had I taken such a liking to him?

On a scale of handsome to pretty, he was closer to pretty. I could see why the coeds took every chance to hug him. I trusted him about as far as I trusted any reporter, the difference being that he let me read his articles before he submitted them. Rare indeed.

"What about the Acropolis?" he asked. We were waiting for a green light at Utica Street.

"Huh?" The guy I saw out the window made me lose my train of thought.

"Santa?"

Across Utica was a Marine Midland branch bank. It had a popular money machine. For a while after five o'clock there was usually a line, as on that Tuesday evening. And there in the line stood Dingleberry.

"Lookee there."

"What?" Makepeace asked.

"My friend the prosecutor. Dingleberry."

"Whoa. Look who's standing beside him. Mouse talking to cat."

"Yes, indeed," I said. "Deep in conversation. Mr. Josh Nachman. When the bad guys are talking to the cops—"

"He's a lawyer."

"When Dingleberry's talking to the guilty party and the guilty party doesn't have his own lawyer present, then the Dingle's a cop. A very sly one."

The light changed and the driver behind us honked.

"Pull over there." After the Grand Prix stopped, I fiddled the rearview mirror until I could see Josh and Dingleberry. "My guess is the Dingle knows almost as much as Byzant."

Makepeace flipped open his little note pad. "His name again?"

"Hmmm, not sure. When we got intro'd, I had other things on my mind. I call him Dingleberry."

"What's that? Football talk?"

"A dingleberry is that little ball of shit that dries in your ass hairs and stings when you pull it out. Why don't you huddle out of the cold and listen hard."

They stood second and third in line by the time Makepeace nestled near them against a low brick wall. Josh, much shorter, wore a gray coat. I put Dingleberry in his early thirties, say five years out of law school.

They went into the booth together and kept chattering. Then they shook hands before they went separate ways.

Makepeace hurried to his Grand Prix. "Not much. A word here and there from Nachman. They both got cash and didn't pass anything between them, far as I could see. One thing from the D.A. guy. Only time he raised his voice. 'I can't wait for the cops to bring me cases.' Emphasis on 'cops.' And his first name, when they shook. 'Soon, Wayne,' was how Josh left him."

"Making progress," I said. "Thanks."

We followed Josh's car down Elmwood and east on North Street two blocks to Main. He turned right into the parking lot of the Anchor Bar. Its sign read, "Where Mama Teressa served the first Buffalo chicken wing."

I was a regular, though not during the season, when I ate carbohydrates. Mama Teressa once snapped me arm in arm with Frank, her husband. She had me sign a glossy blowup, then she framed it and put me on the wall between Milton Berle and Frank and Miles Davis and Frank.

"My, don't I get lucky. Stop," I said to Makepeace.

He pulled in behind Josh. "What are you going to—"

I got out of the Grand Prix, so I didn't hear the rest. Leaning on my cane, I pretended I was leaving the bar. Walking toward Josh, I kept my head down. When we got close, I looked up. Appeared startled. "Well, lookee who."

He kept walking.

"Hey, bozo," I called.

"Yes?" Josh looked as though someone was squeezing his internal organs. He smelled of alcohol. "You? Go back to work." His face was flushed. His sparse hair needed combing.

"Josh, your plan's working. Guys are crossing the line as we speak. But I want to know why Byzant doesn't take me seriously. Why not give you the once-over in that little room? The whole tape-recorder and good-guy-bad-guy number like I got."

"Been there twice."

That stopped me. It didn't say Josh wasn't a killer. It did say why Byzant wasn't doing it my way. He'd already done it. When?

Josh was breathing heavily. "You stay away from my little girl."

"I haven't gone—"

"Yesterday!" he shouted.

"I asked her a few questions."

"Hit her when she's down? Heartbroken? Won't get away with treating my girl like that."

"Like what?"

"See how fast you graces turn to new whores! Another man's daughter. Is your heart so hardened by sin?"

"By sin?" Those "graces" again. Who were they? He'd babbled about them on Sunday at Rich Stadium. And another man's daughter? Cramer?

He pointed a finger. "Fornication. Lies. Godlessness. Those rules minister well to humanity's eternal needs, young man. A reason they last so long."

"You sure know a lot of big words, Josh."

He smiled. At least, he tried. He opened his mouth and bared his teeth. "You stuffed that football, knocked out that window, set the fuse, and threw it through."

Wow, the details. Had he been watching? Or had Dingleberry told him at the bank? "Byzant thinks I put the nicotine into the Kahlúa, too?"

"He's going to put you away for a long time."

"Won't that hamper your efforts to kill me?"

"Huh! They'll know where you are." He turned away.

"Since you killed my teammates—"

That made him wheel around, mist in what was left of his hair. "Does this not expose you for what you are? You graces let your own die rather than restore what is ours. Stop the strike!"

"You stop killing."

"No. I have better things to do tonight."

"What? Like kill the rest of ten?"

That set him off. His belly began quivering. "Well put, Santa." Then his head began shaking. His eyebrows went up up up. A wide grin spread over his face.

"Well put." He clapped me on the shoulder and walked in the drizzle toward the bar's front door.

"Josh, I can help."

He called over his shoulder. "No, you can't."

"I know the whole story."

"No, you don't. No, sir, you don't." He opened the red door and walked in.

In that mind, sweaty, fevered, slurring, Josh wouldn't last two questions into any confirmation hearings in Albany. I could see him getting off a murder charge, too. By reason of insanity.

*　　*　　*

I figured to stop by Cramer's. But much as I'd taken a liking to Makepeace, that didn't make us running buddies. I had him drop me off on Elmwood on his way to teach his evening class. At Village Green, the big bookstore, I bought the Boston, New York, and D.C. papers. Even a day late, they had better strike stories than the *Buffalo News.*

Opening the *Globe,* the others tucked under my arm, I strolled up Elmwood. The sidewalks were crowded but not so that I couldn't read while I walked. A block before I needed to, I turned left at the grocer's on the corner of Delavan. Past the bus stop, along the windowless side wall of the grocer's, the crowds were gone. Except for two men who rushed up behind me.

"Arkwright," a voice said. "Hold on there."

Papers flew as each grabbed one of my arms. Byzant and partner. But not the same partner as on Sunday night.

My heart began thumping hard. "Evening, officers." Take them both on? Cut and run? I could probably hobble faster than they could sprint.

They helped me lean into the wall, arms spread, palms flat. "Spread your legs." Byzant, in coat, tie, and topcoat, helped me with his left shoe.

My heart started slowing. Wait them out, it told me. They have the guns and the badges.

Byzant was checking under my collar and every buttonhole. A pat-down? What was he checking for, fabric and stitching?

"Any weapon that small won't do you much harm."

Nothing. He kept feeling.

"What're you looking for? A microphone? A radio transmitter?"

"Quiet, asshole." Byzant jangled a set of handcuffs. "Cuff him."

The partner was downright clumsy at it.

"C'mon, man. That's much too tight."

"Sorry." He loosened them. Sorry? Since when did a cop say sorry while he arrested you?

I tried to crane around to get a better look at the partner. He was much younger and much larger than Sunday's. Dressed in a sweater and jacket. Grinning, he gave me a little wave. I'd seen that grin and wave often: a Bills fan.

"Hiya, Santa," as though he'd known me half his life.

After relieving me of my wallet, Byzant grabbed my neck and forced my face against the cold brick.

What Byzant did next I can guess only from what I heard. "I smelled a controlled substance on your garments," he said.

"How do you know that?"

"My training and experience." The last word was a little muffled. He stuck a hand into the right pocket of my jacket. "And what do we have here?"

"Wow." The partner said it like a rookie, truly surprised.

I tried to twist around, but the partner had his hand on my lower back only inches above my cut.

Byzant dangled a baggie. The seal had a blue line and a yellow line. You pressed them together, and the bag was airtight. In the baggie I saw an orange plastic pill vial. It had a label and a white snap-on lid.

One thing I knew for sure. Byzant had brought it with him. He held it to my eyes.

"Recognize this, Arkwright?"

"Yes indeed. It's the one I gave you two nights ago. I took the last pill while we were chatting. Remember you asked what it was and why I was taking it? The scrip can't be refilled, so I let you keep it."

The partner asked, "What do you think's in there, Captain?"

"We'll let the lab boys tell us that. Meanwhile, Mr. Arkwright is under arrest. Take him over to the car, Vinnie."

*   *   *

It wasn't any marked cruiser, just a beat-up old two-door. Vinnie drove.

Alone in the backseat, I considered an elaborate discussion of probable cause, or even the official reading of rights. Nah.

What about littering? The *Globe*, the *Times*, and the *Post*. Nah.

How had Byzant found me? Makepeace? Why? Maybe Josh had followed me back to Elmwood. Probably had a phone in his car to keep Byzant up to date.

I said to Byzant, "I'm only ten days out of surgery." The same ten days since he and I met. Give me surgery anytime. "Mind if I lie down?"

"Not at all. Go right ahead."

Put my head behind Vinnie and my feet behind Byzant? Then I could kick if I got a chance. No, I was better off with my head behind Byzant so I could talk to Vinnie. "You play college ball?"

He turned briefly to nod. "Two years."

"Running back?"

"I wish. My school's so small I's a defensive end."

"Injury put an end to it?" The odds were excellent.

"Our own guy fell on my knee."

"He did you a favor."

"What?"

"You get to like the applause. But the game takes years off your life."

"If you had it to do over?"

Good, I had him thinking. "It's been a lot of painful work, but it's been fun, too. Those Rich Stadium crowds give me goose bumps when they get going."

He flashed a proud grin. Great. He'd been in those crowds.

Byzant hadn't said a word. Didn't he realize I was getting Vinnie to lose his professional objectivity? Maybe he didn't care.

"But the real reason I'd do it over is the money."

Stopped for a light, Vinnie turned and gave a slow, wise nod.

"I mean, I've invested well. Bought the rest of my life free. I won't be leaving the kids enormous trust funds. But I never have to earn another dime. And that freedom makes it worthwhile."

A honk from behind interrupted me.

"Right," Byzant ordered.

Vinnie snapped around and turned the car right. Right?

I raised my torso enough to see Kleinhan's Music Hall on the driver's side. So we were on Porter Street headed toward the river. Conclusion: they weren't taking me downtown.

Vinnie made rolling stops going through the D'Youville College campus. At the next long stop, I rose again. Yup, Niagara Street. Straight ahead—the Peace Bridge and Ontario. No way they could sneak me handcuffed through Customs. I'd introduce myself and accuse Byzant of kidnapping and carrying drugs. Plenty of Bills fans in southern Ontario.

We'd have to make a choice when we got to Lake Erie. North toward Niagara Falls? Or south toward Orchard Park, where the Bills practiced and played, and beyond to Hamburg, Jack Kemp country? A dangerous jurisdiction for me if there were pills or pot in that vial.

But that was a very snaky route to Jack Kemp country from where we'd started back on Elmwood.

The front had two bucket seats. And down at the lower back of Byzant's seat was a little silver lever. After Byzant got out of the car, either he or I would lift that silver lever, and the front seat would drop forward so I could get out. It had a simple spring and release mechanism. If I didn't pull the lever and tried only to push the seat forward, I couldn't do it. Jimmy or Eddie del could have, but the seat would have needed major repairs.

When Vinnie started up the entrance ramp onto I-190, I said, "I have to move again. Bedsores, you know?"

Byzant sighed. "Go ahead."

It was easy. I put my back against the back of Byzant's bucket seat and slid down until my butt hit the floor and my calves rested on the backseat.

"Hey, what the—"

My hands, cuffed behind me, found the silver lever. I pulled it up, releasing the front seat, and pushed my feet into the backseat. Because I had released the front bucket seat, I could straighten my body.

"You bwufwau—!" Byzant, folded in half beneath me, was shouting, but the shouting was muffled.

I didn't want to listen to him anyway.

Vinnie had driven halfway up the ramp to the Interstate, elevated through that part of town. "Hey, what'd you do that for?"

"Don't slow down, Vinnie." I could see through the back window the cars behind him on the ramp. In a couple of seconds he would be entering the stream of sixty-mile-per-hour traffic. But at the moment, he was going very slowly.

"Where were you taking me?"

Vinnie kept turning his head from me to the oncoming rush of traffic. "I don't know, Santa. Really, I don't."

He slowed down even more behind the car waiting to enter the Interstate. "Thanks, Vinnie. I'll send you tickets to the next home game after the strike." I had been groping for the door handle. It was very small, recessed into the door; luckily, the lock button was right beside it. Handcuffed, I could get out of the car only one way—feet first.

The driver behind us honked. The moment Vinnie hit the gas, I opened the car door. Pivoting on my hands, I pushed and out I went.

By the time my butt hit the concrete, Vinnie's car was gone. What choice did he have on an elevated highway in furious traffic?

I landed on my hands because I was using them to protect my recently fused vertebrae. I had the palms together, left hand down. I was afraid I'd broken a couple of little bones. My left hand burned. I could feel blood and strips of skin and cinders.

Running hard down the concrete ramp was not a wise thing to do, given my back. And given that Byzant didn't seem to be following. Some of the people in the cars I passed looked startled; others looked amused.

Byzant could come after me on foot, but he'd never catch up to me, even if I was handcuffed. If he got Vinnie to take the next exit, it'd be five minutes before they'd cruise back down Niagara Street. They couldn't know I'd be heading for Cramer's, so good luck.

The slow walk on shady West Side streets took me until six-thirty. Twice, I saw patrol cars. But the cops didn't see me.

*　　*　　*

Cramer McKensie lived on one of the cross streets north of Delavan. I kicked the door gently because I couldn't figure out how to knock. Even though the sun had set, I stood against the wall. Not good for Cramer's neighbors to see a gentleman caller in handcuffs on her porch.

The front door opened a crack. "Yes?"

"Sorry I didn't call first, but—"

The front door opened wide. "I thought I'd hear from you after those cops took that computer stuff. That was two nights ago." She sounded more curious than angry.

"Did you give them the backups I made?"

"Course not. I brought them home." She stepped onto the porch. Her bosom stretched tight an oversized, baggy sweater. She was simply a lot of woman.

"Do you have a chisel and a mallet here?"

"What do you want to break into now?"

"Break out of." I turned my back.

"Handcuffs!" She said it so loud that she brought her hand to her mouth and looked at neighboring porches. Then she whispered it. "Handcuffs. And what happened to your pants? I mean, did you escape from prison? Don't they hurt?"

"Nah. Byzant's muscle man put them on me just an hour ago."

"Why?"

"Take them off and I'll tell you."

"I don't know. You look sorta cute all trussed up. And you look much more trustworthy."

I turned to the wall again. "Cramer."

She chuckled. "All right. C'mon. To the basement."

It was her studio. She painted rich people's portraits in an almost photographic style. It blended accuracy and flattery, near as I could tell from the three in progress. The fleshtones glowed.

She also welded frames for the portraits out of twisted, burnished metal rods and wires. Very distinctive, very handsome.

The position I had to hold was awkward, but she torched through the cuffs in about two minutes. While she threw my clothes into the machine, I went upstairs.

In the shower, I scrubbed out all the cinders imbedded in the back of my left hand. Then I put on some clothes she loaned me. Jeans—a bit hippy—and a sweater.

The antiseptic in her medicine cabinet stung something mighty. I tried to arrange the strips of skin as best I could. Then I covered it all with gauze and adhesive tape.

When I got to the kitchen, she stood at the stove, stirring something in a copper pot. "You hungry?"

"Yup."

At the refrigerator, I crushed ice in a plastic bag and used the rest of the adhesive tape to attach the bag to the back of my left hand. While she stirred, phone between cheek and shoulder, she talked to her dad, the good doctor. He told her we'd done everything we could for my hand. Go for X-rays right away.

"Did he ask how I hurt myself?"

"No. He recommended you go back to work. Failing that, go on vacation and take me along. He sounded busy." Our eyes met.

"Typical doctor, huh?" Of course, she'd say no if I asked.

107

"Oh, Father's been super these last six weeks since I moved to Buffalo. Hasn't said no to me yet."

At the kitchen table, Cramer set out chicken soup and a cream cheese on black bread sandwich. The soup was excellent, the sandwich so good I asked her where she bought the bread.

"I made it. So tell me."

I didn't omit a detail.

She asked a few questions but didn't comment until I brought the story up to her door. "You jumped out of the car?"

"Yes."

"While it was moving?"

"It was way below the speed limit."

"You sure do stupid things. Why not let the authorities take care of this?"

"The what? The who? Some nut—Josh, for instance—is killing my teammates. Byzant's picking me up tonight might lead a reasonable person to suspect that your 'authorities' haven't the foggiest. And why was that Vinnie character driving a beat-up old two-door?"

While I finished eating, Cramer got my clothes out of the dryer. I changed back into them.

We sat in her living room. I sipped tea, she sipped brandy. She showed me her sketches for remodeling the whole house, which it turned out Harvey owned.

"Looks like a big improvement."

"Thanks."

"Meanwhile, these walls look pretty bare. Why don't you put up your portraits?"

"I sell them all."

Not a problem I'd ever had. "Want one of my paintings?" A frown, so I added, "Don't worry, I didn't bring any more slides. You plan on doing all this work yourself?"

"I've done interiors before."

"If this football strike lasts, I may be looking for work. So let me know if you need any help."

She laughed. "And when I get done, Father will be able to charge the next tenant twice the rent he could now."

"Harvey never struck me as greedy."

"You've seen his house."

I shook my head. "We always meet in Albert's office or club."

"Well, if you saw it, you'd know. Father's greedy."

"Why do you call him Father?"

"I don't know what else to call him. Until six weeks ago, I hadn't seen him since I was a baby. My mother always called him 'your father.' My stepfather, her husband, was always 'Dad.' So that's what I always called Harvey in my mind: Father. He hasn't said not to."

"So what should I do about Josh?"

She held my gaze for a moment. "You're the authority." Big gray eyes.

"Doesn't mean I can't use some advice."

"I did have a thought." She tugged on her right earlobe and stuck out her lower lip. "Let's say Byzant's doing you a favor to get you out of harm's way because he can't arrest you legally."

"But what about—"

She held up a hand. "It's an assumption. Hear me out. Someone tries to kill you, you don't seem to care, and Byzant wants to stop a fourth murder. Another assumption: a fourth murder by Josh Nachman. Now, let's say Josh did the Kahlúa. Let's say he either set your bomb or had someone set it. That he bombed your teammate's car."

I nodded. "Yes."

"And he did that and ran the computer bookie and all the rest because someone's got something on him. He knows who that someone is."

"No question."

"Think his wife knows?"

I sipped my tea. "That's a toughie. She may well not, if only because she doesn't want to." I reminded Cramer of Charlayne's haggard, made-up eyes, the tremble in her hands. "In any case, I can't imagine she'd snitch on Josh."

"What about Lona?"

"I talked to her, remember? Only yesterday afternoon. Told her how much trouble her dad was in. How much she could help."

"You think she'd give away a family secret to a guy who recently broke her heart?"

"Good point. Any ideas?"

"Remember when you saw what happened to Ronnie's paintings, all slashed? We were assuming Lona did it, and you said she might have been so drunk she wouldn't even remember the next day? Why don't you take her somewhere, get her real drunk, then ask her what you want to know?"

"No, you try. She might open up to a stranger."

"Not me. I'm staying out of it."

You're already in it, lady. "Listen. We both get her drunk. Then you attack her father. Have a fight. As insulting as you can."

Cramer caught on right away. "Then you come in and take her side. That'll confuse her."

"The good-guy-bad-guy routine. Will you help?"

She chewed her lip. "Where would you do it? Some bar?"

"Too public."

"Your house?"

"Not if Byzant's out gunning for me. We could do it here."

"No way."

"You've got a great pretext. Call and say you saw her slides and want to talk about giving her a show at Artists Gallery. Here's the number." I wrote it down.

"No way. It's illegal to meddle with the cops' job."

"To obstruct. We're trying to help."

"That's how you see it. From your rather limited and peculiar point of view."

"What's limited is my income, thanks to this strike. What's peculiar is Bible-toting Josh Nachman being somehow involved in all this."

"Well, I won't do it."

"My teammates are dying."

She stared at me.

So I stared back. "And besides being teammates, we all have something else in common. We all slept with Lona."

"You're kidding."

"Well, Jimmy and I did, for sure. She told me about Shrimp Saturday night."

"And Eddie del Greco?"

"Probably just happened to be in the wrong place—Jimmy's car—at the wrong time."

She slowly closed her eyes. "All right. I'll help you." Opened them again. "Just this once. But it's already after seven."

"Middle of the afternoon for Lona. How much alcohol you got?"

"Plenty. The rest of this brandy. Then there's a whole three-liter box of wine in the pantry."

I laughed. "You want to get her drunk, not tipsy." I stood up. "Where're you going?"

"We need a bottle of her favorite, Stolichnaya, the one-point-seven-five-liter size. A couple liters of Coke to mix it with." I stopped at the front door.

"Yes?"

"Uh, Byzant got my wallet, my cash, my money card. Can you loan me thirty bucks?"

No time at all, I was back with the drink fixin's. Cramer said, "I don't know why I agreed to this stupidity. I obviously have nothing better to do."

"Did you call her?"

"She's coming around ten. Bringing slides of new work. She sounded excited. A little flattered. How long, you figure?"

I held up her brandy glass. "Keep this full of half vodka, half Coke. Toss in a slice of lime; she'll think you're an angel. Give her something salty to munch. Keep her talking about her work. She'll stay excited and breathless and thirsty."

"You can wait upstairs."

"Nah. I have people to see. About midnight, I'll call. Tell me if she's slurring, stumbling in midsentence. Keep track of how long between trips to the john. When she's going every quarter hour, you can start talking about her dad. And try to find out if she's slept with any other Bills."

"Wow. She drinks that much?"

I nodded. "Odds are she'll drop or throw at least one glass."

"What if she passes out?"

"Believe me, you cannot drink Lona Nachman under the table."

"I'll stick to Coke."

"Won't matter what you drink. If she starts speaking in circles, let her ramble. If she starts crying and feeling sorry for herself, milk it. All the terrible things her dad's done to her over the years. All the terrible things her faithless boyfriends have done. Try to connect them all."

"This is cruel, isn't it?"

Your idea, lady.

*　　*　　*

The Louis Agassiz Institute had a bright new student center and an old main building. A second building, very plain, had been built within my lifetime. And a sleek contemporary wing stretched between. Architecturally, a hodgepodge.

The small parking lot was carved out of a gently rising greensward. Beyond the lot, across the Scajaquada Expressway, Delaware Park stretched into fairways, tennis courts, a zoo, jogging tracks, boccie courts, pools, woods. To me, exercise centers, one and all, and I exploited them during the off-season.

I pulled Cramer's long Nissan flatbed into the Agassiz parking lot at a quarter to eight. The lot was full, as it had been the previous night when Makepeace brought me there to use the word processor in the basement. I cruised until I found Makepeace's black Grand Prix. Parked as close as I could.

At the info desk, I talked to a coed filing her nails. Roxanne, her nameplate said. "Evening. Can I do for you?" She had her hair cut short, combed forward. She probably hoped it made her look like Liza Minnelli. To me, it made her look like Napoleon.

"Hi. I'm looking for John Makepeace?"

She pointed her nail file to my left. "On that chart."

In yellow under the heading T/Th 6-8:05, I read, WR 260 Writing for Publication / Makepeace. Room 101.

"Where would room 101 be?"

She pointed. "Through those doors. Last room on the left."

What else did Makepeace teach? I studied the chart for his name. "If Makepeace is up here for only this one course, that's the only one he teaches?" It sounded like a stupid question.

But Roxanne had to think. "He also advises student publications."

So the guy taught only Tuesday and Thursday nights. Made sure the newspaper editors didn't commit libel or run off with the fancy laser printer. Not exactly a labor-intensive job.

I hobbled down the central hall. After all, someone had told Byzant where to find me. If it hadn't been Josh, that left the guy who had dropped me off on Elmwood: Makepeace.

In the last room—shit. Gone. Two students lingered.

One looked way too serious and way too fat. His thin friend, taller than I, had curly hair and wore a dark suit, red tie. He recognized me: the double take, the stare. He didn't say anything right away, which usually meant he wouldn't say anything at all. A tactful fan was a gift.

"Makepeace let you guys out early?" I tried to keep my bandaged left hand out of sight.

The fat guy said, "He always lets us out early."

"Which way did he head?"

The tall guy said, "One looks for him in the cafeteria or in that room off the student lounge."

I learned from them that Makepeace was really a *News* reporter. He only taught part-time, they said, one, maybe two courses a semester.

So wait a minute. The *News* writer thought he was a teacher; the students thought he was a reporter.

What could he make, two thousand for each course? Make it four grand a year. Plus an article a week in the *News*? The guy had to live at home with his parents who fed him. To dress out of *GQ* and drive a '93 Grand Prix?

Maybe it was his big brother's hand-me-down clothes. Maybe it was his dad's Grand Prix. Maybe he had a trust fund.

Maybe not.

I hobbled out to the lot. The Grand Prix was gone. Shit. I should have waited in Cramer's truck and followed him home.

Just for the heck of it, I tried my charms on Roxanne. No, she couldn't give me any home address. Claimed she didn't have it.

Wandering, I spotted Sally the poet through the window in the door to room 115. The prof was thin, stooped, and gray. No wonder Sally looked so bored sitting there.

He wouldn't let his class out right after it began. So I went back to the library, where I'd seen Makepeace's tall student. The library clock said 8:20 P.M. The tall guy sat on a soft green leather couch between the two ranges of current magazines. He looked up but didn't say anything. Could I trust him? "You don't have a class?"

He held up his Writing for Publication text. "At home, the kids won't let me study. So I hang here an extra hour, do my homework."

I sat beside him. "When you think the strike's gonna end?"

"You should know better than I do."

I snorted. "I only know what I read in the papers."

"Can't believe them." The guy was getting a good education. "Listen, what I'm working on'll help end the strike quicker."

"Yeah? Won't matter much, all these guys crossing the line."

"Who?"

He ticked off a dozen household names, but still no Bills. "On the five-o'clock news. And they say—get this—they don't fear for their own lives. They fear for their families' lives. That no strike is worth it."

"Any of them mention Jimmy and Eddie del?"

"Yup."

To the point. "Is John Makepeace a good teacher?"

"Makepeace? He's super. Everyone likes him."

"Even the young ladies?"

"Oh, yes."

"Is he going out with what's-her-name? Sally, the DJ?"

"Sally Hall? I suppose so."

"You know where he lives?"

He shook his head. "I hear the women just show up. Some nights he ends up with a bunch over there, reading poetry and talking about books and ideas. They say he has a great house. You hear them bragging about it in the cafeteria before class."

"Yeah, but who's the last to leave? And at what hour?"

He shrugged. "Can't help you. I got the wife and kids, so no time to sit on Makepeace's floor looking goo-goo at him."

"Can you ask Sally where he lives?"

"Why don't you?"

"I don't want Makepeace to know I'm asking about him. I can trust you not to tell." I stared into his eyes. "But Sally . . ."

"I hear you, Santa."

"She's in room 115 down the hall. Think you can take a chair and go study near the door?"

He smiled broadly and stood up. "Where'll you be?"

"I saw an empty room full of computers upstairs. If I'm not there, I'll be right here, catching up on my reading." I pointed with my chin. "You have *Artforum* and *Art in America* at least."

Looking down at me, he started to speak. Then stopped. Then started again. "That was terrible about Roma and del Greco. And Shrimp."

"They'll catch the bastard."

He raised a fist. "Go Bills."

I thrust my thumb into the air.

In the computer lab, I borrowed a system utilities disk from one of the resident wizzes and went to work on the backups of Josh's data I'd brought from Cramer's. As I had at Artists Gallery, I found patterns to the numbers and matched these to the order in which the program asked for information.

Nothing incriminating about ANSERBAK, the voice messaging system stored on the hard disk. And the real gambling data—no doubt downloaded often from somewhere far away—was stored on an easily destroyed floppy disk.

Did all the big numbers stand for marbles? Matchsticks? If not, a bunch of money was passing through that bookie.

Because Cramer had given Josh's original to the cops, I made another backup and buried it deep in the lab's server. A couple copies under different names while I was at it. In that humongous hard drive, no one would notice or care. And I'd always know where to find them.

Then back to the library. In *Byte,* I found a display ad for ANSERBAK. Under a thousand bucks. About ten, the tall guy returned. He gave me John Makepeace's address on Ferry Street, the old east-west route from the depot to the dock.

Outside, walking toward Cramer's truck, I saw Sally, the DJ, walking through the lot. She wore a long, blood-red coat, open, its belt flapping behind her. She seemed in a rush.

I sat in Cramer's truck for a minute. Makepeace lived on Ferry. The night before—after I'd finally agreed to give Makepeace the story—we'd been driving down Main Street when he told me he wanted to go somewhere private. I ruled out my house and a bunch of other places.

That's when he thought of the Agassiz Institute. But from where we were at the time, his house on Ferry was closer. He'd told me his house was too far. But it wasn't.

As though I weren't already, that made me curious. I started Cramer's truck and drove off, thinking, thinking, thinking.

Makepeace's huge old house had a wide driveway running down the right side. No lights. I parked in front.

One man lived there alone? He must have someone come in and clean. Maybe all the coeds. It had to be his parents' place.

On the wide front porch, I found two mailboxes: Makepeace upper and no nameplate on the lower. No one answered either bell, so I walked down the driveway. No side doors. Past the house, the driveway opened onto almost a parking lot in front of a four-door garage.

Two cars, neither of them Makepeace's Grand Prix. One had a cold hood. The other, a blood-red 1990 Camaro, had a warm hood.

The house extended farther back than the house next to it. It looked patched, as though a staircase had been added on, a little porch at each back door. Later the staircase had been enclosed, leaving a short, wide window on each landing.

Both the first and second floors were dark and curtained. Nothing except a light through each porch window.

Then I heard something. Saw a shadow on the second-floor window. Someone up there belonging to the warm Camaro? Muffled footsteps on wooden stairs. A shadow on the first-floor window.

I stepped under the pine trees to see without being seen. Sally Hall, the DJ, came out. Let the flimsy screen door slam. Wearing the blood-red coat, driving the blood-red Camaro, she backed out of the driveway and purred off.

I climbed the stairs. On the second-floor landing, I read the note Sally had slid into the crack between the screen door and its jamb. "Doctor Silly, Sorry I missed you. I wrote a pome about you in Stat class. Give me a call so I can read it to you. Luv, Sally."

Silly and Sally, huh? Brazen, to leave it where the other young ladies in Makepeace's goo-goo circle might read it. I folded it and slid it back. I tested the door, tugged the windows, fingered under railings and atop doors. Not a key to be found.

What did I expect inside? Except for not revealing his original source—probably Lona—for my phone number and daily schedule, Makepeace had played fair with me. More polite than your average reporter. I didn't think he was into poisons and bombs. But then Shrimp, Jimmy, and Eddie del sure were dead.

And Makepeace was hiding from the *News* and from his students. Why not from me, too? Hiding what? A reason to tell Byzant where to find me? Did I want to know badly enough to break in?

Yup. I put my hand on the bottom left corner of Makepeace's screen door and pushed. After a moment, the last wires gave enough. I reached in and groped for the handle. Found the lock button and pushed it. I caught Sally's note before it hit the ground.

Then the wooden door. It had six rectangular glass panes in the middle. Behind them was a curtain. Between them were thin wood slats.

I tried the lock first. Nope.

I put my shoulder into the door. It bent but didn't give. Thinking of my spine, I poked out a windowpane with my elbow. Waited, ready to skedaddle. But no alarm.

117

So I reached through and opened the door. Sally's note I set on the blond-wood kitchen table. I snapped on a light.

"Anyone home?" The kitchen sparkled. Copper pots hung in rows. Chrome and stainless-steel stove and sinks, polished bright. No food in sight. Rows of shiny ceramic canisters. The place looked ready for shooting by *House Beautiful*. And no one was home.

Makepeace lived on the second and third floors, which had been hollowed out and redone. I know because I snooped. The huge living room had been created from knocked-out walls and ceilings. The kitchen and two smaller rooms led off it.

The powder room had only toilet paper, a hand towel, an empty soap dish, and a candle. Underneath the sink, in the back corner, I found a plunger and an unopened box of tampons.

The study was full of toys: a good ten thousand dollars' worth of audio equipment. Thrice that of computers: hard drives and color laser printers and scanners and CD-ROMS and a bunch of gadgets and gismos I didn't recognize.

I turned on the closest of his computers and called up the hard disk's directory. Felt my way into the subdirectories. No matter that the file names tempted, I was pressed for time. Some I called up. If my meager sample was any indication, Makepeace wrote a lot of games.

They all had the same format. I could take a character, select its knowledge, skills, and attitudes, and then set it loose in a space the author had created for me.

The last one I looked at broke my character's personality into its parts and let my creator manipulate each of them. Emotion by emotion. Idea by idea. Each of the senses in turn.

Could Makepeace be the man behind Josh's electronic bookie? Nah. Houses up and down Buffalo's West Side had computer literacy equal to Makepeace's. Computer wiz had become ordinary computer consumer.

In a desk drawer, I found financial statements. He had accounts with three brokerages. In addition to the usual blue-chip stocks and municipal bonds, he had T-bills, mutual funds, limited partnerships, new issues. Not a sign of his tax forms, though I looked. He had a nasty mortgage, which probably included the remodeling. No sign of rental income from the ground floor apartment.

He couldn't have earned all that. Must have inherited it.

The large living room had a matched pair of armoires that I know cost thirty-seven fifty apiece; I'd looked at one down on Allen Street.

And the art on all the walls. Some local artists. Some embarrassingly bad paintings, no doubt by his friends. And, on an easel, track-lit to do it justice, an original Matisse.

Did the man have an alarm on the door? In a closet, I found it behind some coats. A fancy-looking job in a metal box with colored lights and a key pad. Makepeace simply hadn't turned it on. I couldn't imagine a company insuring an original Matisse without at least that much alarm. Then when an idiot like Makepeace didn't turn it on, it would be his liability, not the insurance company's.

Upstairs and down, Makepeace had *objets* of gold and silver and crystal and ceramic. Some of them were elegant and beautiful. Most ran between oh dear and silly. But they all looked expensive.

The whole upper floor was the master bedroom. In the nightstand left of the bed, the books had titles like *Mansex* and *One-Fisted*. In the right nightstand sat a well-twisted tube of scented jelly, among other oddities.

Off the bedroom, a huge dressing area opened onto a step-down shower. I'm talking a marble shower so big it didn't need a curtain. From the toiletries, the two vanities were his and his.

Two wardrobes. Lots of silk and wool, discreet labels in Italian and French. As best I could tell, none of the shirts had come off a store shelf. A lot of hand-stitching. And the smaller guy, Makepeace, had a sweater and shoe collection to rival my own.

In a shoe box high on a shelf, I found love letters from Scarlet to Carmen. All handwritten on scented paper and dated within the past four years. Most were flowery twaddle. Dearest this and darling that. All they pledged to do for each other. Some, explicit, had no mention of female anatomy but enough buggery to make me

119

blush. Scarlet could always make a living by writing for the rags in the left nightstand. Figuring it'd never be missed, I slipped one of Scarlet's letters into my pocket.

I'd bet the goo-goo dolls didn't venture up there.

So Makepeace hadn't inherited? He'd indeed earned it? When would he come home? Should I wait and hope he didn't bring Scarlet with him?

I found Makepeace's name all over. But not Scarlet's. Nowhere. Maybe that meant he wasn't a roommate—only a boyfriend. He needed to change his clothes and spend time in the bathroom, but he didn't live there.

Back downstairs, I sat in front of the Matisse to think it through. Monday night, Makepeace was too scared to take me back to his house. And Tuesday night he didn't even turn on his alarm? Which led me to the big question: had he told Byzant where to find me? I still had no answers. So what if he came home and found me? I'd let him have it.

Makepeace's kitchen clock next to the wall phone said ten to midnight. If Cramer had kept to schedule, Lona was drinking yet another stiff Stoly and waxing poetic about her own paintings. I called to find out.

"Lona was drunk when she got here."

"What else? How were her slides?"

"I don't want that work on any wall I'm associated with."

"I always knew you were honest. What's her mood like now?"

"She's bear huntin'. And you be the bear, my man. I don't know, though. Times I swear she's ready to rip her clothes off."

"She's like that when she gets drunk."

"Should I worry she's going to jump me?"

I laughed. "Somehow I feel you'll be able to take care of it. Ready for me to come back?"

"If only to get her out of my house, you'd better."

Day

s i x t e e n

In Cramer's living room, Lona waggled her glass at me. "Someone got shit on his shoes." She sniffed. "Stinks in here."

Cramer brought me a glass of herb tea. The fat bottle of Stolichnaya on the floor was only half full. Even given spills, that seemed a medically dangerous amount for Lona to drink in three hours.

"What's shit doing? Break in training?" She had trouble getting the words right. "Staying up pas'is beddy time?"

This Lona I knew how to handle from many a long night. Find the dark spot and plunge in. "Angel Ramirez, your boytoy down in Houston? You told me he was the only guy you ever went with—other than me—who drew more stares than you did."

That set her off. "You, because Buffalo crawls to Bills players. Angel, because he had such a face and supple, tender body." Which I guessed I didn't.

Fifteen minutes more of drivel. I tried to find out if she'd slept with any other Bills, guys I should warn. She wouldn't admit to anything.

Finally, cross-eyed, she got up to go to the bathroom. Not only wobbly. Careening off walls. We heard her slump to the floor. Both Cramer and I sprang to our feet. By the time we got into the hall, she'd already relaxed and was pissing.

Our deal: Cramer'd soak the carpet and toss the dirty pants,

121

panties, and blouse into the machine. I'd wash Lona and dress her in Cramer's bathrobe.

Cramer had a tiny bathroom. The floor was cold. And naked Lona had gone limp, so I dumped her into the tub. Not good for my back.

After turning on the cold water, I sat on the furry toilet seat. After the cold rose to her armpits, I turned it off.

While I washed her bottom, she woke enough to slur, "Why'm I a bath?"

"Because you need one."

She nodded slowly, heavy-lidded. "Got 'ny stuff?"

"Any what?" I stood up and tossed the washcloth in. "Finish washing yourself."

"Drink 'n' smokes, too."

"Yes, your ladyship."

When I returned, she lit up. Yup, back in business. She was drunk beyond drunk. Slowly licking the filter, she had droopy eyelids and a loopy grin on her face.

Her right hand slid between her legs. "Wanna help?" Rubbing herself lazily. "Mmmm."

I heard Cramer coming up from the basement. In the doorway, she offered her white terry-cloth robe. "Here." She put the bleach back under the sink.

Lona stopped rubbing and let her hands float. She raised her right knee and shifted to her left butt, angling her crotch toward the wall. A perverse, willful drunk, she would not stop driveling. "Angel, my Angel, was the kindest, most considerate, humblest boy." Her radiant look again. "You wouldn't believe him. He was warm and caring and honest."

Cramer asked, "Was he your first?"

Lona's eyes went blank; her face went slack. I thought perhaps she'd not heard the question.

Then, "Yes." Maybe she'd been recalling the festivities.

I asked, "So what happened the night your Angel died?"

She took a slow, deep breath. Quite the actress. Problem was, Meryl Streep did it sober.

"He got half my bra off." She patted her left breast. "You

think it's Christmas, the way he plays. So, oh, excited!" She looked up at Cramer. " 'Member being a teenager?"

"No."

"Well, Angel thinks, harder and longer he chews, more I like it. After a while, you wanna say all right 'ready, take my pants off. But who knows what he'd do down there?" She drifted off, mumbled, "Bring a lawn mower and a putter?"

Cramer looked at me. "What did she say?"

I shrugged. "She's gonzo."

"Did you," Cramer asked, "let him take off your pants?"

Her nods were long, slow, and heavy. "Yes."

Saturday, she'd told me no. "Where were you?"

She took a break for a gulp of Stoly. "In my car."

"Your dad's car," I corrected her.

"Wrong again, Santa. Daddy had his own car."

"Big backseat?" Cramer wondered.

She wobbled a nod. "Big very wet. He was very beautiful."

"When did your dad figure it out?" Cramer asked it, but it made sense to me, too.

"Moment I walk through the door."

"So what did he do?" Cramer asked.

Lona took a two-handed sip and held it in. Her eyes crossed. Her mind must have crossed, too, because her nose started running and she didn't sniff or wipe it.

Why was Cramer encouraging Lona to prattle on about an old boyfriend? We needed her to talk about Josh. I gave Cramer a wide-eyed, impatient look.

Cramer saw it and gave a little wave with her left hand. "So what did your dad do when you came home with that look in your eye?"

"Daddy? He made Angel 'n' me the brownies." She slipped a little deeper into the tub.

"Then they had the argument?" I asked.

She blinked but other than that didn't respond. Then her eyes shut.

"Lona, wake up."

"Let her sleep."

"But we haven't even started talking about Josh."

She stood. "As Lona would say, 'Wrong again, Santa.' We've been talking about her father all along. Weren't you listening?"

Hmmm. Not wanting Lona to drown, I drained the tub. While Cramer looked away, I dried Lona's arms, breasts, and back—no problem. For legs and bottom, I needed help. "C'mon, Cramer. She's dead weight."

We got Lona dry and enrobed. Then Cramer could pick her up. In the living room, she laid Lona onto the couch and spread a black-and-yellow afghan over her.

I followed Cramer down the hall to the kitchen. At the sink, she poured the Stoly down the drain.

"It's not going to turn back into rotten potatoes."

"I don't want it around my house."

"Why not?" I hated waste. She had no kids lurking or moms snooping. Her dad wouldn't mind. "When I got here this evening, you had half a bottle of brandy on the fridge and a three-liter box of Chablis in the pantry."

"Well, I shouldn't have. The stuff's poison. See what it did to Lona?" She was washing the decanter. "Made her a quivering, blithering idiot. She urinated all over herself."

Urinated? "She's always like that. It's her specialty. But that's Lona's problem. Not the vodka's problem. I'll let her sleep a little, then I've got to get her back up to talk about her dad."

She pushed off the drainboard and turned to the pantry. "I have this Swedish coffee."

"Sure. I'd love some." It was coming up to 3:00 A.M. on the kitchen clock.

She poured coffee beans into the grinder.

"We never found out if she slept with any other guys, I mean, my teammates."

"I asked. Before you got back. She kept talking about some musician."

Che Guevara. "Her new boyfriend. And we never asked the big question: who's got something on your father?"

"That I also asked."

"All she talked about was Angel Ramirez."

"That's her answer."

"But Angel's dead years. Far away. How's he answer anything?"

"Did she not look and sound and sob like a woman giving a heartfelt answer? Like someone unburdening herself?"

While she zapped the beans, I ran the bathtub scene through my mind again. "Maybe, now that I think about it."

Cramer poured the powder into a white paper filter.

"She told me about Angel last Saturday. It was odd then."

"Odd?"

"Because Lona never says anything about her past. Never uses it to comment on anything. Why start with Angel Ramirez?"

"Because it says who has something on her dad. At least in her mind. Josh just found out she'd lost her virginity to this Mexican. Next morning, said Mexican turns up dead."

"You aren't suggesting that Josh killed him?"

"Why not? You're suggesting he killed three of your teammates. Two of whom she slept with." Cramer pushed the switch and the water began gurgling through the pot. "Many a father of a daughter wants to kill young boys. Many a bookie wants to kill to restore his profits."

"It's hard to believe Josh hates Mexicans that much. I mean, a fair percentage of Reading, Inc.'s, clients are black and brown."

"This isn't black, brown, or otherwise. This is father-daughter. You have any children?"

"No."

"Ever been married?"

"No."

After a pause, "Want a cookie or something with your coffee?"

At least she didn't ask why. "No."

"You think you should go downtown? See if the library's newspaper collection has anything about the kid's death?"

I shook my head. "Lona and Josh lived in Houston back then."

"Meaning?"

"The Buffalo paper won't have the death of a lovesick minority teenager in Houston, Texas. Paper'd be two hundred pages every day, just the obits."

"You have any friends in Houston?"

"What do you want to know?"

"Was it a suicide, as Lona claims? So do you have friends?"

"Danny Howard. He retired from the Oilers last year, asked me to write a recommendation for him. Now he wants to be a commentator with the networks."

"Then why don't you give him a call?"

I looked at the wall clock. "It's way after two A.M., Houston time."

"You want to be polite or you want to stop Josh from killing a fourth? And you're next on the list, he said. He's already tried to blow you up."

"We don't know for sure it was Josh. And I don't know Danny Howard's number by heart."

She handed me the phone. "Call directory assistance."

I started poking numbers. Eventually, I got Danny's answering machine. "Danny? Santa here, up in sunny Buffalo. Get back to me, man. It's urgent and it has to do with el striko, so—"

"Santa?" He broke in. A long, warm pause. "My man. What'n I do?" He had a whiskey slur.

"Hope I'm not waking you."

"Nah. I's rocking here in m'rocky chair contemplating life after football."

"How is it?"

"Sucks, man. Then our paper ran this picture of Jimmy's ancient Mercedes." Another long pause. "Warn't purty."

"No, it wasn't."

"I didn't know Eddie del Greco. But Jimmy 'n' me were tight. I been in that very old but very fine car, Jimmy's wife in the backseat shaking the cocktails. How they taking it in Buffalo?"

"Bunch of guys lit out. What about in Houston?"

"It gave two, three guys reason to cross the line."

"Two, three too many. Listen, you can't tell anyone this conversation even happened until the strike is over."

"I hear you, Santa."

"You got anyone on the Houston papers won't tell anyone?"

"Yup. When you going to call?"

"Fast as I can. What's the name?"

"Barkdull. I got his number somewhere."

Cramer wrote it down. I promised to call Danny back, pressed the button, and then poked the numbers.

After six rings, he answered.

I introduced myself. "Sorry to wake you."

"It's in my job description." A deep, slow, rumbly voice. "What can I do for you?"

"Until the strike's over, this conversation is far off the record."

"Oh, yeah? I'm awake now. Gimme a second, get a smoke." I heard a tap when he set the phone down.

A minute later, "Okay, shoot. This a big story?"

"I find what I want and it'll be in every paper in the U.S."

I could hear his long exhale. "What you want me to do?"

"I need some info probably in an old issue of your paper."

"Hey, no problem."

"Yes, a problem. I need it in the next hour."

Cramer, sitting on the floor, gave me a thumbs-up.

Barkdull agreed to help. "On the condition that if any part of this story comes out of Houston, I'm the very first Houston reporter you talk to."

"Exclusive live coverage." After I told him what I wanted and hung up, I looked at Cramer. "What now?"

"We wait." She must have seen some look in my eye. "Nothing more."

Yes, ma'am.

While we waited, I amused her with a play-by-play of my adventure at Makepeace's upstairs apartment. She didn't get far through Scarlet's love letter before she blushed and gave it back.

An hour later, the phone rang. "Gene Barkdull. This Ramirez suicide wasn't in the paper at all. But our archivist thinks like a squirrel the day before the first heavy snow."

"Saves everything?"

"Not only that, it's all neatly filed and you can walk in at three A.M. decades later and find something all by yourself."

"What'd you find?"

"Your young man. Ramirez, seventeen, suicide, drug overdose."

"Sounds like him. What's the date?" I wrote it down.

"But this is a Hector Ramirez, not an Angel."

"Wait a sec." I let the receiver fall away and told Cramer. "You think Hector and Angel are the same boy?"

She looked at Lona, mouth open, lips fluttering. "Yes."

I put the receiver back to my ear. "Got anything else on him?"

"What I got is a death story that was written but never got onto the page. Easy to edit out the suicide of a young transient."

"Transient? But he lived there, went to high school."

"Listen, I'll read you this thing."

"Wait a sec." I motioned Cramer over. We leaned our heads close, the receiver between us. She smelled good. "Okay, go."

" 'Police today reported the apparent suicide death of a Montgomery County teen. Hector—' "

"Montgomery County?"

"First county north of Houston. 'Hector Ramirez, age seventeen, was found nearly lifeless on the floor of his rented room. He died while being airlifted to Texas Medical Center and was pronounced dead there at seven fifty-five this morning.

" 'According to records, Ramirez was recently employed as a maintenance worker at Houston Intercontinental Airport. Authorities characterized Ramirez's blood as containing a lethal amount of an unspecified poison, presumably a drug.

" 'From information found at his residence, Ramirez had lived in the Houston area only since late last summer. The other residents of his rooming house characterized Ramirez as polite and quiet. He "always had a smile on his face," according to one resident.

" 'Ramirez apparently has no relatives in the Houston area. Authorities are trying to contact the teen's family, who reportedly live in the Kleberg County area.' That's it, Santa."

"Kleberg County?"

"South of Corpus Christi. Basically, it's the King Ranch and its company store, a burg called Kingsville."

Cramer, still listening in, took notes.

"Who wrote what you just read to me?"

"No byline. Sorry. Pretty high turnover on the transient teen commits suicide beat."

"How reliable's that Kleberg County stuff?"

"I'd say the reporter didn't have a specific town. Maybe a rural post number, maybe they don't have a phone. That's why he used the word 'area.' "

"Wait a sec." I put my hand over the mouthpiece. "You have a map of Texas?"

Cramer got a Rand-McNally jumbo number from the next room while I chatted with Barkdull about the strike. When the paper crackled, Lona turned onto a shoulder and went limp again.

"Got a map here," I told Barkdull.

"What for?"

Cramer knew where it was. She put her finger on it.

"Kleberg County." I read around Cramer's finger. "We're talking the southern tip of Texas." To the east was the Gulf of Mexico. To the south the state of Tamaulipas, Mexico.

Barkdull asked, "What are you working on?"

"That the Ramirez kid didn't commit suicide."

"That long ago? What's that have to do with the strike?"

"Sorry. When it's over, I'll tell you everything."

He sighed. "Deal."

I thanked Barkdull and hung up.

From Kleberg County directory assistance, I got three and a half dozen listings for Ramirez. I called out the numbers while Cramer wrote them down.

After I hung up, I asked, "Want to go get some breakfast?"

She thrust up the piece of paper. "When you have all these calls to make? You start on this list, and I'll find something in the kitchen."

"I'm not calling anyone at five A.M. Especially a total stranger."

"But five A.M.'s the best time to get them. In a couple of hours, they'll all be at work."

"They all speak Spanish. And I don't."

"I do. Rusty, but it'll do."

"Then you call."

She pulled the phone to herself. "Say, can you rustle us up an omelet?"

While I walked down the hall toward the kitchen, I heard her poking buttons. Rustle us up? I liked her attitude.

Not twenty minutes later, I returned with a tomato, parsley, and cheddar cheese omelet. She was putting down the receiver.

"Don't you ever sleep?"

She grinned. "Omelet smells great. Why should I sleep? This's too much fun. I'm not just harboring a criminal. I'm furthering your criminal enterprise."

"Give it a rest, Cramer."

"And you can sleep on the plane. I think I found Hector's folks. They live on some farm-to-market road. But *no teléfono. No hablan inglés.*"

I knew that much Spanish.

She stood. "You can call the airlines while I go wash up."

"So when do we—"

"Me? I'll drive you to the airport."

"You gotta come."

"Why?"

"You know Spanish. You have a credit card."

"Great. Now you want me to finance this criminal enterprise."

"Please."

"I have two reports to write and a small but vociferous payroll to meet. Appointments to keep tomorrow at the Albright-Knox and the Arts Council. Now that Ronnie's sewed up those paintings, his opening's still—"

"How do they look?"

"Fine. Better, actually. I've got a job to get back to, buster."

"Hire a temp. Run up a long-distance bill. I'll cover it."

"What are you trying to do? Buy me?"

"Yes."

"I can see why no one's ever trusted you enough to marry you."

*   *   *

After Cramer dressed and packed, she called Becky, her assistant, to figure out how to cover herself at the gallery. Then we roused Lona. Rat's-nest hair, high-octane bad breath, squinty eyes. Probably still half buzzed. Politely call it a hangover.

At the sight of me, Lona blinked and furrowed her brow, which meant she'd gone off the edge before I got back. She would have no memory of the bathtub or the Angel Ramirez story. A nasty, spiteful drug, that alcohol. All I got by way of parting was a stiff middle finger.

Cramer and I stopped off at Albert's office. He was stuffing his briefcase for the flight to D.C., where Lance Bishop had promised a car to meet him.

After I introduced Cramer, Albert told me, "Bad news. The first Bills crossed the picket line this morning." Bad news? Try major disaster. My pride was on that line. Albert didn't even have to tell me who.

"The Puritans?" Alex Lamar and his Fellowship of Christian Athletes crowd.

Albert nodded.

"All of them?"

He nodded again.

I explained to Cramer, "They're a half-dozen guys who have a problem with established authority. They respect it." Those guys hadn't been my best friends. Now they'd be scabs forever.

I asked Albert whether I could borrow some bucks. "Byzant got my wallet." I told him how.

He shook his head slowly. "Speaking as your attorney, I—"

"Don't bother. I'm leaving town. Think I should ask Byzant?"

"No. I'll tell him after you're safely in the air to, uh . . ."

"Texas."

He twisted one side of his mouth into a smile. "I'll pick a different direction to tell Byzant. Why Texas?"

"Here's our theory. Josh Nachman poisoned the Mexican kid who took Lona's virginity."

Cramer jumped in. "We're going to Texas to talk to the kid's family."

"And theory confirmed, we're going to Houston to look for the gambler who knows and who's squeezing Josh."

Albert looked over the top of his glasses.

"Josh doesn't have the brains or the balls to do this on his own."

"Agreed," Albert said. "So what sends you on such a wild goose chase?"

"Lona got drunk last night and all but told us."

"All but?" he asked.

"I said it was a theory. Now add it to the poisoning here in Buffalo."

Albert said, "Poison once, poison again. I can go with you that far. But what about the bombs?"

I had him covered there. "Remember my boyfriend theory?"

"Only if," Albert spoke slowly, "Josh knew about all of you."

"Me, Jimmy, and the Mexican kid, for sure. But Shrimp? Even I didn't know until four days ago."

"But still," Albert said.

"Four out of five isn't bad," Cramer added.

"Know of anyone else Lona slept with? We might warn him."

Albert shook his head.

The door opened and Gus walked in. He and Harvey were the only ones Albert's secretary didn't have to announce.

As usual, Gus didn't waste any words. "The Puritans crossed. You hear?"

We nodded.

"Cocksuckers." Gus looked at Cramer. "I wouldn't say that if it weren't true." He held out yet another unpostmarked plain white envelope.

I took it. My name, again in red and blue crayon. "Oh, no, Gus. When?"

"Saw it this morning, so it musta come overnight."

Albert opened his mouth, no doubt to give some expert legal advice on obeying Byzant: don't open it and call right away.

But I had it ripped open and read in a jiffy.

ROSTER MOVES, ONE BY ONE
I BEG YOU TWO TO STOP IT
IF NOT, THE REST OF TEN WILL DIE

I got this sinking feeling in my belly. The rest of ten will die. My hand trembled when I handed the note to Albert. It wasn't fear; it was anger. Bubbling into rage.

Cramer and Albert leaned close and read it too. She turned to Albert. "Is there anything illegal about my going to Texas with this fugitive?"

"For you? No. For him? Not only will he violate a court order, they'll probably add kidnapping to the list of charges on the arrest warrant."

No one laughed except me. I borrowed two thousand dollars from Albert. He advised me to let Cramer rent the car, keep my name off paper.

Gus drove us all to the airport. We dropped Albert off at West Terminal for his plane to Dulles. On the way to East Terminal, Gus told me that some FBI agents had been poking around the house. Gus had referred them to Albert.

After Gus dropped us off, he drove away in Cramer's truck. Park it in the courtyard at Artists Gallery, she told him. Leave the keys with Becky.

Inside, the TV screen labeled "Departures" gave us few choices. At the United desk, I paid cash and gave made-up Mr. and Mrs. names. Why leave cookie crumbs for Byzant or the FBI to follow?

Cramer and I slept through the flight via Chicago and got off the plane in San Antonio: hot. *Hot.* Credit card in hand, Cramer rented a white Crown Vic with four-wheel drive. Out in the boonies, who knew what we'd get stuck in?

We headed southeast toward the Gulf. The land flattened

during the first few miles. The air was clear, the sky cloudless, the sun lowering. The land was flat as a tabletop. I saw nothing on the horizon taller than the odd stand of cottonwoods or a lonely mesquite. A lot of cows at first. I'd been to Texas but never that far south, never that dry.

Cramer dozed in the backseat. Somewhere between Edroy and Odem, the sun started setting off to my right. The colors muted. I called to Cramer and we watched while she fully woke up. Pink and orange. Gorgeous. We watched it in silence.

After the sun was down, we might as well have been on any other tabletop. Cars and trucks whizzed past at frightening speeds.

We entered Corpus Christi from the north, along Nueces Bay. Oil refineries and storage towers and natural gas plants lined the bay; large ships filled it. Smelled terrible. The hundreds of palm trees were pretty, but they couldn't take away the odor.

Cramer spotted a supermarket. "That's probably our best bet for a local map this time of night."

"Great." I looked forward to applying to a local map the directions Cramer had scribbled back in Buffalo.

"Another hour around Corpus to the Ramirez place."

"Cramer, it's after dark. They *no hablo* English. We *no hablo español* very well. We're dredging up some powerful family memories. Can we let it rest? Catch them first thing in the morning?"

She sighed. "It's against my nature, my better judgment."

"Then tomorrow—some sensible hour—we can drive out there and start knocking on doors."

She growled but finally said, "Tomorrow."

After I parked, she went into the market. Soon she came out, wheeling a full cart. That got me out of the car right away.

"Pop the trunk and help me unload this stuff."

Sweating, I peeked into the paper bags. "You didn't buy dinner, did you? I wanted seafood. But I had something fresh in mind. Like at a heavily air-conditioned restaurant."

The bag she was loading into the trunk was full of clanging metal. "How fresh?" she asked. "How about just out of the water?"

* * *

Hours later, Cramer drove us over the JFK Causeway onto the longest of Texas's barrier islands, North Padre. "Now this first part's all developed. But the next hundred miles south is a national park. We used to come here when I was a kid."

"Where are we going?"

"We're going to sneak into the park, drive for a while, and then hide the car between two sand dunes where we can build a fire and cook these crabs."

The couple dozen we'd caught in Petronila Creek were swimming frantically in a bucket between my legs.

"Why don't we avoid all this sneaking and just go to a motel? Uh . . . Cramer." Why did I pause?

"Now what fun would that be?"

I paused because I'd been on the verge of calling her something. But what? "My dear"? "Honey"? She'd been both from the moment she decided to head south with me. Hadn't given me even a bit of a hard time.

We found two steep, parallel dunes, and in the wind-protected hollow between them the remains of a fire.

She'd bought everything we needed. It was just before midnight when we finally started cracking crabs and dipping the meat into garlic lemon butter. The air was sultry and buggy. We had our sleeves rolled down and our bare feet buried in the sand. "You forgot the bug spray," I said.

"Sorry."

Cramer was drinking her fourth Lone Star. She told stories about her childhood and art school. I didn't try to keep track of everybody's name and who was sleeping with whom. Mouth full, picking away, I nodded. Since her second beer, I'd been laughing almost too much to eat.

Byzant, Harvey, Gus, Albert. All were correct. Getting out of town for a few days was the best thing I could have done.

"Thanks, Cramer."

"What?"

I rose and held out my dripping arms. "I said, I told you we'd need napkins."

"And I told you that's what we have the water for." When she paused, we could hear it. She rose and slapped me on the shoulder. "Race you around the dune."

I held her eyes, level with mine. "You're on."

She grinned. "Ready, set, go."

The Gulf was warm. Seaweed swirled around our ankles. Above, whole waves of stars. Cramer, peeling sweatshirt and slacks, dove in.

I looked into the stars and thought about the third note, the one Gus had brought. The rest of ten will die. That was the line that took my breath away. I knew where I'd heard "the rest of ten" before. I'd said it to Josh in the Anchor Bar parking lot. And no one knew that except Josh and me.

When I got back home, I'd mix a palette with the colors of the sunset Cramer and I had seen that evening. A stunning, saturated pink. And next to it a pale orange strip of cloud. I was still thinking about the blend between them.

Where they met. Cramer and me.

Day

seventeen

ate in the morning, we finally found the Ramirez homestead: no sign, no mailbox, not a marker. A path, dry, rutted, and straight. Take it, Cramer's directions said. Turned out to be the Ramirez driveway, but we bounced along for half an hour before anything bolstered our hope. That driveway ran straight for twenty miles, a cotton field on each side.

From miles away, we saw the top of the barn. The Ramirezes lived in a dusty clearing. A tall cottonwood grew on either side of the house, and a tethered goat nibbled at the base of a fence post.

By the time we chugged in, they'd gathered on the front porch. Two adults and two very young boys. It was a stifling breezy day. Not a cloud to be seen. We waved howdy before we got out of the Crown Vic. The old man stepped forward: skinny, straw-hatted, silver belt buckle. A wary look on his face.

Cramer towered over him. Her Spanish was better than his English, so I only stood and listened. From watching Cramer's eyes and listening to the tone of her voice, I knew she was asking urgent questions.

Turned out we were talking to Hector's parents and nephews. Señora Ramirez, on the porch, gathered the two boys to her long blue skirt. I kept hearing the name Hector. Hector, Hector. The señora's lip quivered and she wiped away a tear.

By the time they got done talking it out, we'd had lunch.

Fresh-squeezed lemonade and *taquitos:* tortilla after tortilla filled with soft goat's cheese and a sprinkling of *chorizo*. The señora hovered and didn't let our plates or glasses get empty.

They didn't have much. No telephone, no TV. But after lunch, I stood with the older nephew on the porch. What a spectacle: the flat land, the huge sky, the breeze stiff in the cottonwoods.

The señora had photos wrapped in Hector's yellowing baptismal napkin. In one, Hector had his arm around a girl who looked close enough to Lona to convince me. My eyes I could trust. For once, Lona had spoken truly. She was beautiful, but Hector was more beautiful than she.

I looked at his sun-creased parents. Where had Hector's face come from? Maybe they'd adopted him from some movie star.

Cramer and I left amid hugs and kisses from the señora, a shake and courtly bow from her husband. The nephews waved us out of sight. We were welcome back any time.

In the Crown Vic, dust swirling behind, Cramer put it all together. "Summer he turns seventeen, Hector Ramirez leaves the hacienda back there for the bright lights, the big city."

"Common enough."

"Indeed. In Houston, Hector finds a menial job at the airport. Saves real hard, sends his parents bucks every week. Every Sunday, the folks go to mass in Kingsville. Hector calls the rectory, has a long talk with them. Oh, he puffs up his job, the size of the city. They aren't stupid."

I defended him. "He sends something home out of every paycheck. He's entitled to crow a little."

"Then during the winter, his whole life changes. He meets Lona. Hector's mother described his voice when he talked about her. The same way Lona talked about him two nights ago. Radiant."

I could see it. "Poor boy, fresh from the cotton plantation, meets beautiful, bright daughter of the white middle class. She crooks her forefinger and says, 'Hey, pretty boy. Come here.'"

Cramer put her finger in her ear and wiggled it. "So Lona finally gives the kid her virginity."

"Josh finds out."

Cramer squinted, as though something hurt. "Josh blows up, makes the kid feel so bad, so guilty, so low, that he goes home and commits suicide."

"Yeah. Sure. Right." I didn't believe it.

She pulled her finger out of her ear. Held it up and the one next to it. "Except for two things. His mother tells me what a sickly baby he was. They finally find out he's allergic to milk and pollen and on and on. This Hector can't even do *cerveza*. Alcohol makes him break out."

"Wait a minute, Cramer. So says his mother. But a couple months in Houston, some bucks in his pocket. Lona's crowd is no doubt faster than the one he ran with back here."

Cramer caught on. "He wonders, 'What's this beautiful Lona see in me?' "

"So he scores some drugs to impress her. Problem is, he does them all at once instead of one or two at a time." I remembered Harvey, in the Blue Note, raising his beer, talking about nicotine. How poisons can in the short run feel very pleasant.

Cramer raised her eyebrows. "And the second thing? Some months after Hector dies, a man comes. So long ago, Mama hardly remembers him now. Speaks *español* like a professor, she says. He asks all the same questions I do."

"Great. We're in the right county to find a man who speaks Spanish as a second language. Hector's mother remembers what?"

"*Nada.* She's crying the whole time. Sitting at the kitchen table and sobbing. She doesn't remember if the guy was tall, short, fat, thin, bearded, *nada.* Wouldn't remember the man at all, except I asked the same questions."

"Did they say anything about where the *Angel* came from?"

"No one here ever used it. Maybe it's Lona's pet name."

"One other thing. Where's he buried?"

"The churchyard in Kingsville, where they used to get a call from him every Sunday morning in the rectory."

"Who paid to get him back there?"

"Good question. Wish I'd thought to ask it."

"Maybe they had insurance." I left a pause. "I won't need your

Spanish in Houston. You can go straight on home if you want."

She stared at me. "Right. Go back and wait for the killer."

"He only kills players."

"So far." Then she curled up, her back to me in the Crown Vic. Looked as though she wanted to get some shut-eye.

I made a short list of people I could spend that many hours in a row with. Gus when we went camping. My sister Grace, as long as she wasn't bragging about me. Not a one of my teammates.

It's not that I didn't trust anyone. Or that I had a short attention span. I could spend three days straight in front of my canvases, swilling beer, pissing into an old turp can. I could spend ten hours straight in front of my TV watching films of the next Sunday's wide receivers.

But I did that stuff alone.

Take away bathroom runs and one short night of sleep front and back in the Crown Vic. Still, Cramer and I had been thigh by thigh since I walked in on her and Lona back in Buffalo. By the time we got to the Houston airport, we'd been together for a few minutes shy of forty hours. Except for Gus and Grace, that had never happened to me before.

And it was her doing, not mine.

Four o'clock, Danny Howard met our shuttle from Corpus. He had thick lips and a peaked head, well battered by running backs and offensive tackles. His smile came smashing and bright. He and Cramer shook hands and said each other's name. "Baggage claim, this way."

She pulled the strap of her big bag. "All we have's carry-ons." So we followed Danny down the long terminal extension into the hub. He and I talked about Jimmy Roma. Whether he should fly to Alabama for the funeral.

"Where they burying Eddie del?" he asked me.

"Back home. Cape Cod."

"You going?"

"It's tomorrow, so I doubt it."

I could hear Eddie del: I wonder how many bits and pieces o' me they found to actually bury? Talk about closed casket. This'll be empty casket.

Then Eddie del would laugh, make the ground shake. I missed him.

In the hub, we took an elevator up to a stinking, stifling garage. It had a low ceiling, oil- and rubber-streaked concrete, and brightly colored section signs. "It'll be easier," Danny said, "if I run get the car. You guys wait here." And off he trotted.

"He's funny," Cramer said. "Lit like a Christmas tree."

In Danny's BMW, I took the back, Cramer the front. He cranked the a/c full blast. We chitchatted until we got on the tollway.

"Now what's the story, Santa?"

I kept it short: "In Buffalo, someone's killing people to try to make the strike end. I got this notion that someone in Houston employs the killer in Buffalo."

"How much is Buffalo getting paid?"

I thought of Reading, Inc.'s, budget. "Between ten and twenty thousand."

"Per dead body?"

Cramer said, "Per month." She shook her head.

He shook his, too. "There's people who'd kill for that kinda payday. So where you think you're gonna find this someone?"

"Who knows? See, we're going backward. Cramer talked to the surviving family. Then we saw the kid's grave in Kingsville."

"What do you want to see next?"

"His dead body here in Houston. Where'd they take him?"

Cramer fished out of her bag the article Barkdull had faxed to Albert. "Says here it was Texas Medical Center. Can you take us there, Danny?"

"It's downtown. We're meeting Gene Barkdull for dinner first."

I was ready. "Where we going?"

"Vietnamese place near Rice. We went there once, Santa."

I didn't remember, but when we got inside and I smelled it, I did. Turned out Barkdull, the *Post* reporter, had chosen the place. He had a long face and a thick mustache. Wire-rim glasses. In his forties, a proud Vietnam vet, he ordered in the native tongue.

After the waitress left, we put our heads closer. It seemed

clear that most of what we needed was the property of one cop shop or another.

I asked Barkdull, "Do you think their logs go back that far?"

"Both city and county cops. No question. I spend hours rooting around." He pulled out a pen and uncapped it. "What exactly do you want?"

"Who else lived in Hector's rooming house? Which cops first saw his body? Who rode in the back of the chopper with Hector?"

"Plus where they are now, so much later?" Barkdull showed me half a grin and twinkling eyes. "You plan on being here till Christmas?"

Cramer said, "We'd also like to know what drug killed Hector."

Barkdull told her, "That may be easiest of all. Remember the article I faxed you said DOA at Texas Medical Center?"

"Yeah. You know someone?"

He stood up. "There's a phone at the door. Back in a sec."

The waitress brought our drinks.

Danny sipped his beer. "Compared to you Bills—Shrimp, Jimmy, and Eddie dying for the strike—the rest of us live in innocence. How you taking it?"

Cramer answered. "He's trying to keep from getting killed."

Danny's eyes bugged out. "You mean the killer's after you too?"

We hadn't told him anything beyond the strictly limited Hector Ramirez chase. Hadn't mentioned Josh's threats. "Thanks, Cramer."

She stared back, not a hint of shame in her eyes or cheeks. "Cramer's exaggerating. I'm not in any real danger."

"Yes he is. Until the strike is—"

"Cramer. Cool it a moment? We'll discuss this later."

"I don't think you have to worry," Danny told her. "I'm saying the union folds its hand after this weekend's scab games. Tell you, I'm glad I retired."

Barkdull walked up. He stiff-armed the table and leaned onto his knuckles. His tie, swinging forward, just missed Cramer's wine. "I got my lady. She owes a friend of mine a favor."

"Who is she?" Cramer asked.

"Nurse." He looked at his watch. "But her shift ends at eight."

Texas Medical Center wasn't far. We all took Danny's Oiler-blue BMW. Barkdull knew exactly where to get out with Cramer and me while Danny solved the parking problem. After normal hours, Barkdull had to ask security to notify his friend's friend.

I wandered into the coffee shop and introduced myself to nurses. Soon I found the Oiler fans among them. One knew I was a Buffalo Bill and was more than happy to change the dressing on the back of my left hand. It looked terrible and didn't feel much better.

She was very gentle. She asked how I'd done it and I told her about Byzant and the handcuffs and my propelling myself out of Vinnie's car. She laughed and said I had quite an imagination.

Back at security, the friend's friend came bearing a file folder. The security desk had a bright lamp. She spread the folder open on the desk, about chest-high, and stepped back.

Danny, Cramer, and I passed the forms around. When we saw something of interest, we called it out and Barkdull wrote it down. We had admissions forms, pathology test results, Hector's official death certificate.

What a gold mine! We got the names of the cops. The address of Mercy Flight, the chopper company, and the operators' numbers. The cause of death: acute barbiturate poisoning, self-administered. We got stomach contents—there were the brownies Lona had said Josh made. Blood analyses, estimated time of death.

We even got one of those indecipherable M.D. signatures. I stepped back and asked Barkdull's friend's friend, "You recognize this handwriting?"

She studied the curlicued scribble. "No."

"Think someone else might? I'd like to talk to the guy."

"Oh, he—or she—won't still be at this facility."

"Why not?"

"Every ER, a case like this gets shuffled off to the lowliest doctor, still a student. At that level, we get a total turnover every couple years. He—or she—was half a dozen generations ago, as far as this ER goes."

143

"Well, he must be practicing somewhere."

Cramer, who looked very tired, chimed in. "And you know how many cases he's had since? You know how much time he gave to this one so long ago? A body comes in. He might even look at it. He orders tests. Someone does the tests, fills out the forms. The M.D. glances at it and scribbles a signature. If he's gone off shift, anyone can sign it."

The nurse said, "She's right."

"Who ran the tests?" I asked. "Any of them still around?"

"Probably. But even at the time, one fluid or tissue looks much like another. Pathology samples have numbers, not names."

"So a kid died on the way to this hospital. And when he got here, you guys took the cops' word for it. They asked questions around Hector's rooming house, took those folks' word for it."

"What's your problem, sir?"

"No one really tried to figure out how the kid died."

She poked the card in my hands. "Says right here, acute barbiturate poisoning."

"Yeah, but what if it wasn't suicide? Did anyone find the bottle the pills came in?"

She shrugged. "That's a police problem. Talk to them."

Day

eighteen

danny insisted we go to his house. Cramer nodded off at midnight, soon as we got there. Danny led her to the guest bedroom while I poured brandy for him, club soda for me in the dark-paneled sunken den.

I remember tucking my glass between my thighs so it wouldn't spill. Then I tried to keep my eyelids open and my chin up.

Next thing, it was crack of dawn Friday. Cramer called from the doorway, "You awake?"

"Hhhhnn." Slowly I rolled over in the blanket Danny had covered me with. I wasn't as asleep as I tried to sound. I'd heard a different tone in Cramer's two words. Think about it. Except for Shrimp's happening to die at the gallery she ran, it was not her fight. She didn't need to be traipsing all over America.

"Santa?" A big woman, she filled the doorway. "I've had my shower and Danny's in now. You're next." She wore her jeans and sweatshirt. Her hair, still wet, was combed straight back off her long, horsey face.

"Yeah, I'm awake." I sat up, vigorously scratched my head. I saw her dad's dark eyes. Every other morning, she'd asked how my back felt. "Listen, I got troops here. Danny, Barkdull. So you want to shuffle on back to Buffalo . . ." I let it hang.

At first, I read in her face: I'll go home. I'll go home. Please let me. Then I read in her face: No, I'd better stay.

But I could've been wrong. "Thanks for your help. I mean it."

"I know you do, Santa. But I've talked to Becky on the phone both days. She keeps reminding me that Ronnie's opening is still on for tomorrow night. I'm gallery director and this is only my second opening."

So that was it. "Tell you what." I stood and stretched. "We fly back to Buffalo tonight. I can still use the phones from there." I climbed the steps and eased past her into the hall. "And if I have to run back down here, why I can run back down here."

"It's safe for you to go back?"

Over my shoulder: "I'm not the worrying type."

"I've noticed," she said while I walked down the hall.

Half an hour later, I stepped out of Danny's shower and wrapped a nappy yellow towel around my waist. Stuck my head out the door and looked both ways.

No one in the hall. I didn't want to put on stale clothes. But the fresh clothes were in my bag in Danny's den.

The den was sunken, down four steps. In the middle sat a group of couches, low tables, and audio and video equipment.

I'd slept there on one of the couches. My bag was down there. And so was Cramer McKensie. She had a glass in her hand. From its amber liquid and the tall bottle in front of her, she was drinking—I squinted—a single-malt.

Because she didn't look up when I came in, I stood still on the bottom step. So there sat the lady who Tuesday night got sarcastic when I asked for a glass of Chablis. Who poured perfectly good vodka down the drain. It's a poison.

And two days later, she drank a single-malt for breakfast?

"What are you doing?"

"Having a drink. Want one?"

"No, thanks. I came for my bag. My clothes."

"You look better without them."

Oh-oh. "Thanks. Where's Danny?"

"He had an early meeting. He'll catch up with us at his office."

"When?"

"When we get there."

"Do you often drink whiskey for breakfast?"

"Never."

"Why today?"

"Because I want to."

"Are you angry at something?"

"Yes."

"Want to tell me what?"

"Not at the moment."

"What can I do to get you to stop drinking?"

She missed only one beat. "Make love to me."

Talk about blindside hits. My heart started thumping. "You're kidding. Cramer, I mean, I like you, but—"

"Danny's gone. We don't need to rush. Let's just do it."

"Cramer."

"What?" She took a sip.

"Cramer."

She gulped the rest of the glass and banged it onto the low table. "I'll stop. I only wanted to see what you'd say."

Right. She looked down.

I'd embarrassed her? I didn't see how. Angered her? What was she looking at?

"There's the paper."

"What?"

"The morning *Post*. It came while you were in the shower."

I picked it off the floor and saw the headline right away. Page 1, below the fold. KILLER STALKS TEAM: BUFFALO QUARTERBACK SLAIN.

My heart sank. It was like I'd got caught. Like it was my fault. "Oh, no."

"Oh, yes."

"Not Greg." I scanned the article.

The Erie County sheriff's department . . . the Buffalo Bills' All-Pro quarterback Greg Bowsk . . . and declared dead early this morning at . . . shot by a small-caliber weapon at close range in his suburban backyard. Bowsk was . . . Sources speculate that somebody known to the victim, NFL Rookie of the Year in . . . holder of . . .

I looked at Cramer. "My first reaction?"

She shrugged. "You want to kill whoever did it."

"Not civilized enough. I want him to lose a few limbs and his tongue and be sentenced to live out his miserable life at hard labor under the hot sun." It'd never happen. My throat got tight and tears welled.

"Go ahead and cry. He was your friend."

Much more than that. "My teammate."

"Well, yeah."

"You don't know the difference."

"Of course. I mean, a friend's a—" She stopped herself, looked at the tall bottle. "No. I guess I don't know."

"You have two categories, friends and relatives? I have three. Friends, teammates, and relatives."

"In that order?"

"Not the point." But she'd never had teammates.

"Catch the final paragraphs, a couple pages in."

I folded the paper back.

Authorities are seeking the dead man's teammate, free safety Santa Arkwright. Arkwright, wanted on suspicion of murder, has not been seen for several days.

A sheriff's department spokesperson says Arkwright is believed to have fled to another state to escape questioning. Both state and federal warrants will follow, authorities promised.

When I looked up, she said, "They just don't get it."

Tight-lipped, squinting, I wouldn't have spoken clearly. I picked up my bag. "I'll get dressed."

I didn't hear her answer.

Stiff-legged, breathing deeply, I carried my bag into the bathroom. Cramer said what? Let's make love; by the way, the cops are looking for you.

A slippery slope, that aiding and abetting a fugitive. Hard to separate what you love: the danger or the fugitive?

I dropped my bag onto the floor and bent to pick socks out of it. The bending brought the blood to my head. Greg Bowsk. I'd been far better buddies with Shrimp, Jimmy, and Eddie del. My generation.

Maybe I'd loved Greg more and not known it. Until losing him felt like losing a son. I slipped to the floor and sat there in my yellow towel, head between my knees.

And I cried for Greg Bowsk.

*   *   *

Eight o'clock, we met Barkdull at Danny's tenth-floor office in Memorial City. Twelve miles due east rose downtown Houston, backlit by the low sun. Between lay a sea of green treetops under a cloud of smog.

The morning papers from around the country were spread out, all open to the story about Bowsk's death. Screaming headlines.

And then the tabloids: CARNAGE IN BUFFALO DUE TO NIAGARA FALLS. NFL CITIES SET FOR SIEGE. CROWDS GATHER. SLAUGHTERED BILLS ALL VIRGOS.

And my favorite: THRILL KILL CHILLS BILLS.

Barkdull called the *Post* and got the unedited wire service reports faxed over. They didn't add anything. Reading the details, I saw Josh walk up to Greg. Shoot him. Walk away.

Then I had this vision of Josh—minus limbs and tongue, of course—given drops that eroded his eyesight permanently. And then sentenced to that sunny hard labor.

I spent an hour phoning my teammates. Except for Alex Lamar and the other Puritans, they were angry and scared. Who was next? Alex Lamar didn't care. Greg's death was God's will. Alex, at least, was sure heaven awaited.

The guys talked about Greg Bowsk. How he'd pulled out the Jets game. The time in practice he'd won a bet by heaving the ball into a bucket of Gatorade sixty yards away.

Most of my teammates were leaving town. They all—every one—warned me they'd had a call or a visit from Byzant, et al., about my bodily presence in the hours before Greg got shot. The warrant was carefully phrased: "presumed armed and dangerous."

I told them where I was in those hours. Well witnessed, reading death certificates in Houston. Neither armed nor dangerous.

Time to turn back to the Ramirez kid. Danny Howard issued legal pads and showed us the phones. Barkdull and Cramer, in Danny's office, took the cops. He played himself, a *Post* reporter doing background research. We played his assistants. Danny, in the conference room, took the chopper company. I got the rooming house.

By noon we'd found one of the two cops—in Cozumel on vacation. Again, Cramer's Spanish helped. The cop remembered nothing, but he did have a current precinct house in Sacramento, California, for his old partner. Barkdull got as far as the old partner's captain, who barked that the guy was walking his beat and would get back when his shift was over.

When I wasn't thinking about Cramer and sex or about Greg Bowsk and death, I found who had owned the rooming house when Hector Ramirez died there: Texas Commerce Bank. Great. It wasn't even in business anymore.

After lunch, Barkdull left, sorry he couldn't help more. Cramer sat by herself, silent. Something more bugging her than Ronnie's opening at Artists Gallery. Must have been Greg Bowsk, though she'd never even met the guy. All her banter and good vibes were gone, as though they'd drained away. She announced she was ready to go home.

Danny asked, "What's your next move in Buffalo?"

"Obviously, Josh is going to keep killing unless I do something. Anything. Four teammates down. Six to go."

"Ain't your gig, Santa. You ain't responsible."

"Oh, yeah? Maybe I can get Sister Charlayne to stop alibiing Josh. Maybe I can get Lona to tell me more of the Angel Ramirez story. Maybe I can get Josh to rat on Mr. Big. Maybe I can get Captain Byzant to arrest Josh."

Cramer snorted. "Maybe."

"Maybe I can get Dingleberry to ask a grand jury to indict Josh. If not for murder or gambling, maybe for cooking Reading, Inc.'s, books."

Cramer snorted again. "Maybe."

Danny said, "Santa, you'll be lucky to stay out of jail. If not that, the morgue."

*   *   *

Cramer McKensie caught me by surprise. Danny, claiming he had work to do, let us borrow his BMW. We'd go back to his house, get our stuff, then return his car and take a cab to the airport.

But next to me in the front seat, Cramer took a long slow breath. While her chest rose, her eyes widened and her grin lit. "Let's fly back in the morning."

"What? But before, you—"

"That was before. I hadn't finished thinking it through. You been to Houston's art museums?"

"Many times." Bottom level of the parking garage, I eased the BMW into the blazing sunlight.

"Rothko Chapel?"

"Many times."

"The commercial galleries?"

"I've showed my slides around."

"And?"

"I'm doing fine with Geraldo in Buffalo. I don't have much good work stacked up unsold." A lie, but why tell her?

We drove downtown anyway. We stopped at two galleries, then drove into the near suburbs, that artsy part of town north of Rice University and south of River Oaks, the old-money neighborhood. In no time, we visited a dozen galleries. Several of them should have been ashamed to have the word "art" on their doors.

At first, Cramer and I kept our distance. I kept thinking I shouldn't be enjoying myself. I should be doing something to avenge Greg. Maybe Alex Lamar was starting to rub off on me.

Then Cramer touched my elbow. "Oh, look on that wall."

"And look there," I said. Bluebonnets galore. We fled.

Outside, at a corner, I grabbed her upper arm when a driver made a sudden right into our path. In the next gallery, instead of wandering separately, we stayed side by side and looked at everything together.

Back on the pavement, Cramer said, "Getting thirsty?" She pointed across the street.

There stood an unornamented one-story white building surrounded by a caliche parking lot bleached by the sun. No sign except in the high small windows. A neon Carta Blanca in the one; Dos Equis in the other. Which meant *cerveza*. Which meant bathroom.

We clasped hands and ran dancing, dodging cars, across busy Bissonet. That was the best way to avenge Greg. Run, dance.

Inside was as cool and dark as the outside was hot and bright. Three-sided bar. A few tables and chairs. Half a dozen booths along the left wall. A dozen people, all male, were drinking beer. A kid was pumping quarters into the video game.

In the a/c, my sweaty skin felt clammy. I straightened both hands and placed one atop the other in a T. "Time-out."

"Me, too. If you get back first, order me something cold."

"Same here."

And then she was gone, heading toward SEÑORAS. I walked to the bar, feeling free-floating, unattached.

The bartender looked up from washing glasses. "What'n I git ya." Not even a question.

"I'd like you to pour four bottles of your most expensive beer into a pitcher and take it over to our booth. One glass only." I laid two twenties on the counter. "The rest is for you."

He was wiping his hands. "Yes, sir."

I sat in a far booth. Rule Number One in the players' handbook read, Don't start a romance during the season. No problem. Except this wasn't the season—this was the strike. Except this wasn't the strike, either—this was murder.

The bartender came with the pitcher and a glass. He emptied his tray of chips, salsa, napkins, and a plate of limes. "On the house," he said.

Amazing what forty bucks'd get. Then Cramer returned, face washed, hair combed. "Great. I'm parched." She slid into the booth across from me.

I poured. So who'd returned, the Nordic icicle, cold and silent? Or the tropic tease, warm and laughing?

"We need another glass."

"I thought we'd share this one."

"In that case." She came around to my side. Put her shoulder and thigh smack against mine. "It's freezing in here."

I did the chivalrous thing, put my arm around her.

Cramer looked me in the eye. "I'm having a wonderful time."

Oh, boy. What was Rule Number Two? Then I remembered. In case of emergency, ignore Rule Number One.

Day

nineteen

Our plane landed in Erie. Looked like a gray, cold afternoon. The plane, rolling slowly to the gate, was continuing northeast to Buffalo, and we'd bought tickets to Buffalo. But I was no fool. Not after those stories about armed, dangerous Santa wanted for questioning, suspicion of murder. Warrants already issued, said my teammates.

But Cramer wasn't wanted. I asked, "Listen, why don't you continue on home? I'll get off here and drive back."

Cramer's eyes flashed. "Screw you."

Even though the seat-belt light stayed lit, other first-class passengers were rising.

Not me. "What? Go on home. It'll save you time. It'll—"

"If that Byzant joker is waiting for you? And you don't show and I do? Then he's going to want to talk to me instead. Gee, where is Santa? I'll be there all night lying. I'll miss Ronnie's opening. What are you trying to do? Set me up?" The plane stopped. Standing, Cramer yanked her bag out of the overhead.

"Cramer."

No response. After stepping past me, she strode up the aisle. The stewardess got a nod, at least.

What was Cramer so touchy about? Was I the lout? Byzant would question her for five minutes. She'd tell the truth. As far as

I cared, she could tell Byzant everything we'd learned in Texas. No copyright on the info. I couldn't see any harm in telling Byzant. Couldn't see much good, either.

But maybe she didn't know that. Maybe I shouldn't have assumed Cramer knew much about cops.

I put on my sunglasses and caught up to her at the top step. "Sorry. I didn't think that through."

No response. She clattered down the steps and strode across the tarmac toward the terminal.

I kept up with her. "You want, we can each rent a car."

She stopped and swung around. Hands at her knees, she held the straps of the heavy carryall. "I'm exhausted. This's not the time for your sensitive male number. So can you drive?"

"What's the problem?" My best no-nonsense voice.

She shut her eyes. Tight-lipped: "I have something on my mind."

Again, she caught me by surprise. Not another word all the way to Buffalo. I hadn't expected that she'd be the one to turn Danny's den into a one-night stand. Off the thruway, I headed east on Genesee, away from town.

Cramer opened her eyes. "Where you going?"

"Thought I'd stop by Reading, Inc.'s, fund-raiser out in Clarence. See if Sister Charlayne wants to hear about our trip."

She stared ahead. "Well, all right."

That turned me off, a Cramer so chummy for three days and then an icicle. "What's bugging you?"

"I have a lot on my mind."

"Tell me?"

She scrunched up her face. "I've got this idea and I need to think it through. And if I tell anybody before I think it through, I might mess it up."

"So what can I do for you?"

"What you've been doing. Don't bug me and keep driving."

* * *

I expected a mob. That fall fund-raiser always got praised in Reading, Inc.'s, annual report as one of the successful events of the year. The monthly newsletter had photos and breathless accounts of the action.

No mob. Fifty cars, tops, in the lot. There were the promised tent, the live country-music combo, the cider, the hayride, and the softball game.

Among the cars, I recognized Josh's gray Oldsmobile and Sister Charlayne's Toyota. I didn't want to barge in. I might strangle Josh. Too, there could be at least one cop in the crowd.

So Cramer and I stood a way off. The tent could hold a couple hundred. But there were more musicians than guests milling in front of the cider. No one danced, though the band played on.

The field was set for softball: bases, lines, and pitcher's mound. But no players. The hay wagon stood empty. We walked up to a teenager who held the horses' reins. He pointed to the crest of a hill. "They're down yonder."

I followed Cramer. Not a steep hill. A few trees, dark green leaves turning red and orange, a week or so from peak color.

At the bottom was a flat field, part of it fenced in a square. Maybe forty people sat ten to a side atop the log fence. Another forty stood around, leaned against the top rung.

Cramer and I sat on the crest and watched. In the middle of the field stood a cow. A lazy, cud-chewing beef cow that didn't care a whit that almost a hundred people were calling to it.

I saw Josh and pointed. "There's the little runt."

Cramer noticed Sister Charlayne. "She's so small. And more frail than she looks in the paper or on TV."

"What are they doing?"

"In Texas, it's called cow-patty bingo. Rural politicians do it all the time as a fund-raiser. I didn't know they played it up here too."

"You mean, the cow—?"

"Yep. See the thin lines painted in the grass? You make a grid out of them. Sell squares. Commonly, the first square the cow poops on wins third place, second poop wins second, and third poop wins first. You know, lets the suspense build."

"So our Josh is in more deep do than he knows." I scanned the crowd. "I finally figured something. Before, I never came to Josh's fund-raisers, but I thought, well, someone must. After all, they raise a lot of funds."

"How much?"

"Oh, I'm sure he reports this one as twenty thou, minimum."

"So?"

"So you can't tell me that motley crew down there gives more than two hundred each. For a family of four, that's eight hundred bucks. They don't have that kind of money. Those're mostly students, their families."

"What are you getting at?"

"Yet another of Josh's scams. He probably takes whatever cash comes in today and gives it out as cow-patty prizes. Pays for the tent and the band and the hot dogs. Then he reports that he took in twenty thousand over expenses."

Cramer caught on right away. "So he takes a large but legitimate donation from someone who happens to run that bookie-in-a-box, say a twenty-thousand-dollar donation."

"Try this. A certain percentage of the gamblers just write checks straight to Reading, Inc. Oh, that Josh's a fund-raiser, all right."

"Deductible donations. Reading, Inc., stays legal and stays afloat, nay prospers."

"And someone paying to keep the box at arm's length has ten times that squirreled away in Switzerland or the Caymans."

Cramer knew not-for-profits. "And who's going to come all the way to Clarence to match names on checks to names of cow-patty players?" She sneered and spit the words. "Every little fund-raiser put on by every not-for-profit group?"

I looked down at the cow-patty bingo. "I'd like to talk to Sister Charlayne in private. Same with Josh, but afterward."

"Someplace private?"

"Yeah. Where no one can hear him scream."

"What are you going to do?"

"Break both his knees and ram my fist up his butt."

*   *   *

Not an hour later, we parked across from the Nachmans' in the Heights. "Josh will come home," Cramer warned.

"Nah. Remember out in Clarence they came in separate cars? I don't expect to see him for a couple of hours, until they take down the tent." When we'd left Clarence—right behind Sister Charlayne's Toyota—people still were dancing and hay-riding. "These fund-raising events, Josh runs hands-on from beginning to end." I kept checking my rearview. "Here she comes."

Sister Charlayne pulled into their drive. She and a bulky woman about her age got out. They chatted a moment, touched each other, and parted. Finally alone, Sister Charlayne trudged to her front door.

Cramer said, "Poor woman looks ready to collapse."

"I don't doubt it." After giving her a chance to get in and get her coat off, I opened my door. "Coming in?"

Cramer didn't move. "Going to shout at her?"

"Don't intend to. She may shout at me."

Cramer turned the rearview and checked her face.

"What're you looking at? You don't wear any makeup anyway." As it came out of my mouth, I knew it was the wrong thing to say.

She sneered. "I'm trying to see whether I can look myself in the eye."

I held my tongue. At Sister Charlayne's door, I knocked. Cramer stood with her hands in her pockets and shivered.

Sister Charlayne opened the door. "Yes? Oh, Santa." Not good. Eyes red, skin slack, hair still windblown.

"Hi. This's Cramer McKensie. She's a friend."

A genuine smile in Cramer's direction. A glare in my direction. "Yes, Josh told me you had a new one already." New what? My, word did travel.

"I'm afraid we have some bad news."

"Haven't you done enough already?"

"What happened?"

"You haven't heard? The governor suspended Josh's nomi-
nation."

"No." Cramer let the word die away. She sounded relieved.
Why? Except for the fact that he should have been in jail, the
Josh/Sister Charlayne team would have been dynamite in Albany.

"Did the guv give a reason?" I hadn't seen a local paper in
days.

"Something about 'pending further review.' In the papers,
you so fouled Josh's reputation. Bearing false witness. That awful
food poisoning and . . . People being what they are. Dwelling in
sin. The Bible says that . . ."

I'd never heard her ramble so. "You going to let us in?"

"Never again, young man."

Young man, huh? Where was the genuine, sincere Sister
Charlayne I had known for years? "Cramer and I've been to Houston."

Sister Charlayne pushed her brows together. "Yes?"

"Where Josh lived before he moved here and met you. Where
Lona, in high school, lost her virginity to a Mexican kid. Josh put an
overdose of barbiturate in the kid's brownies. He never woke up."

"Josh wouldn't."

"Then, last week—"

"No," she whispered.

"Last week, your husband started killing again."

"No," she repeated.

"The Mexican kid's death got ruled a suicide. Someone found
out but didn't tell the cops. Told only Josh."

"No!" A scream. Where was her sharp tongue? Where were
her deeply held convictions?

"Then when you wanted to start Reading, Inc., Josh said, 'Oh,
honey, I'll raise the funds.' "

That drew her lips tight. She squeezed her eyes shut.

"And what did Josh get when he tried to raise money? He got
a turnout of poor folk like today. You know what Josh'll say got
raised out there in Clarence? Maybe twenty thousand dollars.
Know where that money comes from?"

Not a muscle moved.

"I told you Monday. It's Josh's price for letting a computcr bookie run in the office. All Josh provides is the filing cabinet and the electricity."

Expecting Cramer to jump in, I looked at her. She shook her head, staring at Sister Charlayne.

"Then the strike hits. No one's betting. Payments to Josh stop. Thus, Reading, Inc.'s, 'donations' stop. Houston orders Josh to stop the strike. Who knows who dreamed it up, who wrote the first-and-ten notes? Who knows who poured the nicotine into the Kahlúa? Blew up Jimmy's car. Shot Greg Bowsk. Who knows? But Josh is responsible."

Hand to her mouth, Sister Charlayne rubbed slowly. As though she'd had a few drinks.

"Then I find the book, give it to the cops. Houston orders Josh to put me next on the list. Sunday night, he tries to blow me up."

I couldn't get her to look me in the eye, but I could look into hers. Too calm. What was she on?

"Josh says, 'Look the other way, and we keep Reading, Inc. Ask questions, and we could lose it.' You made a choice, and it's killing you."

That finally set her off. "Killing me? You're—"

I clasped her upper arms and lifted her straight up.

"Santa? Let me down!" She wriggled and kicked.

I carried her into the living room.

"Santa! This instant! How dare you!"

Cramer followed us.

I did what Sister Charlayne demanded and marched into the bathroom. Didn't matter what she said. And she was too little to do more than kick. I pawed through the medicine cabinet. No luck.

Cramer asked, "What are you looking for?"

"Won't know till I find it."

In the bedroom, fending off Sister Charlayne, I found coat and purse. She screamed louder, so I figured I was getting warmer. In her purse, I found a thin orange plastic vial. I held it up.

Cramer came into the doorway. "Oh, no."

"What?" Sister Charlayne put her hand to her throat.

I pushed open the white plastic top and shook out a few. "Says 'Wallace' and a number: 1001. 'Miltown 400,' it says on the label. Twice daily, fourteen days. Isn't Miltown an industrial-strength anti-anxiety pill?"

Cramer agreed.

"Let's see. Dated last Monday. So one on Monday and two on Tuesday, Wednesday, Thursday, and Friday. Maybe two already today." I looked at her eyes. "Maybe three today. Still, there ought to be sixteen, maybe fifteen left. But you know what?"

She looked down and began to cry. "I'm so ashamed. I've never taken a pill in my life. It's like I'm not good enough."

I rattled the orange vial and shook out every pill. "But only half a dozen—"

Sister Charlayne slapped my hand, knocking the pills to the floor. Letting out a cry, she collapsed onto the bed. She buried her face.

"Only half a dozen left. You're way ahead. So you are a very upset lady, more than a little fuzzy-headed about how much trouble Josh is in. Too many of those things in you to do what you should."

Muffled: "Josh's in the hospital." To hear, I had to put my ear close. "Was when Greg Bowsk was . . ."

"What?"

"ECMC." Erie County Medical Center. "I took him in for bleeding."

"Don't give me that. He was in Clarence this afternoon."

She was sobbing, so I strained to listen. "After the bleeding stopped, they took some pictures of his insides and let him out this morning."

I could call Albert or Harvey to get that verified. "Stop excusing Josh." I knelt beside the bed and put my hands in front of me in prayer. "Sister Charlayne, please. Tell me who Josh owes. With luck, we can leave Josh's name out of it. You could go to Albany after all." I tried for her eyes, but she wasn't giving them. Wailing, could she hear me?

Cramer touched my shoulder. "I think we got our answer."

I couldn't stop. "You claim to be a Christian, yet you let Josh get away with murder."

Sister Charlayne sobbing, Cramer tried to pull me away. "You're done, Santa."

No, I wasn't. I raised my voice. "You're the one protecting Josh."

Cramer pulled me out of there. I took a last shot. "So it's up to you now, my dear," I called over my shoulder. "It's all up to you."

When Cramer shut the front door behind us, we could still hear Sister Charlayne sobbing and wailing in the bedroom.

* * *

The art places in Buffalo had worked out schedules to not compete for the same Saturday crowds. Martha Jackson's son did afternoons. The Albright-Knox did late afternoons. Artists Gallery and Geraldo and the other commercial places did early evenings. Then the gallery hoppers still standing would end up at Hallwalls, where the shows didn't get cranked up until after midnight.

So early evening, no time to swing by her house, I got Cramer to Ronnie's opening right on the dot. Mobbed, as she had predicted.

After parking the rent Chevy blocks away, I stayed out in Artists Gallery's shadowed courtyard.

Shrimp, Jimmy, Eddie del, Greg, and I had had our last laugh together in that courtyard. I could put my fist through car tops. I could eat bricks. Or I could wait to see if Cramer found Lona and sent her out.

I waited. From the sign over the door, Ronnie had retitled his show: "A Stitch in Time."

Soon, Cramer made her way out the door into the overflow crowd. Lona came out behind her. No coat; she held her purse tight to her belly. Cramer pointed in my direction. Whatever she said next worked. Lona threaded her way down the steps and around cars toward me.

"What do you want, shithead? Your name's in all the papers. And not the sports page."

"So I've heard. How's Ronnie's opening?"

"Cut the crap. One phone call from me and there'll be cops all over here. Now what do you want?"

"More Angel Ramirez."

"What about him?" She dug into her purse and brought out her favorite curved flask, covered in leather.

"Real name: Hector."

A cloud passed her lovely face. "How do you know that?" She unscrewed the metal top and let it dangle from its leather strap. Took a long swig.

"I saw his picture. He's gorgeous as you said."

"Where'd you see—?"

"At his mother's house."

She stared, put her hand to her heart, swallowed.

"In South Texas, on Thursday. Then I went to Houston and saw the file at the hospital where they took him."

Lona took another long swig.

"Has Josh always been prejudiced against Mexicans?"

"He's not," she snapped.

"Then why was he so angry? Because Angel got to screw you?"

She didn't answer.

"Angel's mother told me a man came to see her, asked some questions about Angel's death. Did the man come to see you?"

"No."

I didn't believe her. "Did the cops talk to you?"

"No."

Definitely a difference. That "no" I believed.

Metal top secure, she shoved the flask back into her purse. "I can't stand it that they're still getting away with it."

"Getting away with what? Angel's murder?"

Her face was reddening. "It's in all the papers. Everyone in there's talking about it. Who's next? Who's next? I need . . ."

"What? What do you need, Lona?"

She drew back her arm. She'd hit me before. That time, she lowered it. "I need to call the cops. Tell them where to find your lousy ass." Raised her eyebrows and added, in a sarcastic tone, "My civic duty." She stomped back toward the crowd on Artists Gallery's porch.

"You won't."

"Maybe," she called over her shoulder. "Maybe not. But you can't take the chance. I finally got one up on you, you shit."

*   *   *

They're still getting away with it, Lona said. And if I wanted to keep getting away with it, I had to skedaddle.

At a pay phone blocks from Artists Gallery, I called Gus.

"Welcome back. You being careful?"

"As I can. Seen Byzant?"

"He popped me."

I hooted. "What for?"

"Not being real cooperative."

"I can imagine. Seen any FBI?"

"They come visit. Not my favorite little boys."

"Think they're listening in?"

"Count on it."

"Then find a private line, get back to me at the taxi stand."

In the rent Chevy from Erie, I drove to Yellow Cab, my favorite greasy spoon on Elmwood. Only a couple of customers, but sometimes a cop stopped for coffee, so I went in through the kitchen door. While Sunny, the cook, broiled some redfish, we chatted.

When Gus called, I told him, "I need to know where Josh Nachman is. Try his home number. If he's not there, tell Sister Charlayne you're some guy on TV and make up some emergency. Whatever, find out where he usually hangs on a Saturday night."

Next I called Albert. Got his machine and left a terse message. "Was Josh in ECMC when Bowsk got shot? ASAP."

Was Albert even back from Virginia yet? Had he and Lance Bishop been able to persuade the owners to cave in? The player reps?

In his cramped little office, Sunny had the past week's *Buffalo News,* all opened to Yellow Cab ads.

While I ate Sunny's fish, rice, and broccoli, I read Makepeace's articles—Wednesday, Thursday, and Friday.

He had added a number of unattributed details of Jimmy's

and Eddie del's bodies and the investigation that I sure hadn't known. Who else was Makepeace talking to?

On Friday, Greg Bowsk gunned down, Makepeace added something else: my name. In the midst of the "most extensive manhunt in Western New York history," he announced, the cops questioned me, but I "fled."

The little shit. Looking back, why had I trusted Makepeace?

Trusted him? I'd burglarized his upstairs apartment before I left. Should have ransacked it. Maybe he'd figured that out and figured he owed me nothing.

Finally, Gus called back. "Near Gondolas and Garlic?" Our name for one of our favorite Italian restaurants, over on Grant Street. "You know that dog-and-pony show?" The OTB place.

"Sure."

"Treat yourself to a brew in the 'hood."

So I paid Sunny and sallied forth. One of my favorite nights: foggy and chilly, trying hard to rain. Late enough that the OTB place was closed.

In dark glasses and knit cap, I slouched into the nearest bar. Scanned the TV and the patrons—no Josh. Elbow on the bar, I mumbled, "Draft."

On the TV, a couple of Latin guys in the 150-pound range were beating each other up. Saturday-night fights.

When the barman laid down my draft, I laid a ten next to it. "Keep the change."

He didn't touch it.

"Josh Nachman been in here?"

He frowned.

"Short guy, good-sized gut. Balding straight across."

He shook his head.

"No hurry. I owe him a penny after last Sunday's Bills debacle." I nodded toward the TV.

His face cleared. "Oh, know who ya mean." He picked up my ten. "He was in here earlier, see some guys. But he left."

"Any idea where he went?"

"I ain't his mom." He walked away. Little birdie told me that was the easiest ten he ever made.

Pulling the cap lower, still slouching, I tried another bar and another. No one seemed to recognize me. Nor had they seen Josh.

At the next bar, a guy had seen Josh "earlier" at another bar across Grant Street. That was the bar where I should have started. Everyone there knew Josh. They expected him back "later."

I walked out, not seeing any reason to draw attention. It had begun to rain. I crossed the deserted street and picked the front wall of Marconi Meats because it had a rolled-up awning to wait under. The plate-glass window was spattered with signs: kielbasa $2.49, Virginia ham $4.29, wings 10¢ each.

Not a pedestrian on that foggy, gray night. A yellow Buick splashed past—not Josh's gray Olds—and kept going. Then a truck that looked like it had been in a wreck and been resurrected with mix-and-match spare parts chugged past.

Josh might walk up, more likely drive up and park close. If he was alone, I'd catch him before he went in. If he wasn't alone, I'd follow him in and ask him to take a stroll.

The next car came from my left. It caught my eye because it slowed down. A little Tercel was parked just to my left, but there was room in front of it and behind.

It was the funky patched-together truck, which must have circled the block. Back again. But why? Plenty of empty spaces. It was a white pickup, well rusted. A red hood. A dark blue passenger-side door.

Wipers blurred the figure inside. It slid into the spot behind the Tercel.

Then its engine roared, its wheels turned, and it came straight at me. Someone in those bars had recognized me.

I wasn't at my most mobile. Huddled and cold. Hopping from one foot to the other. Also, where was I going to jump? Two seconds, and it'd have me pinned.

So I bent slightly at the knees and sprang up. My idea, if indeed I had one in that split second, was to slide my fingers between the brick and the rolled-up awning. Grab the awning, pull my feet up, and let the truck pass beneath me, through the glass, and into Marconi Meats.

Good plan. I bent, sprang, stretched, opened my hands to

166

grasp. And got my thighs slammed into by the front of the red-and-white truck.

It wasn't able to pick up that much speed across ten feet of concrete. So it didn't crash through. The low wall holding the plate glass stopped it. And all stretched out, I couldn't have made much bigger a target.

I let go of the awning, dropped my hands to the hood, and tried to wriggle free.

The driver's door opened. Sure enough, Josh Nachman came out. I got few details of his face because I couldn't stop looking at the black thing he pointed. He came closer, the gun wobbling.

"Josh, you can't—"

"She is the innocent. You will not do that to her."

"Lona?"

Then an explosion. The gun went off and the plate glass cracked on my right almost at the same time.

"You have taken from her all you—"

"Lona, Josh? Is that your problem? You kill any guy who—"

A second explosion, that time to my left. I dropped down.

Shoving the truck, I got it to rock enough for me to wriggle past the grille. After my feet landed solid, I slid under. Josh was shouting something, raving. Something about love.

Hot under there. The engine was still running. Smelled thick exhaust. I curled sideways and slid again and got going headfirst. A couple of scrunches—banged my head, my cheek burned—and I could reach for Josh's legs.

Two shots spent. Four more, max, and he'd be mine.

He was crouching to see under the truck. If he had any sense, he'd glance a shot off the concrete and let it ricochet.

I reached out, grabbed his ankle, and yanked.

He went down onto his butt. I still had to pull myself out from under the truck, so I let go of him.

How long did it take? Four seconds to slide out from under the truck and get to my feet. Josh had as long, but he was ranting about purity and grace. Trying to point the gun, but his arm shook too much.

We each got one blow in. I used my fist to knock the gun out of his hand. He howled and used his shoe to kick me square in the balls. The gun flew away.

I wished my balls had.

I doubled over and Josh ran south. He wasn't a fast runner, tubby, waddling, holding his right hand in his left. But then I couldn't run at all. Hands at my crotch, gasping, I leaned against the truck and watched him disappear into the fog.

Above, a window opened and someone called out. Across Grant Street, a couple of guys came out of the bar but just held the door open and stood there. The guys who'd recognized me and told Josh?

I took a big gulp of rainy air and limped over to the gun, a little thing. I picked it up by the barrel, about as long as my middle finger. Not real accurate if he had missed me. But then Josh hadn't fired point-blank as he had at Greg Bowsk.

I stuck the gun into my pocket. If I ran into Josh later on, maybe I could return it.

*   *   *

Outside the Wilson Farms corner of Elmwood and Auburn, I huddled in a phone booth, still short of breath and grunting from the pain. Know the crazy thing? I had a Harvey Laurel codeine scrip waiting at the Rite Aid on Bryant, not six blocks away. Did I dare go pick it up?

Nah. I wasn't in that much pain.

Gus answered. "You be one popular item. Since your last call, Byzant's come visiting, warrant in hand."

"So he's listening in now."

"I suppose you could be cute and say howdy."

"Too busy calling plays."

"I'm ready."

"Ball's in front of the show." The show was what he and I called the movie theater up on Hertel. "You're split wide right." That was football talk for being the pass catcher who starts the play near the right sideline. "Post thirty and over." In thirty minutes,

Gus was supposed to go down the alley along the right side of the movie theater, turn left, and look up. "No tellin' who you meet." Which meant I'd be there.

"No tellin'."

"And run your own pick." Slip past the defender, meaning Byzant. But I needn't have added that.

Not given to sentiment, Gus grunted and hung up.

* * *

Feet dangling from the show's fire escape, I heard Gus scuffing down the alley.

He looked up. "Your cheek looks like day-old burger meat."

"Josh persuaded me to scrape it against a sidewalk." I slid to the ground.

"You sure keep busy." Gus followed me over the fence, through a backyard, and down a drive to the Chevy. Inside, he asked, "What you want me along for?"

"Makepeace. Little shit's in this up past his common sense."

The lower floor of Makepeace's house was dark. The upper floors, where he lived, were lit. Around the back, only one car, Makepeace's Grand Prix. Cold engine, so he'd been home for a while.

Gus yanked me into the dark under the pine trees. "Lookee there."

My head snapped up. The open porch window was lit. So were the curtained windows on either side.

"Two shadows on that curtain, Santa."

On the right, the living room, as I remembered.

"He has coeds over all the time."

"On the other hand."

"The boyfriend. Yes. I'll go knock. You go around front."

"Anybody tries to slip out?"

"Keep him close and give a holler. Even if it's a she."

Bottom of the stairwell, a thick metal door had replaced the flimsy screen. Locked. Beside it, a buzzer on a shiny brass plate and a speaker grille. Such was Makepeace's reaction to getting

broken in on. Or the reaction of his insurance company. I gave
Gus a moment to get around front.

I buzzed. The speaker behind the grille came alive. "Yes?"
"Santa here."

Long pause. "Where, uh, where have you been?"

"Down south. Houston. I've got more to the story."

Another long pause. Would he call Byzant? I heard a buzz, so
I pushed the thick metal door. It opened.

On the second floor landing, Makepeace closed and latched
the wide window. "What happened to your face?"

"Scraped it."

"Can I get you something for it?"

Did it look that bad? "I'll tough it out. Listen, can I come in?"

"Sure." He held the door. "Something to drink?"

"Juice or soda. Yeah, something wet would be nice." I nodded
toward the living room. "You here alone?"

"Yes." He opened the fridge. "What about apple juice?"

"Great." By the time Makepeace brought my juice and his
wine, I'd looked into the computer room. No one. In the powder
room, I looked at my cheek. Not pretty.

I pushed past Makepeace and opened the front door. "You
don't lock this?" I pulled the door wide.

"Usually. Guess I forgot to."

I nodded into the hall, top of the wide front stairway. "Mighty
dark."

He rushed toward me as fast as the two full glasses would let
him. "What are you doing?"

On the landing a dim light, and to the right a locked door. I
thought about the layout of his apartment and the stairwell and
the shape of the house. There was no space for a room for that
door to lead to. "Where's this go?"

"It's a broom closet. I haven't opened it in years."

Probably enough space for a closet. At the bend in the stairs
was a window right above the front porch where Gus would be
watching. I walked down to the window and raised it. "Gus?"

"Yo."

"Any business?"

"Been mighty quiet."

I shut the window and dashed back up.

Makepeace stood in his doorway, legs spread. "Who were you talking to?"

"Whoever's in here with you must be hiding up in your bedroom and I don't want him slipping out."

"What do you mean? I'm here alone."

"Right." I stepped past him.

He let me. "You sure seem to know a lot about—" He set the drinks on an end table. "Were you the bastard who—?"

On the stairs, I turned. "Yup." Gave him my biggest grin.

Shit. No one was up there, not on the bed, not in the bath, not in the closet.

Back downstairs, Makepeace waited. "Satisfied?"

"No. Who's your other source for those articles?" I stared at him, tried to bore through his skull and root around until I found the truth.

"Wayne Hall. The guy you call Dingleberry."

"Why's he talk to you?"

"Remember that DJ at school? The one whose poetry we're putting out? She's his little sister, and it seems he blabs at the dinner table."

That made me stop. The woman of the blood-red Camaro. "You knew that when we saw Dingleberry talking to Josh on Tuesday night."

He gave a shake to his head and shoulders but didn't deny it.

"And you called Byzant after dropping me off later that night."

"No." He raised one hand. "I swear, Santa."

"One other thing. A part-time teaching gig and the odd news article do not pay for this."

"Thank you."

I stared back and waited.

"You see, I have a friend."

"The one who fits all those clothes up there?"

He nodded. "When you broke in here, you didn't find anything." He followed me into the kitchen. "What'd you come back for?"

"To see which side you're on."

He leaned on the back door. Cocky son of a bitch. "Tell me something I don't know."

"Sure. Ten years ago, Josh Nachman killed a Mexican kid down in Houston and almost got away with it."

From the look on his face, it surprised him that I knew. What surprised me was that he knew, too.

*   *   *

Where had the second shadow gone? Makepeace's house had no side yards. The driveway ran down one side. The other side butted against the church lot next door. A high chain-link fence separated the two. Bushes grew between the house and the fence so thick that I couldn't push through.

Gus and I walked down to Ferry Street and around the fence onto the church lot. The church building kept me from going all the way along the fence on that side. We had to go around the church, back onto Elmwood Avenue, and past the church to the M&T Bank. Behind, in the bank's parking lot, sat a couple of cars—people who didn't want to feed the meters on Elmwood while they dined at Rigoletto's or the Greek place across the street.

Where the bank parking lot met the back corner of the church's outside wall, Gus and I found a gap wide enough to edge through.

So we did. It was dark under the pine trees. Quiet. We walked back along the chain-link fence until we were across from Makepeace's house, dense with those bushes.

Except one narrow gap, overgrown with bushes, led to a side door. It looked well used.

Gus rubbed his chin. "Purty crafty."

"Yup. From Elmwood, it looks as though a car's driving in to use the money machine. But the guy parks and stays in the shadows along the church. To that gap in the wall. He walks along under the pines . . ."

"To this screen door."

"Which leads up to the door at the top of the front stairs." I loved it. "Makepeace told me it was a broom closet, but it's enough space for a narrow stairway."

Gus caught on. "And while you're searching up there and I'm standing like a fool in the front yard—"

"He slips out this way."

"But who is he?" As usual, Gus was right on target. "And will he come back after he thinks we're gone?"

To find out, Gus parked himself deep in those pine trees behind the church.

*   *   *

Let common sense reign. I hated cops, but.

So I held a quarter in my hand at the row of phones outside the NYNEX switching office on Elmwood.

Should I cover my ass?

Indeed I should.

At the leftmost booth, I found the number in the blue pages. Quarter into the slot, I poked the buttons.

"Detective Bureau."

"Captain Byzant, please. This's Santa Arkwright."

"Hold, please."

After about a minute, which seemed like twenty, I hung up.

At the next phone, I dropped in another quarter and re-poked.

"Detect—"

"Santa again. Byzant?"

"Captain Byzant is not on duty, sir. May I—"

"Then I'll call you back in ten minutes, and you give me a number." I hung up.

I hated waiting. I started pacing. I started fantasizing.

When I called again, I got a number.

Byzant was waiting. "Arkwright—"

"I'm not going to stay on this phone very long."

"Arkwright, where are you?"

"Get real, Byzant. You going to listen or—"

"You're in a lot of trouble, son. You were told—under penalty of law—not to leave Buffalo. We have warrants for—"

I hung up, hard.

*   *   *

For a couple of minutes, I let Byzant stew. Then I went to the first phone and called back.

That time, he listened. And listened.

How long did it take to trace calls?

After a couple of minutes, I hung up and drove over to Main Street, where I called Byzant from the Metro station. Then downtown and the Convention Center. Then the Hilton.

By the time I was sipping an iced tea at the Hyatt-Regency bar, phone in hand, I finished. Byzant would never get me on withholding info: Josh and the rest-of-ten note, Angel Ramirez and the spiked brownies, Makepeace and his scented missives from Scarlet, even the truck-and-gun number over on Grant Street. I spun out the Josh-jealous-of-boyfriends theory. Not once did I refer to that bullshit when Byzant and Vinnie kidnapped me.

And finally, Sister Charlayne. "I rattled her this afternoon. She wants to do the right thing. If you take her in and start her detoxing from those pills, she may stop alibiing Josh."

"What are you going to do about your own problems? You're subject to arrest on sight."

"Josh confesses to murder and attempted murder. Four bodies, Byzant, in Buffalo alone. Better yet, Josh gives you the guy down in Houston who's pulling the strings, you personally give that guy to the FBI, and I don't figure I have any problems. Mayor's gonna pin a medal on me while you hold my coat."

"You better be right."

"Is that a threat or you only being your usual patronizing self? Why don't you try helping me?"

"The bureau is doing everything within its purview to—"

"Asshole." I hung up and sipped my iced tea.

*   *   *

Before ten, I took Gus coffee and a couple of doughnuts. No one had come. No one had gone. But he hadn't begun to exhaust his patience. I said I'd check back in another hour.

From there, I drove the Chevy down Essex Street past Artists Gallery. Nary a car was left in the big courtyard.

Since Byzant knew I was back in town, would he have someone watching for me twenty-four hours? My house, my phone, of course.

But Artists Gallery? I stayed in shadows, quiet for a while. Nothing.

I moved slowly.

On the porch, I knocked and waited. Slowly, the door opened.

Cramer. Was she alone? She didn't say hello, didn't say anything.

I held up a check I'd borrowed from Gus. "This is to cover your Texas expenses."

"They're already covered." She opened the door the rest of the way. "What happened to your face?"

"Had an affair with a sidewalk."

"You might as well come in. I'll pour some salt on it."

Yes?

Smoke still hung in the air. The ashtrays and baskets were overflowing. Many butts had been stepped out on the concrete floor. Empty glasses and beer bottles were scattered around the edges. Bunched napkins held once-bitten crackers and cheese.

"It was a zoo in here," she said.

"Cops?"

"One asked me questions. He and his buddy hung out to the bitter end. They said for protection. But they're gone now."

"Ronnie still around?"

"He got so drunk he had to be carried out."

"His paintings turned out terrific, all sewed up."

She raised her eyes. "You know, I agree. So did the crowd." At the sink in her office, she ran hot water on a cloth.

"You sold some." I'd seen red dots.

"Two big ones. A bunch of little ones. Next week will tell,

175

second looks." She rinsed out the cloth and turned to the swivel chair where I sat. "How'd you maul your cheek?"

"Crawling under some old truck Josh rammed into me."

"Josh?" She was so close, dabbing at my cheek. "Why were you under—"

I winced. "He pinned me to a storefront and took two shots."

"Shots with a gun?"

"Yup." It really stung. "Ow!" What I really needed was a hug and kiss.

"I'll make it hurt worse, you do something that stupid again. Santa! This killing has to stop."

"I'm working on it." I didn't mention that the gun was in the trunk of my Chevy.

She threw the cloth into my lap. "Here. My hands aren't steady enough." From a high cabinet, she got a box of gauze pads, a roll of thin white tape, and a bottle of disinfectant. "You want something to drink? I'm having wine."

"You want to get drunk or get Josh?"

She wasn't to be teased. "Get drunk. What about you?"

"I'll take some juice."

Washcloth in hand, I followed her into the main gallery, where the food and drink table looked trashed.

"Know why I don't need your check?" She poured my juice before she answered. "I got paid to get you out of town. By Father."

"Harvey?"

"Remember Tuesday, before we left? I called Father to ask what else we could do. He explained someone was trying to kill you. That for your back, he prescribed sun and palm trees." She smeared disinfectant onto a gauze pad. When she gave it to me, her hand trembled. "He said you'd never go on your own, so anything I could do to get you out of town, he'd pay my expenses. So I thought, why not?"

"Is this why you were brooding on the plane coming back?"

"Yes. I'm apologizing."

I sat on a stool and pressed the pad to my cheek. Quite bracing.

Cramer's face was changing. Wait. I knew better. My perception of her face was changing. It didn't look better, didn't look worse. But it sure looked different. I thought of the off-seasons I'd prowled the world's art museums. Some I returned to year after year. So many world-class paintings and sculptures I had to look at for hours to finally begin to see. Why any less with Cramer?

"I was two when Father divorced my mom. She moved to San Antonio and went to nursing school while Nana looked after me."

"You told me that Friday night. You never saw your father."

She nodded. "He sent his support checks to the agency in Austin and they sent us a state check for the amount minus their service charge. So we had an official record."

"And otherwise you never heard from him?"

"He was busy. Med school, starting a practice. But every Christmas and birthday, I'd get a hundred-dollar check, always folded in half. No card. Mom would deposit it in my college account. When I got to be a teenager, I'd cash it and buy clothes or art supplies."

"What are you getting at?"

"Before I'd cash the check, I'd look at it. I had no visual memory of this guy. He got *nada* from me and my mom, no letters, no pictures. But he felt guilty enough to keep sending these hundred-dollar checks twice a year. I'd rub the check, smell it, read every word and number, looking for some sign of him. I think that's why I took this job in Buffalo. To find out who this guy really is."

Cramer was looking at a spot on the floor, speaking in a monotone, and almost wringing her hands she held them together so tightly. She looked up at me. "Did you see the papers?"

Makepeace's articles in the *News*. I nodded.

"I think Father wanted you out of town so you wouldn't see those articles until it was too late."

"What makes you think that?"

"Father's signature on the checks when I was a kid. His handwriting was all I really had of him. And I had to give that up when I cashed the check. It wasn't really a signature. It was an H and an L and a design scribbled through and around them. His curlicue signature was all that was left of his art, my mom said." She took a deep breath. "Know where I saw that signature?"

I did. But I let her tell me. No wonder she was shaking.

"Thursday night. On Hector Ramirez's death certificate at that hospital in Houston."

* * *

Cramer called her dad but got his service. Which didn't mean he wasn't home. So we walked to the Chevy. Driving up Bidwell Parkway, I asked, "Where'd your dad grow up?"

"Sonora. A couple hundred miles west of San Antone. Know his real name? Herve. Herve Laurel." She gave it a heavy accent.

"But didn't Hector Ramirez's mother say the man who visited spoke Spanish like a professor rather than a native speaker?"

"He could have used Castilian. The pure mother tongue, to a Tex-Mex speaker, isn't regular Spanish."

"Good point."

"See, Father graduated first in his high school class. Science scholarship up the road at San Angelo, a little state school. Says my mom, school scared him. So he came home that first summer and talked his high school sweetheart, my mom, into getting pregnant. He would quit school and labor on some ranch and do his art at night. But no. His family supported all three of us and kept him in school, and he kept getting A's in all these hard science courses. Then he got accepted at medical school, going places. My mom and I seemed a burden, she says, so they divorced."

"And that's the last you saw of him? At least until you moved here?"

She nodded. "Not even one of those checks since I turned eighteen. But my curiosity wouldn't quit. I found him in a medical directory. So after a quarter of a century, I picked up the phone and said, 'Father, this is your daughter.' "

"What was his reaction?"

"At first? He cried. We both did."

On Elmwood, I parked in front of the M&T Bank. Only half a dozen cars sat in the bank's back lot. While Cramer waited, I ducked through the gap in the wall. Behind the church, I slipped into the darkness under the pine trees. "Gus!" I hissed. "Gus!"

"Over here."

"C'mon. You can go home. I've been talking to Cramer. Makepeace has nothing to do with any of this. You know who's got Josh by the short hairs?"

He tiptoed up to me. "Don't shout. And don't tell me nothing. I been waiting here and waiting, and finally, 'bout half an hour ago, I hear someone coming from the parking lot. I get way back under the trees so he don't see me."

"Yes?"

"But then I'm so far back I don't see him."

"Sure it's a he?"

"No."

"Big guy, little guy?"

"A dark shadow. Sorry, Santa. Once he's upstairs, I think I hear shouts. But there's no window on this side, so it coulda been the wind diddlin' the pines."

Half an hour? Too long to suggest that we go back out to the parking lot, feel hoods, take down the license of the hot one. I looked at the side door. "Screw Makepeace's personal life. Let's go."

"I'm staying."

"I tell you, you don't have to."

"But what if he comes out ten minutes after you leave? You sayin' I've been wasting my time?" Gus could get so stubborn.

I wanted to tell him, Yes, you've been wasting your time. He raised his hand as though he wanted to show me some proof. So I asked, "Guess who?"

"Guess who what?"

"Who signed the death certificate of the Mexican kid who took Lona's virginity. Same kid who Josh probably poisoned."

He looked confused. "But that was long ago."

"Harvey signed that death certificate."

Wasn't often I could make Gus's jaw drop, but I did that time. "Doc Harvey? How'd you—"

"Cramer recognized her dad's signature at the hospital in Texas."

"Doc Harvey, huh?" Gus and Harvey never saw each other except on Monday afternoons. Then they acted cordial, respectful.

"Now will you come with me? I need your help."

Gus shook his head. "I don't believe it." But he followed me back to the Chevy, Cramer waiting patiently inside.

Turned out Harvey lived a couple streets north of Delaware Park in the high-priced neighborhood. I parked at the curb.

The house was dark. "He's either sleeping or not here," I said.

"Once again," Gus replied, "master of the obvious."

To make sure, the three of us took the long, winding stone path through tall trees to the front door. After ringing, we peered into the windows.

Gus whistled. "Fancy place."

"You should see the upstairs," Cramer said.

What you don't know about your personal physician. Deep inner needs? Childhood traumas? A fortune in gambling? Holding a whole city hostage?

"The guy's come a long way from Sonora," I said.

No response, so we strolled back toward the car. I kicked leaves.

She kept looking into the treetops. "If I hadn't gone to Houston, you'd never have recognized that signature on your own."

"You're right. Harvey doesn't sign his scrips like that now."

"My own father? It can't be."

Why not? I would have asked. But I knew her answer: Because I don't want it to be.

Back in the Chevy, Gus asked the commonsense question "What will we do when Doc Harvey comes home?"

"You guys wait here," Cramer said. "I'll go talk to him."

I snorted. "No way I'm letting you go in there alone."

"What? To protect me? Father wouldn't hurt me. He'll tell me the truth."

"I'll bet you believe in the tooth fairy, too."

She raised her voice. "He wouldn't dare hurt me. He's my father. I'll bite his head off unless he has a good story for all this."

"Going to shout at him, too?" I asked.

"Probably. He may shout back after he hears what I have to say."

"Which is?"

" 'Father, can I trust you?' "

"Hmmm."

"Then another one. 'Tell me you're not a murderer.' "

I looked over her shoulder at his house, deep in the trees. "That might do it."

"Lady has a point, Santa. I don't believe Doc Harvey's any daughter killer."

"I'll let him convince me of that."

"Even so, you can handle him. Why don't you two go in. Gimme the car keys and I'll stay here in case."

Cramer said, "You both stay—"

"I'm going in."

Gus changed the subject. "Why'd Harvey moonlight as a bookie? What's he do, run ads in the medical journals? Who're his clients? How's he collect?"

I shrugged. "Don't know."

"You guys got nothing. I be doing more good watching Makepeace's side—" Gus stopped, face frozen. I'd seen it happen before when he got an idea. "Santa, I'm staying put, right here. Know why?" He leaned forward. "Let's say, against all my guts, you're right. Doc Harvey's got a bookie gig. Remember he's also your personal doc? How you think the National Football League's gonna look on that? Consortin', I do believe."

"Consorting with known gamblers, Gus. I didn't know. Albert didn't know. How could we?"

"You think that lame excuse gonna fly at NFL? You do need me lookin' out for you. Try this: you write checks to Doc Harvey."

"That's a retainer for medical services, not gambling debts."

"Oh, right. Try this: you're tight with Josh Nachman, who ran the book."

"Gus, I didn't know."

"Um-hmm. Try this: you been boppin' his daughter for months."

"That doesn't mean anything, what her father does." Although guys had been investigated by the league for far less.

"Try this: you been writing Nachman, alleged bookie, a thousand-buck check every couple of weeks for years. So happens you tie it into INTs and fumble recoveries."

"I write checks to Reading, Inc."

"So do the man's other gambling clients. Add it up."

"I get your point." I didn't mention that I had in the trunk the gun that probably killed Greg Bowsk. I could see how from a certain point of view—say, Byzant's—I was in a fair amount of legal trouble.

The NFL spelled it out in lectures, pamphlets, slogans taped to our lockers. Pool: the person keeping track donated the service and all the bettors equally shared any risk. Book: the person keeping track charged, usually 10 percent, and didn't share any risk.

As players, we were welcome to hug and kiss the person who happened to run your office pool. But bookies would give us an incurable disease and a chilling prognosis: banishment from the game for life.

Cramer had been sitting in silence, watching her dad's driveway. A couple times she rubbed a forefinger under her eyes and swallowed hard.

Until then, Reading, Inc., had solved my problems. I needed to give something back to the community that I wouldn't mind getting publicity for. To keep the NFL happy, it had to appear squeaky clean. And Reading, Inc., had so appeared until I started feeling up filing cabinets.

Gus added, "Albert's going to earn his nickel getting you out of this mess."

"He's here," Cramer said. "Just pulled in."

"Let's go." I grabbed the handle.

"No. I'm going alone. This is between my father and me."

"Boys and girls," Gus said. "Calm down. Let the doc get settled."

The three of us followed Harvey's progress. Soon half the house was lit.

She pointed. "He's in the master bedroom. Now that light's out." After a few moments, "That's the light in the den. A desk in there. Medical books. A TV. Phone. A bar. I think he spends a lot of time in there."

"If he's settled, let's go knock. Both of us." I passed the car keys to Gus.

She sighed. "All right, all right."

I slammed the door and hopped around the hood. Took Cramer's elbow and we hurried. The front stoop was lit. The door chimes sounded cathedral.

Cramer, breathing hard, put her hand to her chest. "I can't stand this. Why did he do this to me?"

I was going to mention a few teammates he did something to, but I held my tongue.

When Harvey opened the front door, he saw Cramer first and he smiled. About to speak, he saw me. His smile froze.

"Howdy, Harvey."

He nodded, slowly.

I saw the cathedral. The foyer, very narrow, went up and up. At least three stories high. Low down, people level, it had marble and tall framed mirrors.

"Santa. Cramer." He paused, then stepped out of the doorway to let us into the echoing foyer. "It's good to see you two. But what are you doing back in Buffalo? You know the police have—"

Cramer stepped right up. "We have to talk, Father. Something's, uh, disturbing us."

"And you want my opinion?" He bowed his head. "One of the perks of fatherhood. Take off your jackets." He herded us down the hall and into a room with a high ceiling and walls of books all the way up.

It had tiny lamp tables next to big stuffed chairs. A desk spread lightly with papers. At its edge, framed snapshots and a Little Ben clock that said 11:22. A computer and printer stood off to the side.

The whole spic-and-span number reeked. When people lived in a museum, what were they hiding?

Harvey wore a maroon robe over light gray slacks and a blue dress shirt, open at the collar. He peeked under the bandage on my left hand and the one on my cheek, murmuring his approval. He bent and twisted my hand and decided I probably hadn't broken anything but still should get an X-ray.

I shrugged. Many a Sunday evening I was in far worse shape.

"I'm very concerned, Santa, that you came back to Buffalo. Until they settle this strike. You don't want to spend the rest of it in jail."

"No, I don't."

"Cramer, dear, you'll pour drinks?" He shooed her over toward the bar. "I'll have a whiskey. Santa?"

"Soda water, Perrier, anything."

"Nonsense. I'm his doctor. He'll have the same thing I'm having. You both look a bit peaked."

"No drinks, Father. This won't take long."

"What?"

"Sit down."

In the few minutes it took, Harvey sat stone-faced in one of his overstuffed chairs, wing tips up on a hassock. He treated us as a shrink treats his patients. Nodded and said "I see" a few times.

Cramer, at his desk, did most of the talking, starting from the banquet at her gallery when Shrimp got killed. She took it chronologically, almost all of it about Josh and me, and didn't leave out anything important.

Finally, stone-face blinked. "I see." They must practice that phrase in med school.

I added it up. "So either you're the man and Josh shields you, lets you stay at arm's length. Or you shield the man from Josh."

"What? What do I have to do with it?" More incredulous than angry.

Which made me angry. Such anger often welled in me on Sunday afternoons, so I knew how to focus my breathing and let the anger drain a little.

The chess master thinking forty moves ahead, Harvey asked, "Remember the old joke? What's the difference between God and a professional ballplayer?"

"Sure. God knows he's not a pro ballplayer."

"Exactly. You've taken all that imaginative energy you throw into your game and thrown it into this crusade. You have to solve everyone's problems. Even if they don't have any. All that presumption and arrogance, paranoia and fantasy, work on the field. But they don't work out here in the real world."

I asked, "And you didn't know about Josh's electronic bookie? Say a couple million a year?"

"That's an office pool at a big steel plant or insurance company. And it's a pool you're talking about, a couple million."

Cramer asked, "Did you know Josh Nachman was a—"

"Except for the odd sports banquet, I don't know the man."

Cramer let out a sigh and slumped back in her chair. Her lower lip trembled.

"Now?" I asked her.

She nodded.

I turned to Harvey. "You're lying."

He pointed a finger. "I resent that, Santa."

"Years ago, you let Josh get away with murder."

"I what?"

"Harvey, we saw your signature on the death certificate in Houston. Hector Ramirez. Texas Medical Center."

Bingo. In silence, he blinked. His eyes wandered. But, wow, was he quick. He charged right back. "I was in Houston. I signed many death certificates. So what?"

The door chimes rang. Harvey excused himself. "We'll get back to this," he warned at the doorway.

Cramer kept her voice low in her throat, quavering. "He did it. Damn him, my father's responsible for all those deaths, all that—"

"Do you think he realizes how much trouble he's in?"

"Certainly acts like he doesn't."

"But he's been getting away with it this long. M.D.s get to feeling invincible anyway."

She put her hand to her forehead. "I'm shaking. My whole insides are—"

I touched her elbow. "Just hang in there. We'll get out of here and . . ."

"And what?" She gave me a hard stare.

"Much as I don't think it'll do any good, I gotta call Byzant."

"Then what?"

Harvey came back alone. "It's Gus. He has to talk with you," he said as he passed me.

Down the side hall, Gus met me halfway, almost dancing. "Remember at Makepeace's I was too far into the trees to see the guy? So I went out into the parking lot, found the hottest car engine. Wrote down the license." He wagged his fist. "It's right here."

I put my arm on Gus's shoulder and walked him down the hall. "Meaning what?"

"I got antsy out there, so I spied on you guys sitting in the den, made sure you was all comfy. Then I peeked into Harvey's garage. And there it was. Same car as at Makepeace's. But the garage door was locked, so I couldn't see the license."

The more I thought about it, the more my grin matched Gus's.

"Santa, hurry!" It was Cramer. "He's on the phone. Hurry!"

We scampered. When we got to the den, Harvey was setting the phone down. He still had that stone-faced look, which I could not read.

I said to him, "Speaking of bets, Gus and I have a little wager going. What's your license number?"

"On what? I have three—"

"The car you drove home tonight."

He shrugged. "Three letters. Three numbers."

"Mind if we take a look? It's a serious bet."

He took a moment, then by his smile apparently decided that getting us out of his house was the thing to do. "Let me get your jackets." He headed for the door, taking off his maroon robe.

We followed. Cramer, looking confused, stayed shoulder to shoulder with me. Gus held his fists low and bounced on the balls of his feet. His eyes gleamed.

In the hall, Harvey traded his robe for a navy blazer. While we put on our jackets, he led us through the kitchen into the laundry room. He flipped a switch beside the back door. The backyard lit up, the garage door rose, and the garage lights went on. Above us, three TV monitors showed the inside of each car.

Harvey scanned the monitors. "Everything looks all right." He opened the back door and let us out. I heard bolts slide into place when it shut.

The garage sat at the far end of his lot. Harvey led us up the gravel drive through the cool night.

"Who do you think Harvey called?" I whispered to Cramer.

"Don't know." She spoke from clenched teeth. I saw sweat on her forehead. "But he said only two words. 'Destroy everything.' "

If Gus was right, on the other end it must have been Makepeace. The computer wiz. No doubt the guy who set up Josh's electronic bookie, kept it humming.

We caught up to Harvey close enough to the garage to be able to read the license plates. The three cars faced us.

On the right sat a Buick from the late 1980s. It was rusting around the edges, the car Harvey probably drove in winter while salt was on the streets.

In the middle was a pickup imported from Japan. And on the left a Lexus. Harvey swept his arm to encompass them all. "Take your pick."

Gus pointed to the Lexus, its license plain as day. On a white background, three blue letters and three blue numbers flanked a red Statue of Liberty. MCA 372.

Gus put his fist in front of my face and slowly unrolled it. In the M&T parking lot, back way out of Makepeace's, Gus had written on his palm. MCA 372.

A deep voice in the dark. "So who lost the bet?"

You did, asshole. I looked up. "Gotcha, Harvey."

"What does my license tell you?"

Oh, did Gus's wide grin and puffed chest say it all.

"That Makepeace is your computer wiz and bag man. Collections and payments. Teaching new clients how to use their modems to bet on sports."

"I can't see what harm a few betting pools do." Tacitly admitting it?

"To say nothing of Shrimp, Jimmy—"

Immediately, he looked away. "If you children will excuse me." He held up his key ring and started toward the garage. "I have an appointment."

Again, Cramer caught me by surprise. She stepped close to Harvey and blew up. Blew up? Erupted. "You call yourself a father?" she shouted. "You're a killer! A vicious—"

And Harvey erupted right back. "You don't know anything about me! Nothing! You come here and think—"

"I came here looking for a father and—"

"A father? You came looking for a meal ticket, you—"

"A what?"

They both shouted at once, mouths not two feet apart, arms gesturing widely.

"I gave you a house to live in. I gave you—"

"You gave me nothing for all my life."

"Life? I gave you life. I—"

"My mother—"

"Your mother was a whore!"

That cranked Cramer up a level. Neighbors' lights went on. I heard windows being yanked.

Once they got to the Texas part, they started slipping into Spanish. *Mi madre* this. *Honra* that. They mentioned money a few times: *dinero*. And love: *amor*. *Matar*. And *confianza*, which I thought meant trust.

I kept my eye on Harvey's hands. If he hit her, even touched her, I was ready to spring.

Panting, they began dry spits at each other. Cramer flung her hands. "Get out of here, you scum!"

"*Puta!*"

Thinking the squall was passing, I started to relax. So when Harvey took off fast, Gus and I needed a beat to react. Then we both made the same wrong decision.

One second, Harvey was spitting contempt at Cramer. The next, he was halfway to the garage and running, keys aloft, searching.

Gus and I assumed he would head for the Lexus, the fastest. But at the last second, he put his right hand on the hood of the pickup truck and hopped around it. Gus and I backpedaled a step or two and headed to our right. But Harvey had enough time to turn on the engine. He must have jammed the gear into second and popped the clutch, because the truck lurched. Then its tires squealed while it shot out of the garage, veering away from us.

Cramer did the sensible thing. She screamed and jumped out of the driveway. But I'd been taught well. On a free safety blitz, the guy closest to the ball carrier closes on him. If not the tackle, at least the initial hit.

And Gus was coming to help from the left.

The truck wasn't going that fast. Still, I had to take two long steps. And take two more while I wrapped my hands around the door handle and jumped on.

Harvey drove faster and faster down the driveway, spraying gravel, in such a hurry that he didn't even turn his headlights on.

The door was locked: surprise, surprise. Soon Harvey would have to slow down for a light or a sign or to avoid a collision. Then I would make my move for the bed, which I imagined much safer and more comfortable.

I never got to find out. At the street, Harvey juked the truck to the right, then swung hard to the left. The tires, sliding sideways, squealed.

It felt like the tires on my side lifted off the pavement. For sure, the door I clung to was no longer at right angles to the ground.

My hands stayed tightly wrapped. But my feet slipped off and started to drag. Then I proved I had a shred of common sense left. I let go of the door handle, tucked my head to my chest, and turned a thump and a skid into a controlled somersault. I took the blow on my right shoulder. During the skid, my back burned, but I didn't break anything.

On my knees, panting, I looked after Harvey's truck. The taillights came on and soon he was out of sight.

I stood, testing my shoulder, when Cramer and Gus caught up to me. "Santa! Are you all right?"

Gus told her, "All right? Boy's standin', ain't he?"

Then Cramer got closer and saw the rips in my jacket. "But the blood! If you reinjured your back? We can go to—"

Gus to the rescue. "Some soap, some water, half a dozen Band-Aids. That's all this boy needs."

"Band-Aids! We've got to get you to a doctor."

"I couldn't agree more." I pointed down the street. "Him."

Day

twenty

Street in front of Harvey's house, Gus tossed and caught the keys to the Chevy. "Old fart's too far ahead to follow." He scowled at Cramer. "He could be up on the Scajaquada by now. East or west?"

"I don't know." Cramer still had that wild-eyed look from screaming at her dad. "He could go to Makepeace."

Gus turned to me. "You think?"

"Sure, Makepeace's, to do a little damage control."

"Let's go."

Cramer had other ideas. "Let's go to a hospital! You're coming off major surgery. You need X-rays and—"

Raising my voice, stressing each syllable, I pointed an index finger. "Cool your jets, lady." A big mistake, overall, but it did shut her up. "A phone, first."

Trotting up Harvey's driveway, I remembered the bolts locking the back door of his house.

The neighbors? I didn't want to have to explain.

But Harvey's garage was open and lit. Full of high-tech gadgets, anyway. And sure enough, a phone. I poked 911 and sang the old refrain, "Erie County sheriff, Detective Bureau."

"Please wait."

Cramer, only halfway up the drive, hugged her elbows, walking slowly.

191

But Gus stood right beside me. "You want Byzant here?"

"I want to be on record explaining and asking for help. At best, he'll slow us down."

Then a female voice: "County Detective."

The magic words: "Santa Arkwright calling Captain Byzant."

"He's not available. How may I help you?"

I told her my story in about thirty seconds.

"Yes, yes," she kept saying. "Yes, yes." She ordered me to stay put until an officer reached me.

"Right. With handcuffs." I hung up.

Gus gave me the keys and helped Cramer hurry back to the Chevy. I tagged along, windmilling my arm. My back felt loose, but the shoulder was getting stiff. No surprise.

Gus put Cramer into the front and slid into the back. She was breathing hard, not saying anything. Then I thought of something. I opened my door.

"What?" Gus asked.

"Gimme a second, guys. I need to put something in the trunk."

Back of the car, after I opened the trunk, I stood still. Tried to center myself. It seemed too big a decision and not enough time to make it. But when in doubt.

I slipped Josh's black gun from behind the spare tire, hefted it once, and shoved it into my jacket pocket.

*   *   *

We had a short drive through Delaware Park and around Gates Circle. Wherever Byzant was, we'd be sure to beat him to Makepeace's.

In three minutes, we turned west onto Ferry. Stone mansions spread on huge lawns. Closer to Elmwood, smaller lawns and smaller houses. Parking was legal on the left side only. We passed a pickup, but not Harvey's.

Middle of the block, I found the one tight space and backed into it. We could walk to Makepeace's at the corner of Elmwood.

No sooner had I turned the key than I heard a *whoo-whoo-whooooo* from behind. I twisted to look out the back window. Red-and-blue flasher. A tan sedan, portable light cockeyed atop the hood, pulled up close. The Chevy would never get out of that tight space.

The siren wound down, but the light kept spinning.

Cramer asked, "Are we arrested?"

"Not yet. Why don't you roll down your window, so we don't have to shout."

Byzant's partner—not Vinnie, not the guy from Sunday, but yet another young one—got out and came around to my side.

Through the open window, Byzant spoke past Cramer. He sounded so polite. "You're under arrest, Arkwright." But he let me see the gun in his hand.

Much bigger than mine, still tucked away. "For what?"

"For starters?" He chuckled. "Try leaving Buffalo. That's contempt of court."

"Byzant, while you're squatting there pretending to be—"

"I heard what you told my dispatch. Now out of the vehicle."

"Dr. Harvey Laurel and John Makepeace are up there." I pointed over his shoulder. "Destroying evidence—probably on Makepeace's computer."

"I believe you, but I got no warrant for that address."

However, he had plenty of backup. I could hear the sirens. "What about Josh?"

"Nachman? I have no proof of—"

"You idiot!" Not the best phrasing. "Harvey's probably destroying the computer stuff, the proof of what he did with Josh. As long as Josh doesn't testify, they're free. Long as they don't testify, Josh's free."

"What'd you do, Arkwright, open a cereal box and find a badge?" He lowered his voice. "Now let the hostages out of the vehicle."

"Hostages?" All three of us in the Chevy said it at once.

Gus, my legal adviser that evening, put his chin atop the front seat and almost whispered, "No search warrant? I saw on TV, believe he can get into that house in what they call hot pursuit."

"Say again?"

"As usual, I'm lead blocker."

Took me but a second to figure Gus.

"Anybody gets lost," he added, "I'll personally escort to that side door you gonna bust down."

My grin spread. "Hey, folks, huddle's over." I clapped my hands sharply.

Gus slid out my side, muttering, "Doin' the man a favor."

I caught Cramer's eye. She dropped hers, but she uncrossed her arms long enough to open her door. Should I leave her alone with the likes of Byzant?

Hey, I needed to follow my lead blocker into the defense's weak side. As soon as I stepped out, I heard more sirens wailing.

Byzant called over the hood, "Arrest them."

"Yes, Cap'n," said his partner, not nearly Gus's size.

Gus—Mr. Do It—did he have moves? He took a misstep, stumbled a little. Trying to catch himself on Byzant's partner, Gus landed atop him.

I hurdled them and took off down the sidewalk toward Makepeace's.

"Now!" Byzant shouted. "Or I shoot, Arkwright!"

Hitting stride, I looked over my shoulder. Byzant was leaning onto the roof to steady his outstretched arms.

Cramer McKensie didn't have Gus's moves. She simply ducked down. Rose a second later, one of Byzant's ankles under each arm. Outweighing him by thirty pounds, she yanked him along the roof and off.

I was gone. Long as I stayed off my heels, ran on my toes, my back would work.

The dozen people I passed stepped out of the way and stared at me. Across the street, past the church, around the corner, I turned into the M&T Bank's driveway and stopped in the parking lot behind.

There stood Harvey's pickup truck.

I danced past it, through the gap in the wall, under the pines, and smack up to Makepeace's side door. Locked.

I took a deep breath. Giving thought to my back, I turned aside and kicked through the lower panel of that door. Yanked some shards and stepped through.

No time to grope for a light switch. Instead, I groped for the stairs and clambered up. Three steps took me to the landing. On the right, the door to the empty downstairs apartment.

A small window let in light, enough for me to find a broom and get off all fours. I grabbed the railing to pull myself up the final narrow flight to the top, the door to Makepeace's landing. Locked.

The outside doors of the house had been built for security. But that inside door had been built for looks: a routed frame around a thin pressboard panel. Thrusting the broomstick, I bashed my way onto the landing and then opened the unlocked door into the brightly lit apartment. Whites and pastels.

On my right, three doors: powder room, kitchen, and, closest to me, the computer room.

In its doorway stood Harvey, mouth agape, eyes blazing. "What the—" What he held made me pause. A quart of charcoal lighter fluid.

Then I heard Makepeace plead, "Five! I need five more minutes."

Squeezing the bottle, Harvey strode into the computer room. "You bitch! Man's here to screw—Told you last week to—Now we torch 'em all—everything!"

"This's my work!" Makepeace backed through the doorway. He wore crinkled black lounging pajamas. Head back, both palms up, he gave a slow, deep moan.

I stepped forward, making Makepeace turn and gasp.

Harvey, backing through the doorway, squeezed the last drop. "Repeat, this's an accident."

Growling, Makepeace charged me low, grabbed my ankle.

Muttering "Act stricken. . . . Keep your mouth shut," Harvey picked a lighter off an end table.

While I stomped Makepeace's wrist, Harvey flicked the lighter and brought it to the bottle's mouth.

Free, I bent forward. "Don't!"

Harvey tossed the bottle, a mass of bright flames.

Launching myself, I screamed, *"Don't!"* Stretching out, my arm strained.

But it arced just under the top of the doorframe.

So briefly, I felt heat as the bottle sailed past my fingertips.

And I got beat. The bottle arced onto the oily carpet. I crashed to the floor and—on all fours—stared. Should I fly in after it? Throw myself upon it? I was trained to.

A line of yellow-and-blue fire snaked away from me. And WHOOSH! The whole room flashed.

I raised my hand and stood. Force my way through flames? Not to rescue computer disks that would have instantly melted or a hard drive merrily roasting.

Makepeace took one look. "I'm outa here, Harvey."

Harvey shielded his eyes. "You twisted piece of shit." He was sweaty, flushed, swathed in black smoke that smelled terrible.

Makepeace vaulted the couch and ran out the door. I didn't bother to warn him what he'd likely run into.

We heard clatter on the stairs. Male and female shouts, Makepeace's among them. Good, he'd slow them down.

Harvey reacted as fast as he had at his house. He scooted into the kitchen.

I followed. In my jacket, I could feel Josh's gun. But I didn't need it. From behind, I grabbed Harvey's right elbow and swung him around. His belly, swinging my way, ran into my right fist, thrusting upward.

"Ooof!" His head fell forward. Wide-open mouth, wide-open eyes, it surprised him to have his wind knocked out.

I clasped my right hand around my bandaged left hand. I put them a foot below his chin and aimed for the kitchen ceiling.

The blow snapped his head back, sent him reeling against the cabinets. His head smashed the glass cabinet door. I was going to hit him one more time, but his hands, outstretching, whapped the glass and shattered it.

Harvey held a pose: shoot me! Then he slumped to the floor. Shattered glass tinkled around his limp body.

I scampered to the back door. It was unlocked. Out on the landing, I unlatched the wide window. Some other time I could sit and enjoy the breeze.

I gave a peek and didn't see anything where I would land, so

I stepped out and hung by my fingers from the window frame. Let go. Dropping: hey, not ten feet. I landed with knees bent and sprang up.

Someone over in the driveway shouted. A cop. He wore a uniform and had both hands on his night stick.

First step I took, the pain shot through my lower back.

But he was the only cop and by the time he shouted something about shooting me, I had hobbled to the shadows under the pine trees. Oh, did my back hurt.

By the time his shouts got closer, I'd rolled over the fence. And then away.

*　　*　　*

I lost myself—head down—in a dark corner of the no-name bar on Elmwood. For my back, I tried a medicinal dose of Johnnie Walker Black. Then another.

What a late-night crowd. The strike—according to local wisdom—was as good as over, the scab games on for one final Sunday. And the killer was still loose and foaming. I couldn't take exception to any of that.

To hear the drunks yat-yat, all of Erie County was going to that game.

Four in the morning, last call, so I had to decamp. What was close? It was risky enough to walk in the shadows all night. Also very painful. What would I do after dawn?

Then—somehow, somewhere—I had to find Josh. If nothing else, to make sure he wasn't looking for me. Would he be at the Sunday game as usual? Why not?

My doctor busy elsewhere, I should have taxied to a hospital. But Nurse Cramer's house was close. I peeked in the dark windows. The living room and kitchen were as we'd left them before going to Texas. So Cramer hadn't been home for almost four days. Was she snoozing in some jail cell?

Her back kitchen door had little panes, as had Makepeace's. I did the elbow-through-bottom-pane number and let myself in. On the couch where Lona'd passed out, I tried to doze. Right. In the bathroom, I found half a dozen PMS helpers with acetaminophen. Maybe in a pinch. But in the kitchen, I found most of a bottle of Tylenol. I'd need them all.

On the landing to the basement, I found a snow shovel. Holding the metal handle, I wedged the other end into a doorjamb and snapped it off. A tad short for a cane, but it would do.

At the stove, I made a pot of Cramer's Swedish coffee. I ended up in the dark living room watching for her. Predawn birds were starting to chirp.

My throbbing back to the wall, I listened, listened. Opening a window, I checked for soft landings in case I needed to bail out. In case Byzant showed up with his pals.

Think. Think in an orderly manner. But my mind raced.

Was Cramer all right? Wasn't she great, taking down Byzant? I felt proud of her.

Gus—atop Byzant's partner—probably had more fun than anybody, even in a paddy wagon.

Had Makepeace's burned down? Harvey still inside?

Dawn came milky and chilly. I moved my chair back a pace into the shadows. Stayed close to my escape hatch. Cold next to the window, so I kept my jacket on. Gobbled another handful of Tylenol.

Who'd Josh go after next? I couldn't take a chance it wouldn't be me. So before that, where to find him? I couldn't go home—another bomb, a sniper shot away from death. I couldn't go much of anywhere until I got Josh behind bars. Maybe the zoo in Delaware Park. I could chain him down in the monkey house.

I mumbled to myself, "Did Byzant tell Josh the news? That Harvey got arrested?"

Yes.

"Think Byzant suggested this to Josh? That instead of worrying whether Harvey and pretty boy will rat on him, it'd be better for Josh to rat on them, first?"

Sure. Divide and conquer was Basic Cop 101.

The black gun had four live bullets. The thing was so light, just a toy. How would it feel to pull the trigger? First I dug out the casings of the two bullets Josh had fired at me.

Sighting through one eye, I practiced on the empty chambers. A tug, then *snap!* A tug—I could feel the cylinder drag—then *snap!* A live round would be next. I put the gun back into my left jacket pocket.

In need of advice, I called Gus and Albert. Gus probably still in jail, Albert in Virginia, I left messages.

"Figure with him," I explained to Albert's machine. "If Sister Charlayne holds her alibis and Harvey and pretty boy don't snitch, Josh walks." I let that sink in. "So it behooves him to act naturally. I'll bet we find him in that stadium, just like last Sunday, at the scab game." No response, so I hung up.

If I had to, I'd taxi to the game.

Twice, Cramer's phone rang. Both times, when her machine cut in, all I heard was a click. I wanted to go out for a Sunday paper. Nah, the debacle at Makepeace's had come down after deadline.

Sometime after eleven, a taxi stopped. Cramer and Gus got out. From her blinking, bleary eyes and his shuffling gait, they'd been up all night, too.

Soon as the front door creaked, I called, "Cramer? It's me."

She appeared in the archway to the living room. Looked pretty good. "How'd you get in here? Oh, never mind." She flopped her hand.

"I need to borrow your truck."

"Why? No, I don't want to know that, either. Spare key's on the hook behind the pantry door."

"How are you?"

"Me? Compared to—"

Gus came in, carrying her coat and his. "There he is!" He held out a palm.

I grunted and slapped it.

They were debating Josh, too. She asked me, "Where do *you* think he is?"

"Let's hope he's in a jail cell because Byzant got enough from Harvey and Makepeace to arrest him. But if not, I think Josh'll be at the scab game."

She looked from Gus to me and back. "See? Well, let's go."

"I see, all righty." Gus pointed a finger. "But you're staying home, now that I got you here."

"Why?" she asked him. "Got a better plan?" she asked me. I turned to Gus.

"Josh won't go nowhere with the likes of you 'n' me, Santa. But the lady here seems to think she can get him to her truck."

"And then?"

"Then," she said, "we push, prod, provoke, corner. Get him to break a law so the cops haul him in. Get him to do something so bad his wife gives up on him."

Gus asked, "And how do you get him to do something?"

She shrugged. "The guy's killed four people in the last ten days. He's obviously at the end of his rope. Bonkers. Feed him a little more rope, he'll have just enough to hang himself."

Gus saw it my way. "But we have to assume he is—as we speak—planting the next bomb or loading a gun or whatever."

"So if we catch him in the act," Cramer said.

"What's so special about us?" I raised my voice. "He'll just walk away from us. That's common sense."

"Of which he seems bereft."

"Good point." I looked from her eyes to Gus's and back and forth a few times. I wanted her with us. "There'll be tens of thousands of people there," I reminded Gus.

"And hundreds and hundreds of cops," Cramer reminded us.

Gus closed his eyes and sighed. Cramer went to get her keys.

He drove her white Nissan flatbed. Cramer crammed into the middle. I got in last, thigh to thigh with her, makeshift cane at my feet.

Not taking any chances, I used a kitchen knife to customize three paper bags from Cramer's pantry. While we zigzagged through the West Side, I asked her, "Are we still friends?"

"After last night?"

I nodded.

That she had to think about. "Yeah." Then all the way down the thruway, she told her story. At the Chevy, Byzant had handcuffed her to the passenger's side door, Gus to the driver's side. All the excitement—her dad, the cops, the sirens—caught up to her and she heaved the meal she'd eaten at Ronnie's opening. So they put her in an ambulance and took her to ECMC's emergency room. After two hours under watch and lock and key, they took her downtown.

"They gave me a pill, calm me down." It must have worn off; just recounting for me, Cramer's voice shook. Knees together, she anchored herself to the truck's seat with both hands. A couple of times she got teary.

Downtown, they wouldn't tell her anything, but they sure had questions. She answered them all, most about Harvey, some about me. "Was I getting angry and frustrated."

"You should have called a lawyer."

"I insisted. They said I wasn't under arrest. But . . ."

"You didn't exactly feel free to leave. I've been there."

"I never realized what stupid idiots cops could be. Are they all like that?"

Gus and I answered at the same time. "No," I said. "Yes," he said.

"I'd never been in trouble until I met you two."

"Get out," Gus said. "This ain't trouble."

I agreed. "At worst, you grabbed Byzant's feet and pulled him down. But after you answered all their questions? They need you on the witness stand, not in the dock. What did they say when they let you go?"

"What you just said. As long as I cooperate."

"See? You got nothing to worry about."

Not from the look she gave me.

When we got off the thruway in Orchard Park, I leaned forward to ask Gus, "How'd it go for you?"

His eyes were bloodshot and baggy, his hair uncombed. "For tackling that cop? They threw the book at me. In exchange for which I could walk, I gave out your biography. It's on tape now."

"Great." I sat back, wedging myself between Cramer and the door, a tight fit.

"My man, everyone got their version of last night. No two the same. Can you dig it from Makepeace's end?"

Cramer wriggled her butt, trying to make room for me. "I saw him, Makepeace. He got put into a patrol car. Father into an ambulance. They did tell me—next of kin, you know—that he's in satisfactory condition."

"What did Makepeace's house look like when you left?"

"I saw some flames licking a window—"

"Engines poured on enough water . . ." Gus shook his head. "To float the 'hood."

Near the stadium, traffic slowed. Again, the scab game drawing a crowd. Fans were so blind.

Cramer put her hand to her right thigh. To pull her coat out, make more room between us? No. To feel my thigh. My jacket.

"Can you move this?"

"Uh, sure."

"What's in it? An ashtray?" She clasped it. "A pipe?"

"Oh, nothing. A gun."

"A—?"

Hmmm. I'd left her speechless. Not the place for Mae West jokes, how happy I was to see her.

"A gun? What are you—? Where'd you get it? What are you going to do with it?"

"Whoa," Gus said.

"Josh dropped it after he shot at me. I thought if I saw him again I'd return it."

"Don't be flip. Now—"

Gus interrupted. "Same piece killed Bowsk?"

"I presume."

We were in the stream of cars rolling onto Bills Drive. Gus downshifted. "Think Byzant could get prints off it?"

"I picked it up from a rainy street. Josh was wearing gloves."

Cramer had crossed her arms high. Breathing hard, squinting. "If you don't use it, why have it? If you do, I never want to see you again. Ever. Is that clear?"

"Yes." Choices, choices. We put on our bags.

A good crowd, at least judging from the number of cars. After Gus parked, I held the door for Cramer. She slid out, her body slow and tired, her eyes neither. Thousands of fans milled in the parking lot, the rest already inside.

The Patriots were in town. Most of their stars had crossed. For the Bills, starting at quarterback was Alex Lamar. The scab. I hoped the Pats whupped him like a stepchild. Turned the Puritans into martyrs.

The paper bags weren't nearly as popular, but we were in fine company wearing ours in the ticket line. The tailgaters roared and whooped and hollered. No union pickets that day. No real Bills, either. But Cramer had been correct—hundreds and hundreds of security guards. Every off-duty cop in Western New York, it seemed.

A different crowd of protesters clogged the gates. The Jesus freaks. A few had been there the previous Sunday. But after three more murders and Makepeace's articles, they'd come out of the woodwork. Wearing signs, carrying them on poles and sticks, they shouted for those who couldn't read: "God hates Buffalo!"

Fans were shouting back, taunting them.

Which made the pickets shout louder for the TV cameras. "Repent! Before He starts killing fans!"

Rows of guards, nightsticks and helmets, stood and watched. None of them smiled.

Cramer said, "I've never been to a pro football game before. Is it always like this?"

"Always," Gus replied.

She pointed. "That's a weird one. 'Christ Bills Strikers.' "

"CBS. In case the networks tune in. Look at that one." I used my cane, the jagged snow-shovel handle, to point for her. " 'Even Satan Punishes NFL.' "

*　　*　　*

Inside, only Gus's idea made sense. Get a vantage point.

David, a local *auteur,* was the guy kept body and soul together by taping our games. I'd borrowed his binoculars the Sunday before to scan the stands for Josh.

Even though David was part-time help, a couple dozen hours per year—not exactly top management—he was a scab for working those games. However, at the moment, we needed him, so I wasn't going to bring it up.

David's was the official tape we studied. Copies to the league archives and our future opponents. So David always had backup tapes, camera, and cords at the ready. And extra binoculars.

He also had a forty-yard-line view from under the upper deck. After we knocked, he let us into his little booth. He slapped palms with Gus and politely nodded a howdy to Cramer.

We turned to the game. Chilly, overcast, no wind. A perfect day for football.

To me, it felt eerie, out-of-body, still. Looking down on my life rather than living it. Below and beyond stretched the stands, though only two-thirds full and muffled through the glass. There sat the fans, about a third of whom wore bags. There spread the field, the scabs wearing Bills whites, Patriots reds.

And there stood I, watching from above. Shuddering, palms sweating. Like because I wasn't where I should have been, I was in big trouble.

I slid open the window, but still the fans sounded muffled. Far away instead of right on top, where they were supposed to be.

Cramer stomped her impatience. "How do we find Josh in this mob?"

"If he wants witnesses to how normal a day this is, he's not wearing a bag. He wasn't last week."

"Oh, that cuts it down to about thirty thousand."

While David tended his camera, Gus and Cramer used binocs to study the end zones and far stands. I eyed the near stands, section by section, row by row. Seat by seat, until I went cross-eyed.

Then Cramer and I switched. She took the near stands while I put the binocs on the private suites hanging under the upper deck across the field. Some glare off the windows, but no Josh.

By the end of the first quarter—scab Bills 17, scab Pats 3. Lots of Alex Lamar, but no Josh.

What made sense? Gus suggested that he stay put with one pair of binocs. I'd take the other and Cramer and I would roam. But how to keep in touch?

David, busy with his camera, wasn't sure what we were doing. But he reached under his shelf and brought out two walkie-talkies.

Gus and I grinned, tested the things. No problem. Cramer pushed me out, waved bye-bye to Gus.

All the second quarter, Cramer and I stayed close but kept moving. We looked not only for Josh's face but also for his body below one of the brown paper bags.

We looked and looked, even during half time when the concourse was wall-to-wall fans. Score was 30–6, favor the ersatz Bills. Alex Lamar was giving an outstanding performance, judging by how often the stadium announcer boomed out his name.

Cramer stomped and growled. Declared she was ready to strangle Josh.

I didn't see Josh's face or body, finally. Early in the third quarter, the fans still milling and waiting in line, I stood against a concrete pillar, Section 22. Leaned on my stick, looking fans up and down.

Then I saw a bandaged right hand. When I knocked the gun out of his hand over on Grant Street, Josh's forefinger must have caught. Which was why he howled and why it was splinted and wrapped. But it was Josh, short and tubby and wearing a bag. Waiting for the elevator in a crowd but alone, best I could see.

I pushed the walkie-talkie button. "Gus." Let up the button and brought the grille to my ear.

Crackly: "Yeah?"

"Spotted him taking the up elevator in Section 22."

"Be right there."

"Wait a sec." I whistled and waved to Cramer, who hurried with the flow of the crowd toward me. I pointed for her.

Her anger swelled her chest, gagged in her throat, and made her eyes bug out. She started straight for Josh, but the elevator door opened.

Josh spoke to no one, seemed alone when he stepped in.

Hurrying there, Cramer stabbed the button over and over.

I told Gus, "Let's see where he's sitting. Depending, you could get here quicker."

"Which way'd the little turd go?" she asked. "I'm going to . . . to—"

"What?"

"I'll make sure he commits a crime and gets caught this time!"

We took the next elevator up.

"You look right. I'll go left." I told her his jacket was standard-issue: blue silk, red-and-white Bills logo front and back. And his pants—creamy chocolate polyester—didn't match.

We got off and took a step in opposite directions. And stopped.

There he was. Josh stood outside a private business suite. He was talking to a burly guy, no bag, wearing a coat and tie. The burly guy had a foot on the concourse, a foot on the stoop, and a hand on the doorknob.

Between there and me, fans were striding to their seats. Josh looked my way. In my bag, not twenty yards off, I felt invisible. While I thought about what to do next, the burly guy stepped into the private suite.

Cramer snorted. She took off, striding, slicing her right shoulder against the flow of the crowd. Why? To get upstream of Josh, keep him between us? But she kept veering right until she stopped in front of him.

What? I took a step forward, then stopped.

She started talking to Josh.

"Let her play it," I muttered to myself. But I began edging their way. Both of them in bags, I had no clue what they talked about.

In a minute, Josh put his hand into the pocket of his Bills jacket and seemed to press up against her. He shouted near her ear. She started, jumped away, but he pulled her close. She struggled, but not much. What? Did he have a gun? Some other threat? Then he opened the door and held it for her.

She turned my way, but I couldn't see her face through the bag. Other than the burly guy, who else was in the suite?

I started across the stream of hurrying people. Eye on the suite's door, I got Gus. Counted from the end down the row of doors. "Can you put your binocs on it?"

"Got it."

As best I could with my stick, I started dancing and dodging through the crowd. "He's wearing a team jacket."

After a second: "Glare on the right side, clear view of the rest. Maybe half a dozen people in there."

I relaxed. "One of them's Cramer."

"What?"

"She went in with him. He may have a gun or—"

Gus let loose a string of vulgarities and blasphemies. "Don't see her. See him. Wait. That must be her sitting next to him. Stupid bitch."

"Doing what? He won't hurt her—other people watching."

"You be asking the wrong question, my man. Will she hurt him? I learned a lot about her last night."

"What're they doing, Gus?"

"Talking, looks like. Now Josh got the others, uh, waving his hand. They're all looking at him. Now moving toward the door."

"Josh and Cramer?"

"No. The others."

Sure enough. The door opened and the burly guy came out. Two other men followed him, one with a woman who looked old enough to be his mother. Last came a babe, dressed like one of Josh's pros. No one went anywhere. Just shut the door behind them and waited as though they were ready to go back in.

"Gus, what's goin' down in there?"

"Did Josh and Cramer leave?"

"No!"

"Then they're behind the—I mean, the one window slid open, it makes the other double-thick. Glare's so bad I can't see."

"Then I'm going—"

"Wait! There she is! Going for the door. There's Josh. He grabbed her. No, he hit her. A bottle? He—ugh, the glare!"

"I'm going in." I was halfway to the door.

"See them again. Against the back."

"Is she—?"

"Her head's hanging, wobbly. But she's moving. His arm around her. Feeding her? Something."

"Can you tape it with David's spare camera?"

"Just a sec." After a moment, he came back on. "It's rolling. David wants to call security."

"What can they do? If Byzant had enough to arrest Josh, he already would have."

"You better get in there. At least get her out."

I slid the walkie-talkie into the jacket's right pocket. Slapped the left where the gun was while I limped on my stick to the stoop up to the door.

The burly guy barred the way. "Hey, this's a private box."

I took off my bag. "I got an appointment."

He blinked and gulped. "Santa?"

I gave my United Way booster-banquet grin. "Make sure no one else goes in. Will you do that for me?"

"What's with the cane?" Ah, the reflexes and instincts of a gambler looking to beat the odds.

"I'll explain later. Now move."

So he stepped away.

The door opened toward me. I stepped up and peered in. A small room—I was in the back corner. Down front, sliding plastic-glass windows, one of them open as Gus had said. A shelf for elbows and drinks. Coats and a purse. Portable TV tuned to the Miami scab game the network was carrying. A row of stools. Behind, two rows of raised stadium seats.

I stepped in and shut the door behind me.

No more echoing corridor. The crowd noises came through the open window, hanging high over the midfield stands. The field spread below; Pats had the ball.

To my left, the wet bar. I heard a muffled gagging and grunting. Josh—bag off—rose from behind the bar five yards away and pulled Cramer up with him. Her bag was gone, too.

"Welcome, ogre." At least I think that's what he said.

His bandaged right hand bent Cramer's right arm high onto her back. The pain had bent her forward, tilting her head away from him. His gloved left hand was at her mouth. As Gus guessed, feeding her?

Josh pushed her, stumbling along the wall toward the windows. "You move toward us, she's dead." His voice quavered. "Fornicators. Perverted my daughter."

Cramer's eyes looked glazed, concussed. And they said a lot: fear. Her mouth forced open, saliva dribbled down her chin. She was gagging, trembling all over, trying to wriggle free, trying to grab him with her free arm.

What? Josh had something to shove down Cramer's throat? Nicotine? I had to assume so. I also had to remember the guy was crazy.

What did the hostage negotiators always do? Stall. "Cramer, it'd be good if you quit struggling. We'll have less chance of an accident here." It'd also get Josh to relax a little.

They stopped in the low end, the corner next to the windows.

"If you're counting on Harvey protecting you now, what's he going to do after you kill his daughter?"

Dropping Cramer's arm a little, not stuffing her mouth so hard, Josh shook his head. "He cares nothing for this girl. About what he does for the neighbor's chattel. That dead soul. Whenever I think who's going to hell, I think Harvey. He's already there."

Cramer, I noticed, had gone almost completely limp. "He loves Makepeace," I said.

"To Harvey, that's about as important as pissing."

"You're going to get caught, Josh."

"Caught? Caught is easy for you graces. But stopped? Never. Now fly out this window."

"What?"

"Fly. You're Superman. Put your arms out and fly." It had to be sixty feet, the drop to the concrete stands below. With my luck, I'd survive by landing on my sore back and end up paralyzed for life.

Instead, I drew his black gun. "I need to return this first."

He stared at it. "How did you—? Oh."

One more time, Cramer surprised me. In a split second, one sight of that gun, she went volcanic. Her free hand grabbed the hand Josh had forced between her jaws. In the same motion, she pulled her head away.

I had the presence of mind to fire a shot into the plastic-glass window, well to the side of them. Both layers just spiderwebbed and with luck the bullet would miss the fans, fell some scab.

But the explosion in the small suite startled all of us—Josh and Cramer especially, not knowing where I'd aimed.

Cramer yanked away, screaming. Josh kept her arm high. Twisting, she lunged toward me. Josh lunged after her. I put the next bullet into his forearm, almost point-blank. Howling, he let go of her, dropped something.

Cramer writhed into a seat, grimacing, still screaming.

"What's wrong?"

She held her shoulder and screamed.

I dug my fingers into her right shoulder: yanking away from Josh, she'd dislocated it.

Poor kid. The walkie-talkie in my pocket kept squawking, no doubt Gus giving me advice. Keeping the gun on Josh, I sat with my heel on Cramer's ribs, toe into her breast. One hand training the gun, with the other hand I tugged her forearm. I tugged and tugged . . . then *pop! pop!*—clear and sharp.

Right away, she relaxed and stopped screaming. She put both hands to her head and groaned. Closed her eyes and dropped her head forward.

A hard pounding on the door. Muffled shouts. More squawks from Gus.

I scooped up what Josh had dropped. A cylinder, an inch long, quarter inch across. Clear glass, open at the top, Old Spice logo in red script. Nicotine? Cramer'd be dead, had she bitten, had she swallowed.

Blood rushing into my head, I stopped thinking. Nicotine, the cocksucker. I put the gun against the bridge of Josh's nose, the Old Spice to his eye. Dump it into him, say he did it to himself.

"Please, no." Josh stared cross-eyed at the gun. "Good God, please." He cowered and tried to slide away. I would never forget his eyes, his wagging jaw. I'd never seen anyone so terrified. "Please."

I couldn't pull that trigger. All I really wanted Josh to do was stop killing. And that was out of my power.

More pounding. The door handle rattled. Had I locked it?

So I compromised. I aimed at Josh's kneecap.

Cramer was still gasping. "Pull that trigger, you're no better than him."

"You're right." So I brought my heel down onto Josh's kneecap. Hard. He howled and grabbed it. Rolled away from me.

"You coward!" Cramer yelled. "You child!" She rubbed her shoulder.

"All I did was save you."

"All you what? You weren't such a bad shot, I'd be dead!"

Oh yeah? "Listen, the chance you took coming in here—"

"Was a great way to provoke him. Besides, I was so angry—"

I would have kept discussing it. But the door flew open and security cops burst in, guns drawn.

They spoiled the whole rest of that day.

Day

twenty-one

albert finally bailed us out late that Monday afternoon. Gus, Cramer, and me. We'd spent most of the day together, but not where we could speak a private word to each other.

Gus's videotape, it turned out, had a pretty clear view of what happened. The threat on Cramer's life, my shot in her defense, Josh's lunge forward with the Old Spice vial. Then, somehow, split second before I shot him point-blank in the forearm, nothing got recorded from then on. Thanks, Gus.

A mob of media in magistrate's court. The magistrate himself, taking pity, let us exit through his chambers. On the back fire stairs, Albert translated the legal mumbo-jumbo for Cramer. "From now on, you tell the grand jury and the judge the truth and that's all you have to do. You're free to go." Same with Gus.

For a beat, Cramer stared at Albert. Her relocated right shoulder, taped, made her dress bulky and lopsided. The lump on her crown wasn't visible. Looking pale—pain, no sleep—she turned and stomped off, clattered down the stairs, not a glance, not a goodbye. I let her go.

Albert drove Gus and me home. Out front, the porch was still a blown-up wreck. Gus spied a mobile TV unit parked up the street. Media types loitered across Ashland, officially staying off the property. Nice of 'em. No one noticed us.

212

So Albert drove us around the block to Norwood. We could get home through the backyards.

Yawning, Gus opened his door. "Long day." Neither of us had slept well, guests of the county.

I turned in the front. "Why don't you hit the sack?"

He sniffed. "Why don't you hit the shower?"

How long had it been? Danny's, Saturday morning, after he roused Cramer and me off his sofa. "I hear you. No doubt I need one."

"No doubt. Don't wake me." Gus got out and crept away into the shadows between the houses.

Albert kept his engine running. "Listen, it won't be official until tomorrow, but this football strike is over. Lance Bishop caved in."

I hadn't wanted to ask. "What a waste. Just like '87. The players lose again."

"Another theory: we should thank Nachman. The strike would have lasted months."

So I could add it up. The strike cost me a quarter million in lost salary, 15 percent of which would have been Albert's. The strike also cost me four teammates. "What happens next?"

"You go back to work tomorrow, what else? Take months for Dingleberry and the feds to sort out just the facts. For starters, they'll need some kind of ruling on Nachman's injuries."

"Bottom line?"

"Here's what Dingleberry finally agreed to. If the facts bear out your version of the truth. For you, no felony indictment. A misdemeanor gun charge, of course. We'll pay the fine."

"Civil suit?"

He shrugged. "Not up to Dingleberry what someone files. You do have tempting assets."

"And a fine attorney. What about the NFL? I consorted with gamblers."

Albert snorted. "I can help the NFL look the other way. There's precedent."

"Dingle say anything on Harvey and Makepeace?"

"Again if the facts bear out your version. He wants arson and some kind of murder indictments. Early lab reports say it was indeed nicotine Josh had, enough to kill that whole section of fans."

And kill Cramer. I clenched my jaws and made a snarly noise.

"The gambling slash criminal enterprise, Dingle tells me, is a little dicey without the evidence they torched. That's federal court, anyway."

"What do you predict?"

"You know better than to ask. Harvey's already retained excellent counsel. Notice he made bail today hours before you did."

"But you'd say . . ."

"I don't predict squat when it comes to judges and juries. Dingle's hope, however, is the wife nails Nachman. The videotape finally cracked her. She spent the better part of today pouring her heart out. Claims Nachman did the murders but in thrall to Harvey. So Nachman cuts a deal to testify against Harvey. And Makepeace cuts a deal, et cetera."

"In exchange for which Sister Charlayne won't be prosecuted?"

"That's the system, Santa. Same for you, I assume?"

Had I learned, almost killing Josh? Yeah. If something inside hadn't stopped me, what? I'd be facing a murder charge. Could I trust myself, either?

"Albert, those jokers killed my teammates. Of course I'll cooperate."

"Hhhmnf."

"You sound worried. What's the down side to testifying?"

"Harvey's lawyer gets to attack your character. And he has budget to learn some of the . . . uh, shall we say murkier areas of your life-style."

"What do you mean, murkier?"

"Even I don't know. But what they find will be in the papers."

Ignore that remark. "I love your worst-case scenarios. What's the best case?"

"The wife sets 'em on the right track to get enough evidence to nail Nachman and Harvey and Makepeace. The state won't need you."

I grunted. Opening my door, I slid out of the car. "Don't count on it."

"I'm not. Nighty-night." He waved and drove down Norwood.

After showering, I put on jeans and a bulky red sweater. Found one of my old birch canes and hobbled out to the barn. Phone was ringing when I walked in. Answering machine full. I yanked the plugs on both.

Under the skylights, Gus's jungle had never looked rosier. His rodents and reptiles and fish had never acted livelier.

I sat on my stool, barely moving.

The birds were covered, but I could hear the rustle of the rodents, the gurgle from the bank of a dozen eighty-gallon tanks. A small splash when a turtle—name of Rocky Colavito, still not in the Hall of Fame—decided to take a swim.

Not my nature to just sit there. I slid a reggae CD into the box and got to it. My canvases. I'd started them before training camp began. Hadn't got back, even after the strike hit and before the first-and-ten nonsense started.

Nonsense—is that how seriously I took it? I'd never put a bullet into a human being before. Sure was effective.

I rubbed the five canvases, seven feet wide, twelve feet high. Thickly layered blues and greens inspired by the summer sun through the skylights onto Gus's tanks.

On the table, the palette was crusty, but I could soften it up. I picked a bottle of linseed oil off the shelf. Pried open a turp can. Everything smelled right.

What about that sunset in Texas? That unforgettable vivid orange and pink. How would they look against the blues and greens? Terrible.

So I squeezed out some colors into two piles and dabbed around until I had those sunset colors in front of me.

The blues and greens were cold. That sunset vision wasn't. Wielding wide brushes, I started laying orange down low. Then pink up high. Gray, my favorite, above that. I didn't give much thought to it until I heard a knock, hours later.

Couldn't be Gus, fast asleep.

The media types knew where my property line started. Over

the years, we'd had injunctions and court orders to draw that line clearly.

Byzant? The FBI? They'd better have a fresh warrant.

After turning off the reggae, I swung open the door. Cramer.

At first glance, she no longer felt the way she had when she stomped off that afternoon. She had her furry collar rolled up. Her breath billowed toward me. "I didn't call, so please tell me to go away if you have friends over and—I mean, with all the people out front, I—"

"No, no." I took her elbow and shut the door behind her.

The big painting was hard to ignore—five panels, a total of thirty-five feet stretching around two sides of the studio, floor to ceiling. She stood rock-still.

"You want me to hang your coat?"

"Sure." Awkwardly, she shrugged out of it. She wore a bright yellow dress, soft, billowy, no frills. Right side bulky.

"How's your shoulder feel? Your head?"

Distracted by the painting, she shrugged.

I waited, letting her look. One good thing: I could paint over the mess I'd made.

Finally: "I'm overwhelmed. Do you always paint so big?"

"Sometimes."

"When I looked at your slides last month, I didn't note the dimensions."

"Aren't you the one who hates abstracts?"

"But at this size, I'm very taken. I mean, it's that sunset in Texas." She turned her head. "All of it."

"In a way."

"I certainly didn't expect to, but I love it."

Little do you know, lady, but I'm going to give it to you.

That was my first reaction. My second reaction: why does Cramer all of a sudden like abstracts? More to the point: why does she all of a sudden like my abstracts?

Trust me, Gus would say.

Then Cramer went wide-eyed, virgin to Gus's jungle and critters. I showed her around. She said the common names of many.

"Something to drink or eat?"

"Sure. I'm not hungry, but the doctor said I should eat."

"Want to help?"

She slightly raised her taped arm and winced. "The one-winged woozy wombat reporting for KP. Where do I start?"

Turned out she liked reggae, too. Lucky her. I cranked it up. In silence, we chopped salad veggies and curried some couscous. The freezer had enough haddock, so I defrosted two helpings' worth in the microwave. Outside the studio door, I set the hibachi on the asphalt. Got out the charcoal and lighter fluid and made like Dr. Harvey Laurel.

Cramer set plates, forks, and napkins on the low coffee table. Two of each. In no time, I brought in the haddock and put a good-sized slab on each plate. Sprinkled on some dill and parsley and tucked in a lemon wedge.

I pulled a stool to the low coffee table and sat with my back to the painting. Then I offered Cramer the couch across from me. Her eyes kept straying over my shoulder.

She ate a forkful of couscous and said, "Mmmmm." After her first bite of haddock, her eyes widened. "This tastes delicious. Do you do floors, too?"

Yup, the same Cramer. Looking into her eyes was the best thing I could remember from the three weeks of football strike.

She got right to it. "We had a problem yesterday. Wasn't hard to pull the trigger when it came time, was it?"

"No."

"That's the scary part. No wonder we have so many murders. And you'd come to save me?"

"Yes, I did."

"But what if you failed? It wasn't as though I didn't trust you. I had to save myself."

"I didn't see any other way. What made Josh hit you?"

"I told him I'd slept with Lona. Gave him the hairy details."

I let that sit.

"I think I understand why you had to hurt Josh. It was still a beastly act."

"Yes, it was."

"Do you feel better now?"

"No."

"See?"

I saw a lot. Seemed she and I were teammates. But as Gus'd say, take it slow, Santa.

After dinner, I slid in another reggae CD. I drew two low stools to the bank of fish tanks. The fish got pretty active after I fed them. I also turned off most of the room lamps to let the tank lights do their thing.

"Oooooh," she said. I took her hand to help her sit on the stool. She pointed to a goldfish.

"Red Schoendienst. Infielder, St. Louis Cardinals."

"What?"

Elbow against Red's fish tank, head against my hand, I stared. Cramer looked wan in the shimmering violet-and-emerald light. No doubt I looked wan to her. When we did look at each other, we sure stared hard enough to notice.

Trust is always such a leap.